One Hundred

One hundred moments of us

JON RANCE

hera

First published in the United Kingdom in 2024 by

Hera Books
Unit 9 (Canelo), 5th Floor
Cargo Works, 1–2 Hatfields
London SE1 9PG
United Kingdom

Print ISBN 978 1 80436 861 9
Ebook ISBN 978 1 80436 860 2

Look for more great books at www.herabooks.com

Printed and bound in Great Britain by Clays Ltd, Elcograf S.p.A.

1

To Kristin. For all the moments

1999

No. 1

Charlie

The girl in the refectory

The first time I saw her was in the sixth form refectory. I was between classes and waiting for friends when I looked up from my book and there she was – the most achingly beautiful girl I had ever seen. I hadn't known girls that attractive actually existed. I had seen models in magazines, actresses on the silver screen, and I imagined that in the bright lights of London there might be girls as incredible as that, but not in Southampton, casually standing twenty feet away from me. I tightened up and could feel every nerve ending, bone and muscle in my body. I was aware of the air between us as if it was a physical entity.

She had just walked in and was looking around, probably for someone she knew, or perhaps she was waiting for someone. She had long, straight, dark hair and was tall and slim in a way that suggested good genes rather than unhealthy fad diets. She had the most incredible face with dazzling green eyes and dimples on her pale cheeks. I was seventeen years old and hadn't ever felt that overcome with lust before. I had been attracted to other girls, and I had even kissed one, but they were ordinary in comparison. This girl was a dream I didn't even know I had, and all I wanted to think about for the foreseeable future.

For a ridiculous moment, I thought about walking up to her and saying hello. Was that even possible? Did people do such things? I couldn't just approach her and start quoting

Shakespeare, could I? *Shall I compare thee to a summer's day?* No, you definitely couldn't compare her to a summer's day! She would laugh in your stupid face. I could barely feel my feet, and even if I had the courage to walk up to her, what would I say? What could you say to someone as perfect as that without just dying on the spot?

I watched her as secretively as I could from behind my well-thumbed paperback. What sort of person would keep her waiting? If she were my girlfriend, I would make a point of being early to everything. She looked at a silver watch on her perfectly formed left wrist, and then casually gazed around the room. She was wearing a pair of faded blue jeans and a white shirt, which she had half untucked, as though it were a passing thought. On her feet, she had a pair of blue Adidas Gazelle trainers, and I wanted to rush out and buy the same pair just so I would know what it was like to wear that pair of shoes. To somehow, rather pathetically, feel closer to her.

It was October, the first term at sixth form, and I couldn't believe I hadn't seen her before. We must have been studying wildly different subjects and therefore been on completely different schedules to be so far removed from each other. Time seemed to slow down as I watched her, hoping she might catch my eye for a split second. Just her knowing I was alive would be enough but imagine talking to her and hearing her actual voice. It was all so fucking unbearable, like walking a tightrope over the Grand Canyon.

I was trying to imagine how she might speak, the way she might laugh, and how her eyes would sparkle when she did. I thought she would have a posher accent than mine. I had no basis for this theory other than she looked better than me and her skin glowed with a freshness that mine didn't. At seventeen, I had a few spots, a greasy forehead and then, of course, the red hair. Flame red! A proper ginger. I had been called names all my life, and the endless jokes about my pubic hair being the same colour. *Does the rug match the curtains, Talbot?*

Finally, after about five minutes of her standing there and me covertly spying on her, I made a decision. I stood up! I was going to walk up to her and introduce myself. I had to grab this moment because this felt like one of those tipping points. This was my Everest!

I pushed my chair back, my whole body alive in a way it had never felt before. A sudden silence filled the refectory, and I took a step forward at the exact moment she smiled the most wonderful smile I had ever seen, and then strode forward until she was face to face with a boy I instantly recognised as Scott Laird. They stood in front of each other, then he kissed those ruby-red lips, and a piece of my heart broke off and fell through my body, probably lost forever in my intestines. I was crushed in a way I hadn't even realised it was possible to be.

Scott Laird was the best-looking boy in the year and by far the coolest. He wore the trendiest clothes, had the perfect haircut, and was aloof to the likes of me because he only existed to a particular group of people. Scott Laird had an aura about him, knew about nightclubs in London, and somehow managed to always look like he was about to appear on the front cover of a magazine. Scott sang in a band and drove a pristine Volkswagen Beetle. I didn't stand a chance.

They stood together for a moment, and then they walked off, hand in hand, the perfect couple. Bright young things! Everest was left unconquered, and as far away as the actual Everest. I sat back down in my chair, slumped in my seat, daydreaming about her, and that one day I might get to be with someone like that.

It wasn't until days later I found out her name was Ash.

No. 2

Ash

The boy with the red hair

We were at the first sixth form party of the year at a nightclub in town and it was packed to the rafters with excitable girls and boys wearing so much Lynx deodorant it was surely a fire hazard. Luckily, my best friend Lilly was there, and I spotted her walking towards the bar, looking fabulous in a red dress she had bought from Topshop at the weekend.

Tonight was one of those nights when I found myself wondering if Scott and I were well matched. When it was just us, and all the things that came with dating him were gone, it was fantastic. The problem was that it was hardly ever just us. When Scott asked me out during the first week of college, I couldn't believe it. When he looked at me with those intense eyes from underneath that rock-star-in-waiting haircut, it made my skin tingle and I felt more alive, a deeper part of the universe than I ever had before. Yet, I also knew he was too good-looking. Chiselled features, brooding eyes and a body that was far too muscular for someone who spent most of his time playing guitar in his band, Apple. He was too popular, too cool, too much of everything, and I just wasn't.

'Hello, you,' said Lilly when I joined her at the bar. 'Band night, is it?'

'Something like that,' I said, looking across at Scott and the band. They were huddled together, smoking, drinking, a gaggle of girls looking on starstruck. 'What's up with you?'

'Sara's getting off with that boy with the glasses again, and I think I'm going to dance.'

'Sounds like a plan. I could use a dance.'

'Being an Apple groupie not really your thing?' said Lilly pointedly.

Lilly had never taken to Scott. She thought he was too full of himself, not that interesting, and the fact he always called her Billy really got under her skin. We shuffled up to the bar, waiting to catch the barman's attention, when I noticed a boy next to me. I only noticed him because he had the reddest hair I had ever seen. I didn't know his name, and we didn't share any of the same classes, but I had seen that hair before. He was close to me, shoved up against the bar, and when I looked at him, he gave me a sort of half-smile. I smiled back and, for a moment, I imagined what it would be like to be with someone like him instead of Scott. The boy next to me was good-looking, not rock-star handsome like Scott, but handsome enough, and he had a kind smile and incredible blue eyes. He had on a Beatles T-shirt, looked nice in an unthreatening way, and if I were with him, I probably wouldn't have to share him with the world. The boy looked like he was about to say something, his mouth opened in slow motion, his eyes flickered, but before a sound came out, Lilly spoke.

'Let's dance. I can't be bothered to wait for this barman who is clearly blind!' she said, making sure to shout the word 'blind'. The barman looked at us for the first time that night, and probably the last. Lilly grabbed my hand and dragged me towards the dance floor that was already packed with sweaty young bodies jumping around to Pulp's 'Common People'.

I looked back for a moment, and the boy with the red hair watched me walk away until he noticed I was watching him, and he self-consciously pivoted back to the bar. A noise went up from the dance floor as 'Live Forever' by Oasis started playing. I glanced across at Scott and he was talking to a starry-eyed girl in a short chiffon dress, a cigarette glued to his lower lip. He had the ability of looking perpetually posed without even realising it, or maybe he did.

There wasn't much room on the dance floor, and we had to squeeze ourselves in before it instantly swallowed us up. I wondered if Scott would come looking for me soon or even cared where I was. After 'Live Forever', the DJ played 'Country House' by Blur, and I continued dancing, and that's when I noticed the boy with the red hair again. He was dancing nearby with friends. He looked across at me and when I looked back at him, he glanced away. Funny boy. The way he danced, curiously not self-conscious or trying to look cool, but with a freedom I wished I had. The way he couldn't stop looking at me but could never hold a smile for longer than a second. I turned back to Lilly, and we danced the rest of the night away.

No. 3

Charlie

There she goes

Scott Laird's band, Apple, were playing a gig at a student pub near college. It was a pub I had been to a couple of times before to watch bands and to hang out in the garden. It was one of those eclectic pubs with a variety of levels and rooms where all sorts of things seemed to be happening all at once, and I never quite knew where to place myself. I arrived early with Sam and Gavin, eager to make sure I didn't miss a moment with Ash.

'Pint?' said Sam, standing at the bar.

'Pint,' I replied, eagerly scanning the busy bar area for her.

Gavin was in the toilet as usual. At eighteen, he already had the bladder of a middle-aged man with prostate issues. I heard the opening bars of a band already playing in the downstairs room below us, the dull bass of a song I didn't recognise vibrating on the floor. Once we had drinks, and Gavin had returned from the toilet, we headed downstairs to see what was happening. I had made a particular effort with my appearance, which I knew was sad considering Ash didn't even know I existed, but maybe tonight she would notice me. After the college party, when she had definitely smiled at me, I had a small sliver of hope, but that was weeks ago now, and I needed something to give me a boost. A reminder I wasn't wasting my life hoping to get the attention of a girl I had a zero chance of actually dating.

We walked past the music room where a band of five skinny, long-haired students were thrashing around on stage, making an almighty racket. It was all noise, hair and a room full of terrifying goths jumping in unison, so we continued outside into the garden. It was unseasonably mild for the time of year; the sky was the colour of denim, a sprinkle of stars embroidered upon it. I scanned every group and subgroup of people until I finally saw them together. Scott and Ash, our very own Damon Albarn and Justine Frischmann power couple.

Scott was looking cooler than usual, and definitely like a proper lead singer. Tall, Liam Gallagher haircut, a tight Fred Perry polo shirt in black and yellow, dark blue jeans and white Adidas Sambas. He had a cigarette loosely held in one hand and a bottle of Red Stripe beer in the other. The band, friends and family surrounded him, but there was only one person in that group who grabbed my attention. Ash had on a pair of khaki combat trousers and a white crop top that showed off a flash of creamy stomach – that flourish of flesh did so much to my mind and body, a million words couldn't begin to succinctly describe it – and over that she had on a blue Adidas tracksuit top. She looked fucking incredible.

'What time is Apple on?' said Gavin, before taking a drag of his cigarette.

'About nine,' I replied.

'Do you think they're any good?' asked Sam.

'No idea, but fuck me, Scott looks the part,' replied Gavin.

'Imagine being in a band,' said Sam wistfully. 'It would be sex on tap. I play guitar, fancy a shag? Oh, go on then. Oh, you're a singer, you must need a blow job.'

'I think it takes some musical talent,' I replied.

'And you would know, Mr Only Plays Guitar In His Bedroom,' said Sam, laughing.

'At least I can play,' I said defensively, before adding, 'a bit.'

'Yes, I can see you fighting the girls off with your three power chords!' said Gavin, and he and Sam laughed hysterically. Banter was our preferred method of communication. It was our love language, the basis of most of our conversations, and the tent poles that held us together. Gavin had a birthmark that looked vaguely like a third nipple, which had given us hours of banter-fuelled laughs and him the nickname Thripple.

I looked back towards Apple, and I noticed Ash wasn't there anymore. I turned, looking desperately around the garden, and that's when I saw her striding purposely towards us. We were blocking the entrance to the pub, so anyone who wanted to go inside had to walk past us. I was suddenly alive, tingling all over with excitement, and my skin felt hot and cold all at once. Suddenly from inside I heard 'There She Goes' by The La's start playing. The nearer she got, the more beautiful she looked, and the more nervous I became. A thousand versions of the same conversation sped through my mind in a millisecond, but they were all variations on the same theme. A stilted, awkward exchange where she would ask me something like, could you move out of my way please, and I would say yes, of course, and then I would add, do you remember the smile we shared at the college party? But she wouldn't remember me at all, and would ask could I just move please, and so I would, offering my apologies for blocking her way.

When she was just a few feet away, she finally saw me, and everything in the world seemed to go into sharp focus. I didn't know if she would remember me, but whether she did or not, nothing seemed to register on her face. Time slowed. 'There She Goes' continued playing. She gave us a cursory smile and then walked past. She was a foot away from me and I could smell her perfume that had top notes of something floral, and base notes of THIS WILL DRIVE YOU FUCKING WILD! She didn't look at me and then she was gone, and I had this excruciating pain in my chest because it was clear she didn't know who I was.

'Fuck me,' said Sam, his tongue hanging out of his mouth like a cartoon character. 'Imagine being alone and naked with her for five minutes.'

'You've got no chance,' said Gavin.

'Nor do you, Thripple,' replied Sam, laughing. 'What do you say, Charlie?'

'About what?'

'Ash Oliver. How fucking sexy is she?'

'Very,' I mumbled, but my mind was distracted, my heart deflated like one of those sad balloons you saw a few days after a children's party, wrinkled, dishevelled and flat.

2000

No. 4

Ash

End-of-year break-up

It was the last day of term before summer, and I was supposed to be going to the pub by Southampton Common for end-of-year drinks. It had been planned for weeks, but then I had that stupid argument with Scott and stormed off. I could have gone to the pub anyway, but I was too annoyed, heartbroken, and just sad. I wanted to go home and lock myself in my bedroom and cry for days. How could he be so cruel and so fucking cliched? I also hated myself because I should have seen it coming. I should have known how this story was going to end.

I was at college, and I felt like I had been floating all morning, desperate for the first wonderful day of the summer holidays. It was a warm day; the sky was cerulean blue with candyfloss clouds, and everyone was in a jubilant mood. After the pub, Scott was having a party at his house, his dad was going to barbecue, and they had the pool, so I had been forced to buy a new bikini. It was shaping up to be a great last day of term and a proper bookend to what had been an almost perfect year at sixth form. Then I saw Lilly walking out of the library with a face like thunder. I had known Lilly since primary school, and so every nuanced facial expression or change in her mood was easily spotted.

'What's up?' I said.

'Nothing.'

'Come on, Lills, what's going on?'

She looked at me and then after a moment she said, 'A girl in the library said she saw Scott getting off with someone else the other night.'

'What?'

'Don't worry, I put her straight. I said he'd never cheat on you. Although—'

'What night did she say it was?'

'Thursday, why?'

Thursday night. I was supposed to go over to Scott's house, but at the last moment he had cancelled for a band practice, and then they were going into town to see a new band from Manchester that were being hailed as the next big thing. I was tired, my period had just started, so I agreed, put on my pyjamas and watched television in bed with a packet of Rolos. The next morning, Scott was acting strangely, but he said he was just hung-over, and so I thought nothing of it.

'I need to see Scott,' I said, suddenly aware of my heart that was pumping blood through my body just that bit faster than normal. I had no right to be angry with Scott, or suspect him of cheating, but there was something inside of me that said I needed to be worried. I found him coming out of a politics class.

'All right,' said Scott with his front-page-of-the-*NME* smile. He tried to put his arm around me, but I pulled away.

'We need to talk,' I said coldly.

We walked around the back of the college and found a quiet spot near the sports fields.

'What's going on?' said Scott, turning to face me.

'Where did you go on Thursday night?'

'You know where I went. Band practice, and then we went into town.'

'A girl in the library told Lilly you got off with someone else on Thursday night. Is it true?' I said with a genuine sense of dread, and when I looked at Scott, I immediately knew it was.

His face gave everything away. He might have been a talented singer, an archetypical lead man, but he was an awful actor. His usually pale face had a sudden pinkness to it, like undercooked salmon.

'I'm sorry. I was drunk, and it will never happen again. I swear.'

I didn't know what to do. I was so angry, my chest tightened, the blood pumping faster, my head spinning. I felt so betrayed and so fucking stupid. Other people knew and they would be laughing at me. I started to cry, the worst thing I could have done.

'I'm sorry,' said Scott, reaching out a hand, but I batted it away.

'Just leave me alone,' I said, shrugging him off. 'We're done!'

I went home, throwing myself on my bed and crying hysterically. My first boyfriend had cheated on me, and I felt for the first time in my life the unflinching pain of a broken heart. I knew it was a feeling I never wanted to feel again for the rest of my life, but one I probably would. The worst part was that despite what he had done, I still loved him, desperately wanted him, and would no doubt take him back. I was fucking pathetic.

No. 5

Charlie

Wish you were here

When my parents told me we were going on holiday to Lanzarote in Spain, I was momentarily excited at the prospect of international travel, but then I realised it was during the same week Sam and Gavin were talking about going to Cornwall. We had discussed camping in Newquay, and because of other commitments, there was only a two-week period when it was possible, but then Lanzarote happened, so it meant Newquay with my friends was cancelled so I could spend ten days with my parents. Not ideal at seventeen, especially when Sam and Gavin were still going and – according to Sam's cousin, Andy – Newquay was full of girls sunbathing topless during the day and 'mad for it' at night. The plane journey to the sun-drenched beaches of Lanzarote should have been overwhelmingly positive but was instead tinged with jealousy that my two best friends were probably going to lose their virginities, while I would end up spending some quality time with my parents. Never had the saying 'wish you were here' held so little truth.

'Oh, this is nice,' said Dad, looking out over the hotel pool.

'It's even better than the brochure. Isn't it, Charlie?' gushed Mum.

The pool area of the hotel did look nice, but any joy I could get from the sun-dappled, sparkling blue pool or the comfy lounge chairs was wiped away by the fact Dad was wearing a pair of bright orange Bermuda shorts and a white vest. Dad was so working class and provincial in his white vest, a slip of his belly poking out of the bottom like the world's most disgusting game of peekaboo. He seemed almost proud of his drab English-ness, while I considered myself a little more worldly. I had my Walkman, and so when Mum and Dad walked off to get a spot, I walked the other way, put my headphones on and ignored them.

The truth was, I loved my parents dearly. Dad was larger than life, and always made me laugh. He didn't care about things like fashion and what other people thought, he just did his own thing, which I envied at seventeen, when self-consciousness was my watchword. They had stressed that this holiday was a big deal for them as we hadn't always taken holidays abroad. I knew they had saved up for a while for it, and so I did feel a certain amount of guilt for being in such a strop, when all I should have been was grateful. They wanted one final holiday with their son before I got too old and what sort of monster would begrudge them that?

I found a lounge chair on the other side of the pool and settled in. I was still annoyed about Newquay, but this wasn't bad. I had seen a few teenagers at the hotel loitering around uncomfortably with their own parents. Maybe I would make friends playing pool or perhaps even meet a girl. There was talk of a disco at the weekend, so who knew what might happen? I imagined meeting a Spanish girl and that would be something to tell Sam and Gavin when I returned to England. I was trying to look on the bright side of life. Plus, it was hot in Lanzarote, and they had forecast heavy rain in Newquay for the next seven days.

I had brought along my collection of Beatles CDs, and I was going to listen to them in chronological order. I also had *The Beach* by Alex Garland, a slightly dog-eared paperback I had picked up second-hand which I was looking forward to getting stuck into. I was going to spend the morning reading, listening to *Please Please Me* by the Beatles, while enjoying the weather. I pressed play on my CD Walkman and picked up my book. I heard the beginning of 'I Saw Her Standing There', when I looked up and literally saw her standing there, and my heart went boom! Ash Oliver, in a bikini, was standing opposite me across the pool. I was in complete and utter shock and didn't know what to do with myself. What was she doing there, and more importantly, what was I going to do about it?

At college, I had seen Ash around from time to time, and she had even smiled at me a few times, most notably at the college party before Christmas. Tellingly though, we hadn't yet spoken, and she was still, as far as I knew, going out with Scott. I had gone to the pub where his band had played their first gig. To be honest, they were nothing more than fine and Scott had lost his temper with the drummer, but I spent the entire evening gazing longingly at Ash. Thirty minutes of mediocre Oasis-inspired Britpop, but sheer heaven for me.

Now here she was in Lanzarote, in a bikini, which did all manner of things to my mind and body. Ash Oliver, fully dressed in overcast England, was one thing, but Ash Oliver in a blue bikini in sunnier climes was something else entirely. Luckily, she hadn't spotted me, so I quickly put on my *Abbey Road* T-shirt because I didn't want her to see my underdeveloped chest. This was my chance. Fate had thrown us together on Spanish shores, far from the madding crowd of England, maybe this was when our love would finally blossom. If only I had the courage to walk over and say something. However, while I was hatching a plan, she vanished.

I looked around but couldn't see her anywhere. Perhaps my mind had been playing tricks on me and she had never been there at all. The sun was shining directly in my eyes, and I had forgotten my sunglasses in the room. I tried to block out the sun with my hand so I could see her, but then suddenly the sun was gone, and she was standing in front of me.

'I thought it was you,' she said.

Her first words to me. Bright. Cheerful. Definitely posher.

'Yes, it's me.'

My first words to her. Ridiculously self-conscious.

'I'm Ash.'

'I know.'

'Oh, right. I'm sorry, I don't know your name.'

'My name? Yes, it's Charlie. Charlie Talbot.'

Then she smiled, and the sun moved out from behind her, blinding me once again.

No. 6

Ash

The best medicine

'Daniel, just fuck off!' I said to my little brother.

Daniel was twelve and annoying at the best of times, but in Lanzarote he seemed to be on another level of trying to be an irritating little shit. Ten days with him would drive me insane. Luckily, I bumped into that boy from college with the red hair, whose name was Charlie Talbot.

I wasn't looking forward to this holiday in the slightest because Scott was at home, and I was missing him like crazy. After we had broken up because he had kissed another girl, he spent the next week begging me to give him another chance. He sent me flowers, wrote me a song, 'An Ode to Ash', which he performed under my bedroom window, and I crumbled. Scott had two gigs lined up, and I was going to miss them both, and despite begging my parents to leave me home alone, they forced me to come along. They needed a holiday and wanted to spend some 'quality time' with their 'only daughter' before I outgrew them, which I already had right under their noses. The whole thing stunk of a midlife crisis, but there was nothing I could do about it. So, a last-minute package deal to the Canary Islands it was, whether I wanted it or not.

The worst part of the holiday, though, even more than missing Scott, was my parents. They had been arguing more than ever and it had continued on the flight over and at the hotel. I heard them arguing in their room, while Daniel was playing on his Game Boy, and I was getting ready for the pool, and it made me want to be as far away from them as possible. At home, Mum kept the house ticking over, while Dad would go to work for as long as possible, so he didn't have to spend time with her or us, it seemed. I didn't understand why we were on holiday together when none of us particularly liked each other, but we were, and I was determined to enjoy myself despite them.

I was in the hotel bar with Charlie playing pool and Daniel kept dashing over, pushing the balls, and then running away. Mum and Dad were nowhere to be seen, and I could tell even Charlie was getting frustrated.

'Sorry about him,' I said.

'Not a problem. Next time I'll poke him with my cue.'

'Please do. Preferably somewhere painful.'

'I'll pot one of his balls!' said Charlie, and I giggled.

I don't want to sound like one of 'those girls', but I knew Charlie fancied me because he didn't hide it very well. He was always slightly self-conscious around me, and I would catch him sneaking looks at me when he thought I wasn't paying attention. I got the feeling he could never truly relax and, despite having fun, there was a little space between us where his attraction lived. I didn't mind because we had a laugh, which made the holiday bearable.

I realised, hanging out with him, how it might be to be with someone funny. Scott was many things, sexy and cool being the most obvious, but he wasn't funny. Charlie was hilarious and didn't take himself seriously, which was an attractive quality I hadn't realised how much I craved in a boyfriend.

After our game of pool, we walked across and sat down at a table, ordering a couple of drinks from the bar. It was hot and I was in a bikini with a thin shirt over the top, and Charlie was in shorts and a Beatles T-shirt.

'So, what's it like being a part of the college elite?' asked Charlie, and I laughed.

'I'm hardly part of the elite,' I replied, taking a sip of my virgin cocktail. 'And anyway, I didn't even realise there was a college elite.'

'Spoken like a true elitist!' said Charlie, taking a sip of his shandy, and I reached across and gave him a gentle punch on the arm. It was the first time we'd had any actual physical contact all week. Daniel had suddenly headed off to the pool with a German boy he had befriended earlier, which was a blessed relief.

'And how does this social system work?'

'Well, obviously, like any system of hierarchy, it starts with those at the top. Yourself being included in the top tier.'

'And who else is in this top tier?'

'You know, the best-looking people, the cool people, a few sports stars, definitely Bradley Hughes, captain of the football team, who is both sporty, cool, and tall—'

'Tall? I didn't realise height was a part of being in the elite.'

'Oh, yes, height is very important. Unless you're Colin Micklethwait, who is enormous, but unfortunately near the bottom of the college hierarchical system due to the fact he spends most of his time playing "Dungeons & Dragons" in the quad.'

'Ah, yes! I've seen them. I saw them live role-playing on the common once. They take it very seriously.'

'Hence why they're lowdown on the college cool charts.'

'And where exactly do you fit into this system, Charlie?'

'I'm actually sort of an enigma.'

'Oh, really, wow!' I said with a silly little laugh. 'And why is that?'

'Because I'm an outlier. Neither cool nor nerdy. Not sporty or part of any particular group, but comfortable with any of them. I am a floater, fluttering between different social groups with ease. I am here with you in sunny Spain, having a lovely time, but equally, I could be at a Medieval fair in Ipswich with Colin Micklethwait, fully invested in a fantasy role-playing game. I'm a chameleon, Ash.'

I laughed, took a sip of my drink, and this was how we spent our days. Laughing, having fun, and after a while I stopped missing Scott quite so much and even my parents' constant bickering seemed less awful with Charlie around. I liked the version of myself I was with him. I was confident, lighter, and all the stresses and anxieties of life that were forced upon me and that I forced upon myself seemed to evaporate, and I was the truest, most authentic version of me. The old adage was obviously true, laughter really was the best medicine.

No. 7

Charlie

The sun-cream moment

Ash and I were lying on the soft golden sand of the beach, looking out over the azure sea, sunshine hitting our faces, and we were having the perfect day. It was the hottest day of the holiday so far, our parents were at the pool, and Ash's annoying brother was nowhere to be seen. It was just us, lying on towels, talking, taking the occasional dip in the ocean to cool off, and then my whole world changed in a moment.

'Could you rub some sun cream on my back?' said Ash suddenly, passing me a bottle of factor-twenty sun cream.

Just the thought of touching her actual skin sent shivers of anticipation throughout my body. I had gradually got used to spending time with her. We could have a conversation now without me breaking into a cold sweat, but the thought of actually touching her body was something else entirely. It was a step into the unknown, and I didn't know if I could do it.

'Umm, right, yes. No problemo.' *No problemo?*

I had never rubbed sun cream on anyone before, let alone the most beautiful girl in the entire universe. She was lying down on her front, and I kneeled down next to her. I had to stop my hands from shaking, so I took a deep breath in preparation, and then, from next to us, another couple – French, I thought – started playing music and it only happened to be the Air song, 'Sexy Boy'. I looked across at them in disbelief. Were they soundtracking the moment with Ash on purpose? It definitely added an extra layer of sexiness and tension to the occasion I really didn't need.

'Just let me undo this,' she said, and then she casually unclipped her bikini top and let the straps fall down by her sides. Oh. Dear. Lord.

I looked at Ash Oliver's naked back and took a moment to savour it like you might standing in front of a masterpiece. Like everything else about her, it was perfect. I tried to take a mental photo so I could remember every tiny detail, lock it away in my long-term memory for safekeeping. Her slim, slightly red back sloped away from her shoulder blades, and I could just make out the merest hint of a breast pushed against the sand beneath, which sent my mind into a spin. It was hard to believe that this was reality. That somehow our lives had crossed at that exact moment, and it gave me hope that perhaps we were somehow destined to be together.

I squirted a small amount of the sun cream on my hand and then spread it across her back. Her skin felt so soft, and I could feel the bones beneath and small pockets of flesh. I loved the way her body felt in my hands, the smooth skin of Ash beneath the slippery liquid, and it was almost too overwhelming. I continued rubbing the lotion across her upper back before I squirted some more onto my hands, then went lower towards the top of her bikini bottoms. I rubbed the lotion out until I couldn't see it anymore and I had done most of her back.

'Just a wee bit on the sides,' I said cautiously, and for some reason adopting Scottish terminology, but fortunately not attempting the accent. I wasn't sure how far she wanted me to go, and although I was enjoying it more than I had enjoyed anything my entire life, I didn't want to go too far. I didn't want her to think I was taking advantage of the situation, but I also didn't want it to end. I could have rubbed sun cream on her back for the rest of my life while Air continued their sexy French electronic space pop.

She rolled onto one side, so I could apply the lotion with more ease, but as she did her breast came off the ground and I caught a momentary glimpse of the full shape of her breast and the merest hint of a nipple. I didn't mean to, but I sort of inhaled in shock, trying my best not to get a surprise erection because it was possible given the extenuating circumstances. I wouldn't have swapped losing my virginity twice over in Newquay for the quickest glance at Ash's breast.

'Is everything all right?' said Ash.

'Everything is fine. Almost done.'

I applied more lotion to my hands and then I gradually rubbed it from her back onto her sides. The whole thing felt so overwhelming, and I didn't know how far to go or what she expected of me. She didn't know how much I lusted after her, or she would never have asked me to do it. She probably saw me as entirely sexless, like some sort of asexual eunuch. She was with Scott, who probably knew how to rub in sun cream and make it sexy. She had rolled back again so her breasts were pushed against the beach, but I was so close to them. I rubbed as high as I could and as I got close to them I felt myself getting aroused. I was trying so hard not to, but I couldn't help it. It was all too much, overwhelming in the best possible way, and I had to stop before things literally became too hard.

'All done,' I said, quickly lying face down next to her, my erect penis pushed uncomfortably against the beach. I closed my eyes and tried to think of the least sexy things in the world to temper my arousal: Dad's Bermuda shorts, the Queen and a book I saw in the library about the history of the steam engine. There was a momentary silence. I was breathing far heavier than I should have been, trying not to inhale any sand.

'If you need me to do your back, just let me know,' said Ash.

What could I say to that? Of course I wanted her to do it, but I couldn't bear the thought of it. If I had a good back, muscular and tanned, then it would have made the holiday, but all I could think was how horrible my back was, and I didn't want her seeing it.

'I'm okay, thanks,' I replied.

We lay in silence, listening to Air, and I could still feel her skin on my fingers. I pictured it over and over in my mind, the thought of her breast and of that nipple I saw for a tantalising moment. If being strangers had made me want her with an almost unhinged level of certainty, then touching her body had taken my infatuation to a whole new level. It felt all at once like the most important, wondrous feeling I had ever had, and at the same time the most insignificant because nothing would ever come of it.

No. 8

Ash

It was definitely the vodka

It was the night before the penultimate night in Lanzarote, and I just wanted to get drunk. I was so sick of my parents constantly bickering and I couldn't stand it any longer. They had been snapping at each other the entire holiday and last night was the worst. They had a full-on argument in the apartment, and luckily Daniel was already asleep, but I was in bed and listened to the whole bloody thing.

Charlie and I started drinking early and I think he could tell something was on my mind. My parents, pretending everything was fine, which had become their raison d'être, sat with other parents in the bar, acting like the perfect couple. I couldn't bear it and had to get away.

'Want to go for a walk?' I said to Charlie.

'Umm, yes, sure. Should we take our drinks?'

'One better. My parents have a few bottles in the room. Let's get them first, then we can head to the beach.'

Charlie looked unsure at my out-of-character hubris, but quickly agreed and off we set. We went to my parents' room where I found a bottle of vodka, and small cans of Coke, which we brought along with plastic cups. We headed to the beach, which was quiet at that time of night, and set up camp. We had a shot of vodka each before we diluted it with Coke, sat on the beach, our feet dug into the sand, and we stared out towards the sea.

'Is everything all right?' said Charlie, eventually.

I had been quiet and I'm sure it was obvious something was on my mind. Unlike my parents, I wasn't much of an actor and my emotions were easily spotted dancing across my face like a show troupe.

'Is it that blindingly obvious?'

'Just a bit, but you don't have to talk about it if you don't want to.'

'No, it's just… My parents are driving me crazy. All they do is argue and, honestly, I have no idea why they're still together.'

There was a sudden quietness over us. Before that night, our time together in Lanzarote had been fun and light-hearted, but suddenly, it was darker and more real. I didn't even talk to Scott about my family. I looked out towards the sea, at the waves lapping against the shore, and I listened to them for a moment. They were so loud at night-time when the beach was quiet. It was late but still warm; the sun was on its way down, creating wonderful colours that smudged together like pastels.

'I'm sorry,' said Charlie after a minute. 'That must be tough.'

'Which is why I want to get drunk and forget all about them.'

It was an hour later and dark except for the lights that illuminated the beach from the hotels along the front. People walked past, and a few drunken groups of tourists shouted and sang songs. We could hear the waves hitting the beach but could barely see them now.

'Why do you love the Beatles so much?' I asked.

'Because they're the best band of all time. If you're going to love a band, you should love the best. Who's your favourite band, and please don't say Apple because I might vomit?'

I giggled. 'God no, although don't tell Scott that. To be honest, I'm actually more of a Take That fan. Scott would go mental if I said that to him. He's such a music snob.'

Charlie laughed, then lay back on the sand looking up towards the sky.

I did the same.

'Your secret is safe with me, Ash Oliver, world's biggest Take That fan.'

The sky was dotted with stars, and I was starting to feel a little drunk.

'Although I do have a confession.'

'What?' I said, an excitement in my voice at the thought of a shared secret.

'Despite the fact that most of my friends only seem to like indie music, and Sam is really into drum and bass for some reason, I actually quite like Take That, too.'

I laughed, and then looked across at him. 'Why don't you have a girlfriend, Charlie? You're good-looking, funny, and now I find out you love Take That—'

'Like Take That. I said like.'

'Fine, like. But still, you have so much going for you.'

I looked across at him, he kept staring up at the sky, and I couldn't help but feel that the air between us had changed ever so slightly. We had grown closer on that beach, or maybe it was just the vodka.

'Don't know, really,' said Charlie after a moment.

'There must be plenty of girls at college who would love to go out with you.'

'You would be surprised.'

Even in my drunken state, I detected a tension caught in his voice. There was something he couldn't or didn't want to share with me. I decided to let it go because I didn't want to pressure him.

'Sorry, I'm drunk and being totally inappropriate. Ignore me.'

'I could never ignore you,' said Charlie, and this time, when I turned my head and looked across at him, he did the same.

We looked at each other and there was definitely something there. I could feel a spark of attraction between us that hadn't been there before. Maybe it was the vodka, being on holiday, or his Take That confession, but at that moment, I wanted to lean in and kiss him. The space between us was suddenly like no man's land during World War One, where neither of us dared to enter. A dangerous space full of booby traps and bombs that could easily go off, knowing one ill-judged misstep could be fatal. The air seemed to fizz with excitement, adrenalin, and it took all of my willpower to turn away, but once I did, the atmosphere changed, and I sat up.

'We had better head back,' I said, standing up, my head swirling with vodka.

Charlie stood up, too. I looked at him, smiled; he smiled back and disaster, it seemed, was averted.

No. 9

Charlie

Lunch in Teguise

It had been the greatest ten days of my life, and I didn't want it to end. I constantly willed time to slow down during the day so I could soak in every second with Ash. Eventually though it was the last full day of the holiday and I wanted to do something to mark the occasion. I thought Ash and I could go somewhere for lunch. Sort of like a date, although obviously it wouldn't be a date because that would involve some level of joint participation and agreement that yes, it was a date, and not just two friends eating food in close proximity.

I spoke with the hotel concierge, and they recommended we take a taxi inland to the ancient town of Teguise. I spent ten minutes trying to explain that it wasn't a date, and we were just friends. The lady smiled and said she understood, but then she winked at me, and so I gave up and booked a taxi.

The night before, something had happened between us. I tried to pretend it hadn't because I didn't want to get carried away, and we had been drinking, but it definitely had. We had shared a moment of tension when I thought for a second that we might kiss. Nothing happened, but it felt like it could have happened under different circumstances. If she wasn't dating Scott. If she hadn't been so despondent about her parents' relationship and was therefore emotionally vulnerable. If I had a modicum of courage.

The drive to Teguise was along barren roads up into the mountains of Lanzarote. It was so different from the coast where we had been staying. There were hazy clouds as we left behind the blue skies of the coast, and despite it only being a thirty-minute taxi ride, the landscape was stark, almost moon-like. The thing that had made the holiday incredible was how easy it was being with Ash. All my fears I wouldn't be able to talk to her, that I would become mute or, worse, gabble complete gibberish and she would think I was an idiot, were totally unfounded. I felt like I had known her my whole life, and it seemed impossible to remember a time when we weren't so close. I could be myself around her and I felt like I was getting a proper insight into the real Ash away from the hubbub of home.

We got out of the taxi, and despite the clouds driving up, it was hot, and we walked towards a square full of intensely white buildings. There was so much white, although all the wooden doors and shutters on the windows were painted a bright green. The ancient cobblestone streets were occasionally broken up with trees and there was an old church at one end of the square, overlooking everything. It was stunning. Ash and I strolled around, taking everything in, and then we found a small restaurant and sat outside. The landscape around the town was starkly brown and barren, but inside everything was so vibrant and colourful. It was only half an hour from the hotel, but it felt like a different country.

Ash was obviously more worldly than me and knew what she wanted to eat. She ordered a variety of tapas, rattling off the order like a seasoned traveller, plus two lemonades, and we sat outside watching the world go by. As moments went, it was one of the more surreal ones of my life, so far from home with the girl I had lusted after and dreamed of dating all year. I watched a droplet of condensation slide down the outside of my glass and then settle on the table as our food arrived.

'I can't believe this is our last day,' said Ash, tucking into the tapas.

'It feels like we're a million miles from home,' I said before I took a sip of my drink. It was the best lemonade I had ever tasted.

'It does.'

'When we get back to college, are you going to ignore me and pretend this didn't happen?' I said, only half joking, and forcing a smile.

'Why would you think that?'

'Because you're in the cool group, dating Scott, and, well, I'm not.'

'I think you're cool,' said Ash, looking across the table at me with a smile and, for the tiniest fragment of a second, I felt something again. The same mutual attraction I had felt the night before. It didn't last long because she looked away towards the market. I had to stop thinking about her like that because it was ridiculous and a pathway that could only lead to heartache and disappointment. Instead, I did what I always did when faced with moments of importance or opportunity: I made a terrible joke.

'You only think I'm cool because you've only met Lanzarote Charlie. I'm way cooler here than back home.'

'Oh, really.'

'Fact. In England, I'm like the opposite of cool. I'm anti-cool, but here it's like Clark Kent and Superman. I think it's to do with the heat.'

'I find that hard to believe and anyway,' said Ash, taking a bite of her patatas bravas, 'there's more to life than being cool, Charlie.'

'That's easy for you to say because you are cool. It's like millionaires saying money doesn't make you happy. I'd like to see them living in a council flat in Grimsby.'

'I'm not as cool as you think I am,' said Ash, and then she smiled at me, but it was tinged with something, and I saw the girl who loved Take That but pretended she preferred Oasis. The girl whose parents argued constantly and wasn't quite as confident as she appeared. There were so many more layers to her than I could have imagined, and something had happened between us in the days we had spent together in Lanzarote. At college she was just a cardboard-cutout girlfriend: beautiful, sexy, but largely one-dimensional, but in Lanzarote, she filled out and became this three-dimensional girl, who was actually far more like me, and closer to the sort of person I actually wanted to date than even I could have predicted. She made me laugh, was easy to talk to, and perhaps most importantly of all, made me feel genuinely good about myself. She gave me a confidence I had always been lacking, the missing piece of the jigsaw I had been searching for my whole life.

We ate lunch, while around us people browsed the market and a small band started playing some traditional Spanish music. Like the rest of the holiday, I didn't want it to end. I didn't want to go back to the hotel and certainly not to England, where life would go on, but Ash and I would never be like that again. No matter what she said, I knew that once we were back on British soil, our relationship would change. There were too many outside forces that would make it impossible. As we were waiting to pay the bill, I felt like I had to say something meaningful. She was looking towards the square and she had never looked more beautiful. Her hair was loose, no make-up, and in a white top, bra straps showing over slightly sunburnt shoulders.

'Can I just say,' I said, my voice suddenly hoarse. 'That it's been really nice. This. Us. Together in Lanzarote. I hope we can remain friends because I really like you, Ash. I think you're...' I didn't know what word to finish on. I wanted to say that she was the most beautiful, thrillingly wonderful person I had ever met. In the end I went with: '...really special.'

I didn't know what she was thinking because she just looked at me. She wasn't smiling and I couldn't read her expression at all. She left a long silence before finally she smiled.

'I think you're really special, too, Charlie,' she said, and then she got up and walked off towards the market, leaving me to pay the bill.

I watched her while I was waiting. She was looking at a stall with some locally made handbags, and I thought while I was sitting there how wonderful life would be if she were my girlfriend. I knew it wasn't possible, but I imagined how happy I would be with her. It was such an intense feeling I had to shake myself out of it when the waitress came back with my change.

2003

No. 10

Ash

The man with red hair in Covent Garden

I was in London for the weekend visiting Lilly at university, but she was busy with her boyfriend that afternoon, so I had popped into Covent Garden to do a bit of shopping. Being at university in Exeter was brilliant, and I was loving my course and the proximity to the beautiful beaches of Devon, but the shopping wasn't quite up to London standards. I was supposed to be going clubbing later, although I wasn't really in the mood. I would rather have spent the night in, drinking wine, getting a takeaway and catching up with Lilly, but she had a whole plan that involved pre-drinks in Islington and then heading into Kings Cross. Even in Exeter, I wasn't much of a clubber these days. I preferred the student union and then back to someone's house for tea and toast. I was becoming middle-aged before my time.

I had just walked out of French Connection on Long Acre, and I was pondering where to go next when I stopped dead in my tracks. I couldn't believe it because standing about ten feet in front of me was Charlie Talbot. He was looking in the window of another shop and I could only see him from the side, but it was definitely him. I would know that red hair anywhere! He looked so different from the Charlie I knew from sixth form. His hair was shorter, and he was dressed in a pair of dark blue jeans and a smart white shirt. He was wearing a pair of Chelsea boots, carrying a jacket, and he looked handsome in a way that surprised me.

I stared at him for a moment and all the memories of Lanzarote came flooding back. Had it really been three years ago? We'd had such a good time together, and he had literally saved me. Without him, it would have been such a terrible holiday with my parents arguing constantly, my annoying brother, and missing Scott, but somehow having him there had actually made it one of the most memorable holidays of my life.

Once we were back in England, things were different, obviously. I had Scott, and Charlie had his own life and social circle, but I'll never forget the boy in Spain who made me laugh so much I thought I might pee myself, and who listened to my problems without judgement. The boy who was obsessed with the Beatles and had awkwardly rubbed sun cream on my back on the beach. The boy who had confessed that he liked Take That, and whom, for a moment, I had wanted to kiss.

I walked towards him, but before I reached him, he turned to walk away, and then he saw me. We stood in front of each other, and time seemed to stand still.

'It's you,' I said.

'It is,' said Charlie with a bright, wide smile.

'What are you doing here?'

'I'm at university in north London. I popped in to spend some time at the British Museum, but as you can tell, I'm in Covent Garden instead. What about you? The last I heard you were at university in Exeter?'

'I am, but I'm visiting a friend for the weekend.'

'It's good to see you.'

'You, too. You look... different.'

'Better different, I hope,' said Charlie, his brilliant blue eyes sparkling and with the same dash of uncertainty caught in his voice.

'Yes. Definitely better.'

We smiled at each other, and there was a pause in the conversation. It was one of those sliding doors moments when we could have said goodbye and walked away. Gone about our days and been nothing more than just a passing memory to each other. A side note in a conversation. *You'll never guess who I bumped into?* He was supposed to be going to the British Museum, I was supposed to be getting back to get ready for my night out with Lilly, but there was something about meeting Charlie in Covent Garden in the same way we had met in Lanzarote and how he had smiled at me at the sixth form party that I had never quite forgotten. It felt like we were teetering on the edge of something. Then he said:

'I don't suppose you have time for a drink, do you?'

No. 11

Charlie

You could ditch your friends and spend the night with me

I was standing at the bar of the Lamb & Flag pub in Covent Garden, and I looked back at the table where Ash sat waiting for me. It wasn't that busy because it was the early afternoon, but a few people were milling about, and a lost-looking family of American tourists seemed to be trying to decide, as the Clash sang, should they stay or should they go? I couldn't believe that after all this time I was with Ash Oliver again.

Since I had last seen her, she had grown up, her body had filled out slightly, her clothes had changed and were more mature. Her hair, which was always long and straight, was still long but naturally wavy now and marginally lighter in colour. Gone was the childish sixth form girl I had known, and now she was an even more beautiful woman.

'A wine for the lady,' I said, putting her drink down on the table.

'Cheers. Can you believe it's been over two years since sixth form?'

'It feels like a million years ago now.'

'What are you studying at uni?'

'History, although I have no idea what I want to do with it yet. Teach probably, maybe, I don't know, but at the moment I'm keeping my options open. You?'

'English literature. I want to go into publishing, eventually,' said Ash.

'Eventually?'

'I'm going to take a gap year after uni and do the travelling thing.'

'Ah yes, "the travelling thing".'

I knew at least four people who were going to do 'the travelling thing' after university. Unfortunately, I couldn't afford to do 'the travelling thing'. I would have to get a job and start earning money after university or I would be doing the 'moving back home to live with my parents thing'.

'What's that supposed to mean?' said Ash with a wry smile. 'The travelling thing, in quotation marks. Are you too good to travel, Charlie?'

'It's just, I suppose I'm probably jealous.'

'You could do it, too.'

'If I had parents who could help me, then yes, but I don't. Anyway, I'm sort of ready to get a job and start earning some money. It's shit always being poor, and London is many things, but expensive is top of the list.'

'Do you think you'll stay in London after you graduate?'

'Definitely. I couldn't imagine living anywhere else.'

'And does London Charlie have a London girlfriend?' said Ash, and I felt a little excitement creeping up on me. A tingle ran through my body at the mention of partners like the Thames through London, winding its way through me, overflowing into smaller tributaries.

'No, and what about Exeter Ash? She must have a boyfriend.'

'Actually, I don't. I was seeing someone for a while, but I'm single at the moment and happily so. It's nice spending time getting to know me. Do you know what I mean?'

'I do,' I said, but the truth was I didn't. I'd had a whole lifetime without a serious girlfriend so I was more than ready for some time *away* from 'just me' – in more ways than one.

I couldn't believe we were both single and together in London, and my mind shot back to that moment in Lanzarote. The moment on the beach when we looked at each other and

I felt the spark. I couldn't ignore it or the fact that, in a city of eight million people, we had randomly run into each other in Covent Garden. I didn't believe in fate, but it was becoming increasingly harder to ignore. I felt it in my body, the pull of certainty that Ash and I were destined to be a part of each other's lives. I wanted to believe it, but the thing I thought of most was that, despite everything, she was still out of my league. Ash Oliver, from the well-to-do family, would undoubtedly end up with someone with a proper career, money and prospects far greater than mine. And yet, being together again we had fallen right back into Lanzarote Us. Although now there was a tantalising difference in the make-up of our relationship. We were both single, and if I believed the hype, able to mingle.

An hour later, we were outside the pub. It was November, but warm for the time of year. We both had coats, but we held them in our hands. It was time to say goodbye, but like every moment with Ash, I didn't want it to end.

'It's a shame you have plans tonight,' I said, hoping she would read between the lines.

People walked past us, the noise of traffic and music from nearby bars filtered towards us. I loved how vibrant London was and I could feel its energy rubbing off on me. London had an optimism as though anything was possible, while back home everything felt small and unchangeable, like it would always be stuck and, if you stayed there, you would be stuck, too.

'It is, or we could have done something,' replied Ash, with a flicker of a smile.

Was she flirting with me? Had she read between the lines and liked the subtext? Was I just imagining everything like a massive presumptuous prick? Maybe it was the alcohol, but I felt confident. This was it. What was there to lose in such a situation? It was now or maybe never.

'You could ditch your friends and spend the night with me?' I ventured.

She looked at me, and I think it was clear what I meant. I think the implication was that I was interested in her and wanted to spend whatever time she had left in London together, and possibly engaged in something romantic.

'I mean, I came all the way from Exeter to spend the weekend with Lilly.'

'True, but you can see Lilly again whenever you want.'

'But you're a one-time deal, is that it, London Charlie?'

'Maybe,' I said with a smile, not really sure what I was saying, but I knew as long as she didn't say no, I was still in with a chance.

'How about this? I go back to Lilly's and see what she has planned and, if I can, I'll slip away later?' said Ash with a smile that definitely felt a little flirtatious. We were both playing with the idea that there was an attraction between us: a flickering, scintillating, slow-burning lust that had been there since that night in Lanzarote.

'If that's the deal, then I'm in.'

'Do you have a phone?'

'I don't. I'm against mobile phones. I don't think they're going to take off.'

'Weirdo. Fine, then write your address down on a piece of paper.'

Ash rifled through her handbag and found a pen and a scrap of paper. I wrote my address down and then we stood in front of each other.

'See you later, Ash Oliver.'

'Perhaps, Charlie Talbot.'

We smiled, then she turned around and walked away, and I couldn't stop myself from smiling until she was out of sight, lost within the crowds of people, and vanishing like a ghost.

No. 12

Ash

Is it okay if I kiss you?

It was dark, and I was standing outside a terraced house in north London, debating whether to go in or not. Inside the house lights were invitingly bright and on the corner of the road music blared from a busy pub. The earlier sunshine had dissipated, and a few drops of rain had begun to fall, creating a layer of moisture on the ground beneath me. I took a deep breath, walked towards the front door, quickly double-checking the address on the scrap of paper I had shoved in my pocket earlier, before I pressed the doorbell and waited. I honestly didn't know what I was doing there and what I wanted to happen. I should have been out with Lilly, but after pre-drinks, I told her to go on without me and I would explain in the morning.

I stood and waited, the rain gradually getting heavier, and then finally the door opened.

'Can I help you?' said a tall, thin boy in a green hooded sweatshirt.

'I'm here to see Charlie Talbot,' I said uncertainly.

The boy smiled, then turned around.

'Charlie, there's a girl at the door who says she knows you.' He turned back to me. 'Don't just stand there, come inside.'

'Thanks,' I said, before I stepped inside Charlie's student digs.

It was the typical sort of student house I had been inside a hundred times before. Sparsely decorated, a stained carpet and it smelled strongly of cigarettes and weed. It wasn't long before another boy joined us with a grin on his face, and then finally Charlie walked out into the hallway. He looked the happiest and most surprised of all.

'Oh, hi. I didn't think you were coming,' he said.

'Is it too late? I can go if—'

'No, no, stay, please,' said Charlie quickly, and then the boy who had opened the door coughed dramatically. 'Sorry. Ash, these are my housemates. This is Matt,' he said, looking towards the boy who had opened the door.

'At your service, milady,' said Matt, tipping his head in my direction.

'And this is Tom,' said Charlie, his cheeks flushing red, his voice full of excitement.

'Nice to meet you,' said Tom, eagerly offering a handshake.

We stood in the hallway for a moment before Matt and Tom made excuses to leave and headed into the living room, where I could hear a video game. I looked at Charlie and smiled.

'Are you going to give me the tour then?' I said.

'You want a tour of my crap student house?'

'I do.'

'Fine, but I must warn you, there's a strange smell in the bathroom. We have no idea what it is, how it got there, and it won't go away.'

'Sounds intriguing.'

'I don't think you'll say that when you smell it,' said Charlie, and I laughed. 'So, if you'd like to follow me for the official tour of Number Two Tattenhall Road.'

Charlie took me into the small living room where Matt and Tom were playing a football video game, smoking and drinking cans of beer. They had stacked the empty cans into an enormous pyramid in one corner that was actually quite impressive. It was messy, smelled horrific, and there was a plant that looked as though it had died pre-war. At least in Exeter, I lived with two other girls, who were both quite neat and tidy, and none of us smoked.

Next we went to the back room, which seemed to be equal parts drug den and laundrette, and then the kitchen, which was tiny, cluttered, and there was a frying pan on the side with grease inside that looked as though it had been there for a while. I followed Charlie upstairs to see the bathroom with the strange smell. He opened the door, and it did indeed have quite an unpleasant aroma.

'What is it?' I said, my hand over my nose.

'No idea,' said Charlie, closing the door. 'Tom thinks something died.'

'I think Tom might be right.'

'And lastly, my bedroom.'

He opened the door to his bedroom, and I was expecting another chaotic room like the rest of the house, but I was surprised to find a clean, ordered and lovely-smelling bedroom.

'Gosh,' I said, walking in. 'This is genuinely nice.'

'Unlike Tom and Matt, I actually like things that are clean and smell nice. It's my haven.'

I walked around his rectangular-shaped bedroom and looked at everything. The bed had a smart striped duvet cover, and the IKEA desk was ridiculously organised with everything in its place. I looked at the framed prints on the walls, generic landscapes, nothing too personal, and the wardrobe with everything hanging in the same direction. There was a plant pot in one corner with a tall leafy plant and the room had a wonderful woodsy aroma, possibly from his deodorant or perhaps an aftershave. He had a rug on the floor that was plain but fitted in nicely with everything else and a window to the back garden. The pièce de résistance was an old record player that sat on a wooden table and under the table were about twenty records. Scanning them quickly, I realised they were mostly Beatles albums. I sat down on the end of the bed.

'I never imagined in a million years that one day Ash Oliver would be sitting on my bed,' said Charlie, and now it was my turn to blush.

'Then you wouldn't have imagined sitting down next to her either.'

'I imagined it but didn't think it would ever come true. It was a dream.'

'You remember the Gabrielle song, "Dreams"?'

'Vaguely.'

'Then you'll know that dreams can come true,' I said, and then I laughed nervously at my own stupid joke.

He slowly walked across, sat next to me, and there we were on Charlie's bed. The truth was, I was having doubts about being in that room with Charlie. When I had left him in Covent Garden, I had told myself on the way back to Lilly's house that I needed to live more in the moment. For my whole life, I had lived under this cloud of pressure from my father. I needed to be a certain way, achieve goals, get the highest marks because he wanted me to be perfect. He never let me just be myself, so when I got to university and started questioning who I was, I didn't know. For so long I tried to fit myself into the mould I was supposed to be, and it just wasn't working. The only time when I had felt like I wasn't acting, when I was being my true, authentic self, was in Lanzarote with Charlie.

I knew I liked him and that we had a spark of attraction, but we couldn't have a relationship at that moment. He was in London, I was in Exeter, and I didn't want or need the complication of a long-distance boyfriend in my life. I also knew that, for one night only, I wanted to forget about all the practicalities of life and do something impetuous. Charlie and I sat on his bed, the rain tapping on the window, and I was going to go with the flow. That's when he turned to me, and said with an uncertain smile:

'I realise this is going to sound monumentally shit, but Ash, is it okay if I kiss you?'

I didn't reply. I just leaned in, closed my eyes and kissed him.

No. 13

Charlie

To me, you are perfect

There are certain moments in life so significant that they define you and you can't remember how you felt before they happened. When our lips finally came together, I closed my eyes, and felt in that second every moment of my life was drawn into it like a black hole and when I opened my eyes again, the universe I knew was altered forever.

'I've wanted to do that for a very long time,' I said.

'I know,' she said with a soft smile.

'What do you mean, you know?'

'Sorry, Charlie, but you're a terrible actor.'

'You knew when we were in Lanzarote?'

'I knew from the moment I met you.'

'But you didn't say anything.'

'I didn't want to make it weird between us. I was with Scott and so I left it.'

'But that moment on the beach. Did you feel it?'

'You mean the night we got drunk on vodka?'

I smiled because she remembered. It wasn't just my imagination. 'Yes.'

'I did, but I knew nothing could happen.'

'And now?'

There was a brief pause, and neither of us said anything. It felt like all the words in the English dictionary were suddenly meaningless and the only thing that mattered, that could truly express how we actually felt, was feeling. I leaned in again and we kissed, but this time we didn't stop. My hands were on her body and her hand was on the top of my leg. We undressed on my bed, tossing our clothes on the floor without a thought, and the only noise I could hear was the rain and my heartbeat, and then we disappeared under my duvet.

'Put on some music,' she said.

I got up, walked across to my record player and took out *Abbey Road*. It was my favourite album at that moment. It always felt futile to have a favourite Beatles album because it could change on the toss of a coin, and they each had a special place in my heart. I turned the record player on, slipped on the vinyl and walked back to bed, hearing the wonderfully crisp crackling noise at the beginning, and then 'Come Together' started playing, which felt sort of perfect, before I slid back under the duvet next to Ash.

'Are we going to have sex?' I asked because I just wanted to clarify that we were definitely about to have sex and it wasn't just my imagination.

'Yes, Charlie. We are going to have sex. Unless—'

'No, no, it's good,' I said quickly, cutting her off with another kiss.

Ash Oliver was naked in my bed and when I touched her skin, felt her breasts for the first time, it was almost too overwhelming. It felt like winning the lottery. What would you do with all that money? It was okay to spend time dreaming about it and thinking about all the things you would do with millions of pounds, but actually having the money in your bank account would be too much to comprehend, and that was how I felt in bed with Ash.

Her body was even more perfect than I had imagined. Soft, smooth, and when I was on top of her looking down at her face in the semi-darkness and she looked up at me with a smile, a look of pleasure, of exhilaration, it was a moment I would never forget. Her hair was messy, and I ran my fingers through it, and we kissed with a raw, ravenous passion, desperate to make up for lost time in my mind, but she must have felt something, too, and our naked bodies moved together, slowly at first, pressed against each other.

'You okay?' I whispered in the dark.

'Yeah. You?'

'I'm just really glad you came. I honestly didn't know if you would.'

'Neither did I.'

I slid down her body, kissing every square inch of her, the smell of her perfume heightening my attraction further, taking a nipple in my mouth, and slowly letting it go, teasing her body that squirmed with intensity beneath me. I moved down further, kissing her creamy stomach I had seen in flashes over the years, then my head was between her legs, and I felt her moving, adjusting herself and then moaning, her thighs gripping the side of my head. I waited until her moans became louder and then I stopped, moving myself up until our faces were level again, and then I felt myself inside of her for the first time, and it seemed like the culmination of something special that had lasted since the first year at sixth form. I stayed on top of her, moving slowly at first, our bodies intertwined, moving as one, revelling in the moment, and then gradually it intensified, and we started going faster and faster until eventually we were done in a crescendo of noises and breathless words, and fuck, it was incredible.

I eventually rolled off of her and lay by her side, our bodies touching, breathing heavily, our hearts pounding, her hand still on me and my hand on her. Everything was changed and felt different. Every single cell in my body had been altered, never to return to its original factory settings. I turned on my side and looked at her. A thin sliver of creamy light crept through the curtains and lay across her chest.

'That was incredible,' she said.

'I have done it a few times before, you know,' I replied, and then she laughed, and I looked at her in the darkness of my room. 'You are perfect, Ash Oliver.'

'I am many things, Charlie, but perfect is not one of them.'

'But you must realise that to me you are perfect, and I'll always think that no matter what, until the day I die.'

'That's quite a statement.'

'I stand by it.'

I traced a finger from her collarbone along her breast, over her nipple, and along her stomach, then rested my hand on her upper thigh. I pressed slightly and felt the skin that was warm, soft, and fleshy beneath me. I knew I wanted to do this every single day for the rest of my life. It didn't matter what she said, how she felt, I would always think of her as perfect because to me she was.

No. 14

Ash

Drive. Ambition. Focus.

I was looking at myself in the mirror in Charlie's bathroom. I had splashed some water on my face, and Charlie had given me a spare toothbrush to brush my teeth, and I was getting ready to head back into his room. It was still hard to believe I was there with the red-haired boy from sixth form, and it had been the best, most fulfilling and passionate sex I had ever had. It felt so natural, so right between us. Scott had been my first, and I had always felt slightly disconnected from him, almost as if I was acting the part of the girlfriend having sex with her boyfriend rather than actually doing it. I had been too self-conscious, and whether it was just my age or because of Scott, I could never truly relax. There had been one boy at university, which was good but nothing mind-blowing if I'm honest, but with Charlie, I felt it. Crossing that line from friends to whatever this was should have felt different, bigger, awkward perhaps, but the only thought I had was that it wasn't and instead it felt like something we should have been doing a long time before last night, which in itself was perhaps the only strange thing about it.

As I looked at myself in the mirror, all I could think about was how I was going back to Exeter the following afternoon. Despite how wonderful it had been, and how I longed to do it again, Charlie and I couldn't be together. I wasn't going to change my world and plans for him, and I didn't want him to change his for me. I was going to leave in the morning, and I had to go without any promises because I felt as though if we started something, it would be hard not to carry on. I heard my father's voice in my head. The last time I had seen him for lunch in Exeter, he had told me, despite not being the most effusive father, that he was proud of me because I was focused, had a plan, and that was something he had always wanted for me. *Drive. Ambition. Focus.* Three keywords that defined my father, and he wanted them to define me, too. Sometimes it was hard to see beyond them.

I opened the door and walked the short walk back to Charlie's bedroom. The landing creaked with age and downstairs I could hear Matt and Tom playing video games. The subtle hint of marijuana smoke floated upstairs towards me, while outside the rain continued, and I could hear it furiously hitting the roof. I opened Charlie's door and walked inside, discarding my shirt on the floor, before hopping back into bed again. It was warm, and I quickly fell against Charlie, who instinctively put his arm around me. I cuddled into him, smelling his woody deodorant, our bodies fitted perfectly together.

'What's your plan?' I said.

'What do you mean?'

'After university.'

'Oh, right, that plan. I don't know. History doesn't throw up lots of career choices, to be honest.'

'So, what are you going to do?'

'I know I want to keep living in London. That's about as far as I've got.'

'It doesn't worry you?'

He moved slightly, and we both adjusted our bodies so they could stay together like one of those yin and yang symbols. Curled up together and into each other. Two spoons.

'Not particularly. Something will come up.'

'You mentioned teaching.'

'Maybe.'

Drive. Ambition. Focus.

'I'm definitely going into publishing. It's been my dream for a while. Finish university, go travelling, then work in publishing. It's my five-year plan.'

'Someone's organised.'

'I think you have to be,' I said, feeling his body against mine. 'Otherwise you'll just drift, and who knows where you'll end up. Purpose is the key to happiness, don't you think?'

He reached a hand down and gently caressed my breast. My nipple hardened slightly at his touch, and I felt the urge for him again. I reached across and felt for him with my hand and we both seemed to turn at the same time, and we started kissing. I was tired, but I also knew this was probably the last time it would happen with Charlie. He probably didn't realise it, actually couldn't have realised it, but his insistence that I was perfect had given me something I didn't even know I needed. It was an incredible feeling knowing there was a boy who idolised me and thought I was perfect, and it gave me confidence. Affirmation, I suppose, that I was important to someone in the world. Even if it was only for one night, I would remember him for the rest of my life because he had changed the very core of me.

No. 15

Charlie

P.S. I think you're perfect too

When I opened my eyes, the first thing I did was look across the bed at the spot where Ash should have been. I immediately sat up, rubbing the sleep from my eyes, and that's when I saw the folded-up piece of paper sitting on the pillow. I had imagined her in the morning with unruly hair and perhaps we would have sex again and then breakfast at a cafe, holding hands across a Formica table, knowing smiles and drinking coffee like two people from a romantic comedy. I reached across and unfolded the piece of paper, already knowing that whatever it said, it wouldn't be good news. There weren't many words on the page, and I skimmed them quickly.

> Charlie, thank you for everything. I will never forget you.
> Sorry it has to be this way. A x

That was it. She was gone and I didn't understand what she meant. Why did it have to be this way? The night before had been the greatest night of my life, but yet the morning after was one of the worst. It was gut-wrenching.

I quickly got out of bed, threw on a T-shirt, a pair of jeans, zipping up the fly as I raced downstairs, hoping that by some miracle she hadn't left the house yet or I could catch her at the bus stop. I ran into the kitchen, living room, and there was no sign of her, so I headed outside.

There were puddles on the ground, but it was bright, if not a tad blustery. I ran to the end of the road, my bare feet cold against the pavement, just in time to see a bus pull away. For a moment, I thought about running after it because maybe I could catch it at the next stop, but I didn't. I looked down at my watch, and it was almost nine thirty. She could have left an hour or more ago. I couldn't believe I hadn't heard her wake up. The simple fact was she had chosen to leave without saying goodbye, without talking about the prospect of something more happening between us. I ambled back to the house, closed the front door as Matt came trudging down the stairs in a brown dressing gown.

'There he is!' said Matt, all smiles and cheeky banter. 'Good night, porn star?'

'Yes, it was. The very best.'

'She was properly fit. Didn't know you had it in you, mate.'

'Now you mention it, neither did I.'

'Very nice,' said Matt, disappearing into the kitchen. 'Tea?'

'Please,' I said absently, before I wandered into the lounge, falling despairingly on the sofa.

I lit a cigarette from a packet on the coffee table and thought about Ash and the night we'd had because it was hard to believe in the cold light of morning that it had actually happened. After all this time, it had been perfect. So many times, life disappoints you. You look forward to something and when it eventually happens, it's often not as wonderful as it was in your head, but with Ash, it was. I should have been happy because it had happened, but I think the thing was, it had given me a glimpse into a world I had only ever fantasised about and now all my hopes and dreams were different. You couldn't go back to how things were after a night like that.

Matt walked in with two cups of tea and sat down on the sofa next to me, grabbing a cigarette from the packet, too.

'Are you going to see her again?' he said, lighting his cigarette before he blew three perfect rings of smoke, a party trick he often used to pick up girls.

'I don't know.'

'Why? No offence, mate, but she was way out of your league. Like way, way, way out of your league, in a different sport, on another planet.'

'I know.'

'So, why aren't you seeing her again?'

'It's a long story.'

'That's good because I have all the time in the world,' said Matt, putting his feet up on the coffee table.

I looked at Matt, stubbed out my cigarette before taking a sip of my tea and lighting up another one. Where to begin with Ash Oliver? How could I even begin to tell that story? All I knew at that point in my life was that I was in love with a girl I had just slept with, but that I couldn't be with. A girl I had wanted since the moment I saw her at sixth form, and spent the happiest of times with in Lanzarote. A girl who had cuddled me in bed until we had both fallen asleep and then she had left and said… *Sorry it has to be this way.*

A few hours, five cigarettes and three cups of tea later, I had acclimatised to my new world order. It had been a surreal twenty-four hours, and I needed time to digest, unpack everything and then somehow pack it all back up again. I was still sad and disappointed when I walked into my room and slumped on the bed that still smelled of her. Her perfume, a hint of floral sweetness and something else I couldn't describe. Musk? Was that even a thing? I put my hand on the sheets for a moment as if I could somehow by feeling them still feel a little bit of her. I lay there for a moment, fleeting memories of the night before rushing through my head, then I saw the note I had thrown down in my haste. I picked it up, read it again, and then I casually turned it over and there was something written on the back I hadn't seen the first time. I sat up quickly and read it to myself, and then I read it again.

P.S. I think you're perfect too

2007·

No. 16

Ash

Across the platform

I had finally moved to London when I landed my dream job as an assistant at a publishing house in Blackfriars. After my year of travelling, which had turned into almost eighteen months, I hadn't had any luck finding a job on my return. I rather wilted at home, living with my parents again, which was quite a shock to the system after the freedom of university and my gap year. I scoured *The Guardian* newspaper daily for jobs in the publishing world, willing to do anything to get my foot in the door, but I was beginning to worry I would end up a failure. It was six months after I returned home when I finally got the phone call and then moved to London. The weight was finally lifted.

I was living in a flatshare in Putney with Edith, a girl from Devon, who seemed to be perpetually congested and lived off tea and Marmite toast. She also worked in publishing and my adult life was finally what I imagined it might be: working hard, having fun, a small but close-knit group of friends like something from a television show about twenty-somethings attempting to navigate life and love in the city. Imagine *Sex and the City* but transferred to London and with far less sex. The heady days of university and travelling, throwing off the last shackles of childhood, were over and I was embracing a new adult phase of my life.

I had just been to Westminster to meet a friend for lunch, and I was on my way back to the office, standing on the busy platform of the Underground station waiting for the next Tube to arrive. It was early April, and I was in a pair of trousers with a shirt, cardigan and a heavy coat. I also had a navy scarf loosely wrapped around my neck, my big handbag over my shoulder, and I was waiting for a Tube with everyone else, packed together like sardines behind an invisible line.

I casually glanced across the tracks at the other platform with a similar line of people all waiting for the next Tube going in the opposite direction. I heard the familiar gust of wind and the noise of metal on metal, and then a Tube rushed into the station on the other platform. I watched the flurry of people getting off and on, and then I glanced at the sign on our side. The next eastbound Circle Line train would be there in four minutes. I heard the doors on the Tube opposite close, then it started off again, quickly gathering speed, before disappearing into the black hole of the Underground.

I looked across at the new line of people on the platform. The Tube had dumped off a gaggle of brand-new passengers and I was scanning the crowd, when my eyes stopped because standing on the platform across from me was Charlie. I hadn't seen him since that magical night we'd had together at his student house. Could it really have been almost four years ago? He looked so different from the boy I had left in bed that morning, still fast asleep on his back, both arms over his head. He was wearing a grey suit, his red hair was smartly parted on one side, and he looked so much more grown-up. He was obviously listening to music because two white cords led from his pocket to his ears, and he was tapping his feet.

I didn't know what to do. I looked up at my train sign. *Two minutes!* I didn't know how to get his attention because he hadn't seen me, and he obviously couldn't hear me. I thought quickly and only one thing came to mind. I would look absolutely ridiculous, but it was something I had to do because I desperately wanted to see him again. So, as I waited on the platform with a hundred other people behind the invisible line,

I started waving my arms in the air, trying to get his attention. I looked utterly ridiculous, but I didn't care. I wouldn't see these people again, and it was London, we were used to the occasional oddball on the Underground and today that oddball just happened to be me. I was waving my arms about, and I started jumping up and down. *One minute!* The people next to me were slowly edging away, and then it happened. The man standing next to Charlie looked at me, and I caught his eye.

'Can you poke the man next to you?' I shouted across the train tracks, gesticulating wildly with my arms and hands. The man looked at me and I could only imagine his thoughts. He pointed to Charlie. 'Yes! Just poke him. Please!'

The man gently patted Charlie on the arm, Charlie looked at the man, and then the man pointed across the tracks at me. Charlie finally looked across and that's when he saw me. I was still waving my arms around like an absolute idiot. Charlie smiled, and I smiled back as I felt the gust of wind as my Tube approached. Charlie and I both realised at the same time, and he put his hand up as if to say, *Stop, don't move!* And I breathed a sigh of relief as my Tube pulled in front of me.

No. 17

Charlie

Hey Jude

I was looking at Ash, who was sitting across the table from me in St Stephen's Tavern, the nearest pub to the Tube station. It was hard to comprehend that after all this time we were together again. The last time I had seen her was in my bed before that awful morning when she left without saying goodbye. The note on the pillow next to me.

> *Charlie, thank you for everything. I will never forget you.*
> *Sorry it has to be this way. A x*

So much had happened since then, it felt like a lifetime ago: graduation, getting a job, moving house and, of course, there was Mia.

'I was listening to the Beatles,' I said.

'Still a huge fan?'

'The biggest.'

'What's your favourite Beatles song?'

'You can't ask that. There's too many to pick just one.'

'But if you had to? Life or death.'

She still looked incredible. Her hair was shorter, cut into a bob with some lighter strands running through it. She was dressed smartly for her new career in publishing, and she looked so grown-up compared to the girl I remembered. Twenty-four years old, and she was exactly how she should be: beautiful, successful, travelled, and once again I had the thought that despite how much I wanted her, I didn't stand a chance.

I was working in a generic office job, an administrative assistant for a marketing company that mostly involved editing spreadsheets, answering telephone calls, and making sure the stationery cupboard was fully stocked. It wasn't a career by any stretch of the imagination, didn't pay anywhere near enough for London, but felt easy enough that I still had time during the day to imagine all the better jobs I could be doing. I still didn't know what I wanted to do long-term, and my lack of a plan had left me high and dry on a career plateau, waiting and hoping that something would come along. I felt somewhat lost, and Ash was travelling faster than me, passing me by, and she would keep going faster and faster until she would end up where she was destined to be all along.

'If I had to pick one,' I said, taking a sip of my pint.

'For *Desert Island Discs*.'

'But don't you get eight choices for *Desert Island Discs*?'

'You do.'

'I can have eight Beatles songs then.'

'But you're only allowed one Beatles song on my *Desert Island Discs*.'

'Fine,' I said, racking my brains. I had spent years trying to pick one Beatles song as my favourite and it had constantly changed. For a while it was 'While My Guitar Gently Weeps' and then it was 'A Day In The Life', but if she wanted one at that particular moment, then…

'"Hey Jude".'

'I love "Hey Jude",' said Ash, then she looked across the table at me and smiled a thin, slightly sad smile. 'I'm sorry about the morning after our night together.'

'Me, too.'

'It wasn't the right time for so many reasons. I knew that if I had stayed, it would have been too complicated, and I wasn't ready for something like that at that stage of my life, but it was, and still is, one of the best nights of my life.'

'Me, too, by an absolute mile.'

It was impossible to look at her without thinking and imagining all the versions of her I knew. The girl I had first seen in the sixth form refectory. The girl I had rubbed sun cream on in Lanzarote. The girl I had spent the night with at university. Looking across at her at that moment, she was different in a myriad of ways, but still so much the same. I had changed, too. Moving from university into office life felt like I was finally leaving my childhood behind, and then, of course, I had met Mia. Our relationship was still very much in its infancy, but it had changed me. I liked Mia and we were more alike than Ash and me. Mia was from a working-class family from Manchester. Her dad, like mine, worked in factories, and after getting her degree from the University of Birmingham, she was in London trying to make it in the media. She was currently a receptionist at a production company in Soho, but was ambitious and had a steely, working-class determination. Mia was happy, hopeful, and she made me feel the same. The only thing she wasn't, of course, was Ash.

Ash and I stood outside of the pub, and it was time to leave. It had been incredible seeing her again, and despite everything, I still felt the pull of attraction that lingered between us.

'Please tell me you have a phone now,' said Ash with a delicious smile.

'I do.'

'I thought you said they "weren't going to take off", were your actual words, I believe?'

'Quite clearly, I was wrong.'

'Does this mean we can exchange numbers and keep in touch properly this time?'

'Definitely.'

'Because I don't have the largest circle of friends in London, and I'd like to think of you as a friend, Charlie Talbot.'

'Always, Ash Oliver,' I said, then we took our phones out and exchanged numbers, and in that moment, I knew I had to break up with Mia. It wasn't because I thought I had a chance with Ash, but I had to give it a go. For the first time in our lives, we were in the same place, potentially single, and perhaps with the chance of being together, and whether it worked or not, I had to try. Ash and I started walking back towards the Tube together.

'If I ever get married, I'd have "Hey Jude" play as we walk out of the church,' I said.

'That sounds like it would be quite the wedding.'

'It's just an idea.'

We kept walking, and as we did, I could hear 'Hey Jude' in my head, and I imagined walking down the aisle with Ash. As we walked towards the Tube station, I knew I had to end things with Mia, and soon. The last thing I wanted to do was hurt her, but sometimes in life the stars aligned, fate intervened, and you couldn't let the opportunity pass.

No. 18

Ash

What a view

The publishing house I worked for was in a modern, open-plan office block overlooking the Thames in Blackfriars, and from the moment I started working there, I adored it. The ambience was bookish, intellectual and relaxed, exactly how I had hoped it would be. Cake was often delivered to the office via some means and every Friday morning there was a coffee run. The best thing apart from the friends I had made and meeting the occasional famous author was the view over the Thames. We were near the top of the building, and I would often gaze across the river, watching the boats carrying tourists to the Tower of London or back towards Westminster. I could see the OXO Tower and the Millennium Wheel, and on clear days, Tower Bridge. I had always dreamed of having a career I was excited to wake up for, something to really excel in, and, in publishing, I had found it.

It was the end of another long week, and time to head off home. We had just put the clocks forward, so it was still relatively light outside, which felt thrilling after months of walking home in wintry darkness. It felt warmer, too, as though the brightness of summer was on the horizon, and there was an air of optimism in the office. I was walking out of the building with Callie, another girl who had joined around the same time as me, and Harriet, a senior editor. We were approaching the large revolving doors that exited the building when I noticed a familiar face loitering around outside.

Once outside, I said good night to Callie and Harriet, and I walked across to Charlie.

'Fancy seeing you here,' I said with a smile. 'Outside my work.'

'Pure coincidence,' replied Charlie.

'Really?'

'No, of course not,' he said, looking at me, a slightly nervous smile on his lips. 'Do you have a spare hour or two?'

'Umm, yes, why?'

'No questions,' said Charlie, who suddenly grabbed me by the hand, and soon we were walking across Blackfriars Bridge together. I tried asking him again exactly where we were going but he wouldn't tell me, and instead told me that all would be revealed soon. It was all very mysterious.

Eventually, after a short walk along the South Bank, we stopped in front of the Millennium Wheel.

'Have you ever been?' asked Charlie.

I didn't know what to say. 'Umm, no, actually.'

'Then tonight is your lucky night.'

'But don't we have to book or something—'

'All taken care of,' said Charlie with a smile. 'This way, madam.'

I couldn't believe what was happening, and perhaps more importantly, why? It had been wonderful seeing him again yesterday, and I had planned on seeing him again soon, but not like that and certainly not on the Millennium Wheel. I had often thought about going on it, but I hadn't wanted to do it alone, Edith was terrified of heights, and so I was waiting for the right moment with the right person or people.

After waiting in a short queue, we eventually walked into one of the pods, and we began our journey. Thirty minutes of some of the best views in London. We had to share the pod with twenty other people, but it was large, and we walked to the front of the pod and looked out as we got gradually higher and higher. I looked across the river, and in the distance I could see my office block.

'So, Charlie,' I finally said, looking across at him. 'What's this about?'

'This is something I have wanted to do since I moved to London, and I have never done it. I have walked by so many times, almost done it, but for some reason, I just haven't.'

We were almost at the top of the wheel now, and the views didn't disappoint. We could see all across London and beyond. It felt surreal to be there so unexpectedly with Charlie.

'So, why now?'

'Because,' said Charlie, turning to face me. 'When I saw you yesterday, I knew I would have to ask you out on a date. It's you and me, Ash. When you left me at university, I was gutted, and honestly, I never thought I'd see you again, but then when I saw you jumping up and down at the Tube station, I couldn't believe it. I have always liked you, Ash, you know that, and whether or not I have a chance with you, I don't know, but I knew I had to give it a shot. Then I thought, where do you ask out the girl of your dreams? At the top of the world because that's how I feel when I'm with you, and this was the closest thing I could think of. Oh, god, is that the cheesiest thing anyone has ever said?'

I laughed. 'No, I think it's perfect, actually.'

'So, Ash, what do you say?'

We were at the very top of the wheel now, and despite the pod containing enough people for a decent-sized dinner party, it felt like it was just us. I looked at Charlie, and he looked so handsome in his work suit, his tie loosened after a day in the office, his hair slightly messy, and he looked so nervous. I felt a sudden frisson of warmth and love for him that had perhaps always been there to some degree but was now stronger than ever. There was definitely something between us I couldn't explain and, for one reason or another, we had never quite made it, but now was our opportunity. It was time to grab our chance and see where it might go. He hadn't needed to take me on the Millennium Wheel because I would have said yes if he had asked me at the pub, but I loved that he had. It showed me what sort of person he was, and how much he wanted me. I took a step forward until I was right in front of Charlie, looking deep into his sparkling blue eyes, at his red hair, and I knew I wanted him.

'Yes,' I said, before I leaned in and kissed him, there at the very top of the Millennium Wheel, and this was how *I* suddenly became *we*.

No. 19

Charlie

Sleeping on a hard wooden floor

Matt and I were living in a two-bed flat in Finsbury Park that was advertised as 'compact and bijou' but was, in fact, just fucking tiny. After university, Tom went off travelling and then, on his return, moved to Leeds, and so it was just me and Matt. Matt had a job working at a bank in the city and was doing well, although was hardly home due to the long hours and the hedonistic nights out, which seemed mandatory in the world of high finance. He had his degree in accounting and business and was determined to make lots of money so he could, in his own words, 'drive nice cars and pick up girls'. Matt's ambitions were limited, but I suppose at least somewhat achievable.

'This is the girl from Tattenhall Road?' said Matt.

'Yes,' I said in front of the mirror in our bathroom that was barely big enough for one, and definitely not two.

'The fit one you shagged before she absconded in the morning like a modern-day Cinderella, leaving nothing behind but a note and a broken heart?'

'I wouldn't exactly put it like that, but yes.'

'And she agreed to this date?'

'She did. Now, how do I look?' I said, turning to face Matt.

Ever since the moment Ash agreed to the date, I had been obsessed over every tiny detail in the hope I wasn't going to completely mess it up. This was the chance I had waited for since sixth form and I wasn't going to blow it. I spent ages picking out the right outfit and had decided to go casual on the bottom with a pair of blue jeans, but I had on my brown brogues, so it gave the jeans a slightly more formal look. I had opted for a navy shirt, and over that, my long black peacoat.

'Yeah, you look all right. You just need one more thing.'

'And what's that?'

'Sex spray!' said Matt, reaching across, grabbing his bottle of Hugo Boss Eau de Toilette, and liberally spraying it on me. 'Trust me, one whiff of this and she'll have her legs in the air faster than a pole vaulter on crack!'

'Not exactly what I was going for but thanks. Right, I'm off!'

'Good luck, mate,' said Matt, and then he gave me a quick fist bump and a sturdy pat on the back as I left our flat, and headed into central London.

I stood outside of the pub in Soho we had agreed to meet at and I didn't know if it was the cold weather or my nerves that were barely hanging on by a thread, but I found myself shivering a little. After I broke up with Mia – which I felt terribly guilty about, but I didn't want to string her along knowing how I felt about Ash – I quickly concocted the Millennium Wheel plan. I knew I had to do something big, make a statement, and thankfully it worked, and she had kissed me. She had plans later that night with her flatmate, Edith, and so we agreed on tonight for our first proper date. I gave myself a little pep talk because this was Ash Oliver, and I needed to calm my nerves. I took one final deep breath and then I walked in, and there she was sitting at a table, drinking a glass of wine.

'Is this seat taken?' I said.

'It is now,' she said with a smile.

I offered to get her a drink, but her glass was still quite full, so I got myself a beer and then sat opposite her. She looked absolutely stunning in a green dress that matched the colour of her eyes, her hair was swept up in a ponytail that showed off her long, slender neck, and vintage silver earrings hung from her perfect ears.

'I'm so glad you kissed me yesterday,' I said.

'It was a close call.'

'Really?'

'No, not really. It was never in question,' said Ash with a coquettish grin, and then she looked at me and I looked back at her, and the something that had always been there between us was stronger and more potent than ever.

It was hard to believe the girl I saw in the college refectory all those years ago, whom I always thought was too good for me, was sitting opposite me and we were on a date in Soho. We talked, had another drink, and time seemed to not really exist. We left the pub and went to the Italian restaurant I had booked, which was only a few minutes' walk away. The conversation flowed effortlessly, the food was superb and afterwards we wandered around Central London lost in the moment and each other.

We walked hand in hand through Soho, Covent Garden, and eventually we got the Tube back to her flat in Putney. I was south of the river, a long way from home, and it was late. The dark night sky was littered with stars like tiny diamonds on a black canvas. We stood outside of the Victorian house where her flat was, and upstairs a light was on. People walked past as we held hands, and neither of us could stop smiling.

'I've thought long and hard about this,' said Ash. 'I could invite you in, we could sleep together, and just go with it.'

'I really love the sound of that plan, but I sense an or coming?'

'Or we could take our time. I know we already slept together, Charlie, but I really want this relationship to work, and so I think we need to slow down and let it grow organically.'

'I agree.'

'Really? You agree to take things slowly, even if it means not having sex right away?'

'Ash, I want this to work, too, and whatever makes it work is what I want,' I said, feeling her hands in mine that were a little cold.

'Then this is good night, Charlie Talbot.'

'Or.'

'Or?' she replied with a curious smile.

'I could come in for a coffee, not sleep with you, but spend the night on the floor and then tomorrow we could spend the day together in London doing something fun. If that's what you want because otherwise I'll head off home and return first thing, and we can still spend the day together. I just thought it might be romantic.'

She looked at me and smiled. 'You really want to sleep on my hard wooden floor? I don't have much extra bedding, and there's a spider I've been trying to kill for ages, but I can't seem to catch the little bugger.'

'It could be the hardest floor with no bedding, and literally infested with arachnids, and I would still want it more than anything in the world.'

She smiled but didn't say another word. She let go of one of my hands, held the other, and she walked me towards the front door and up the stairs that led to the flat. Edith had gone home for the weekend, so we had the whole place to ourselves. We got to her bedroom door and then she turned, looked at me, smiled, and then she kissed me. I felt at that moment like the luckiest man in the entire world. Just getting to sleep on Ash's bedroom floor was better than any bed, no matter how comfortable, because it was close to her and that was all I wanted to be.

No. 20

Ash

Relationships like IKEA furniture

When I was eight, I fell over and cut my knee. I don't remember much about the incident, but according to Mum, I was cycling down a hill on my bicycle one moment and then the next I was on the floor crying, blood dripping from a gash on my knee. She immediately took me to the local doctor's surgery and the nurse dressed the wound. I limped out of the surgery with a strawberry lolly and a story to tell, and I've had a small scar ever since. The small scar Charlie was now feeling with his fingers.

It was a bright, warm day, and we were at the top of Greenwich Park, looking out over London. I was in a dress for the first time that year, and it felt good to feel the sunshine on my skin and to have Charlie with me. The night before, he had kept to his word and slept on the floor next to my bed, although I think we were both quite tempted to ignore my little speech and jump right to the bit when we had sex. It was actually quite romantic with him on the floor, and me in bed. We talked late into the night, our voices in the dark, laughing, and asking each other questions about our lives and loves, delving deeper than we ever had before, until eventually we both drifted off to sleep.

In the morning, we went for breakfast at the cafe I had been going to ever since I moved to Putney. We had a lovely breakfast of eggs Benedict, lots of coffee, and then we headed into London and took the ferry to Greenwich. It was something

I hadn't done before, but when I explained to Charlie how I would sit at my desk and idly watch the boats drift by, he said we had to do it. Tourists for the day! When we floated slowly by my office, I looked up and found the window I looked out of during the week.

'Do you have any scars?' I said, casually running my hand along the grass next to me. I had always loved the feeling of grass. It reminded me of school playing fields.

'Physical no. Emotional, probably,' said Charlie. 'I think I was over-protected as a child. Only-child syndrome. Mum was always quite a cautious person, still is, and I think that's probably why I'm quite risk-averse now. Her fears bled into me. What about you?'

'Where do I start?' I said and then left a pause.

'How is your relationship with your parents now?' said Charlie after a moment.

'Fine, I suppose. They still bicker like children, but despite everything, they're still somehow together. What about your family? Any skeletons in the Talbot closet?'

'Not much to tell. Dad has worked in factories for most of his life, still does. Mum didn't work much when I was small but has been a receptionist at a doctor's surgery for a few years now. Fairly ordinary childhood. Small house, small world, camping holidays, mostly.'

I looked out across London for a moment at the view, which was spectacular. The vivid green grass of the park sloped down towards the brilliant white of the National Maritime Museum and then, beyond that, the murky waters of the Thames and Canary Wharf that jutted into the sky like a vast series of mountain peaks. People were dotted about the park, enjoying the sun, and the whole day had a sort of clarity about it. It meant something, and I knew it.

'Do you ever miss living there?' I asked.

'Southampton? No, you?'

'Not really. I think I always wanted to get out, and all the publishers are in London.'

78

'You can be honest with me,' said Charlie, and then he looked across at me with an adorable smile. 'You followed me here, didn't you?'

'Fine, you got me. I only moved here to be with you,' I said, and we both laughed. Silly, youthful, carefree laughter. 'It was super hard manufacturing the day we met on the Tube station platform. Lots of stalking, obviously.'

'Obviously.'

We moved to fill the small space between us, and I rested my head on his chest. I felt his heartbeat as his chest moved me slowly up and then down. I didn't know what time it was, and I didn't care. It was that sort of day. The sun shone on our faces, and we lay knitted together on the grass, silently enjoying the moment, and then from somewhere nearby, music started playing and the voices of people infiltrated our little bubble. We were in our own little world, and nothing was going to upset the balance or disrupt its ecosystem.

From the moment I kissed him on the Millennium Wheel, life seemed to go on automatic pilot. Everything happened so instinctively, that neither of us even questioned it. We went along with it, enjoying every moment of the most wonderful day when time seemed to stand still, and we got to truly appreciate what we were doing as we were doing it. It was one of the rarest things: a relationship that seemed to arrive fully formed and ready to go.

Before Charlie, all my other attempts at relationships were flat-packed like IKEA furniture. I had to unpack the boxes, go through the little bags for all the pieces, read the instructions carefully then go through them step by step, hoping I wasn't doing it wrong, and hoping something wouldn't go wrong, and without fail something would, and there would be pieces left at the end and you would never know how vital they were. Tightening screws with Allen keys, hoping that when it was done it wouldn't look completely rubbish. But with Charlie, it was like getting something bespoke and delivered that was perfect right away and you didn't have to read the instructions because they weren't needed. It felt solid, reliable and like something built to last.

No. 21

Charlie

Three simple words

It was a Saturday night, and I was sleeping over at Ash's flat again, which had become something of a recurring theme in our relationship. We had been dating for four months, and I would stay over at her flat for days on end, only returning home to catch up on sleep, wash clothes and make sure Matt was still alive. Ash didn't sleep over at mine often because her flat was nicer, larger and smelled lovely, while my flat was messy, cramped and smelled like Matt. Edith had a thing for fresh flowers, so the flat always had a natural floral scent, and Putney was more pleasing on the eye than the worst part of Finsbury Park where I lived with Matt. Although, the main reason I stayed at Ash's was that her bed was bigger and far more comfortable than mine. When she had moved in, her parents had bought her a brand-new double bed from John Lewis, whereas my bed had a terrible mattress that, despite being so small, still somehow sank in the middle, and you could feel the springs beneath, so it was like sleeping on a cheese grater.

Ash and I had been lying in bed browsing the channels on television, but all I could think about were my feelings towards her. I knew we hadn't been dating for long, but I loved her. I had known I was in love with her from day one, but the problem was, you couldn't say the words so early in a relationship, could you? I knew she liked me, but I wasn't sure if she loved me,

and if I said it too early and she didn't say it back, it would be mortifying. I had trapped myself into a love corner. On one hand, I knew I had to say it, but on the other, the overwhelming fear that those same three words I felt in every sinew of my body could also be the same three words that would break us apart. There were moments when I felt like she wanted to say it, too, but how could I know? So, I stayed in my corner, pretending everything was fine when all I could think was…
BUT I FUCKING LOVE YOU!

She was in her pyjamas with the sailboats on that made her look adorable, in the crook of my arm, looking up at me, her slightly damp hair that smelled of coconut and vanilla lying against my shoulder. I looked down at her and the words which had been gathering speed the past few weeks were itching to escape.

'What should we do tomorrow? It's supposed to be warm,' said Ash. 'We could take a walk by the river, go to a pub for lunch, and I don't want to be the purveyor of bad news, but my parents have mentioned wanting to meet you. I don't know why I told them about you yet because I knew they'd want to meet you, which is fine, but it's my parents. They can be difficult, and I don't know, it's just something that—'

'I love you.'

The words came out while she was talking like gunshots in the dead of night, creating a sudden vacuum of tension that seemed to envelop everything in the room. It had felt like the words were becoming bigger and bigger in my mouth, and it was at the point when I had to let them out before I couldn't breathe. Ash instantly sat up in bed and looked at me. There was a pause, and we both looked at each other before she said, 'Say it again.'

'Ash, I love you. I know it's soon to be saying it out loud, but I do, and I can't keep not saying it when it's all I want to say to you every—'

'I love you, too!'

'You do?'

'I was just waiting for you to say it first,' she said, then giggled.

'I was waiting because I was worried I'd say it and you'd say something back like "Thank you" or "You're smothering me, you fucking knobhead" and it would ruin things between us, and things are so good. I didn't want to wreck everything with I love you.'

'Oh, Charlie.'

'Love you.'

'Love you, too.'

Then she sank back into me again, her head on my shoulder, and I felt her body in my arms. Her body in those pyjamas with the little sailboats on. She was the first girl I had said the L-word to, and the first girl who had said it back. The words that had been on the tip of my tongue were now back inside of my body, filling my heart with even more love.

'So, what now?' I said after a few minutes.

'What do you mean?'

'It feels like such a big thing to tell someone you love them. We did it and now it feels like we should celebrate.'

'Charlie, you are a funny boy. Is there something you would like to do to celebrate?'

I thought for a moment and then it came to me in a blinding flash of inspiration. When I was twelve, I went to Brighton for the day with my parents. We didn't go to the beach often, and it was a wonderful day that even now was clear and succinct in my mind. We sat on the beach by the pier and ate fish and chips, while trying to keep the giant seagulls at bay, walked The Lanes browsing the eclectic shops, and played games on Palace Pier, sinking two-pence pieces into the classic pushers. I remember Dad playing the Beatles in the car, and I think it was the first time I understood why he loved them so much. I don't know if it was just my age or the day we had in Brighton, but it was the day I fell in love with them. Somehow my love of the Beatles and Brighton had been intrinsically linked ever since, and so it felt right I would take Ash there, and perhaps all the love could overlap like some sort of Venn diagram.

No. 22

Ash

Who is going to make you better?

Charlie and I were standing in front of my parents' house on a dull, grey Saturday afternoon, and I was dreading going inside. The last time I had spoken to Dad about Charlie, his first question hadn't been *What's he like?* or *Does he make you happy?* but *How much money does he earn?* Obviously, this was a problem, as Charlie didn't have a proper career or a plan for one. I was rather hoping Charlie might win Dad over with his personality and obvious love for me, although as we stood outside my childhood home, I had my doubts because, whether I agreed with the charges or not, I knew Charlie was on trial.

'Ready?' I said stiffly.

'As I'll ever be,' said Charlie, and so I pushed the doorbell and we waited.

I knew my father in particular intimidated Charlie. Charlie had grown up in far less salubrious surroundings than me, and it was something I didn't care about, but I knew it bothered him. We waited and finally the front door opened, and my father was standing there, and just behind him, Mum, in a long black dress.

'Ashley, darling,' said Dad.

'Hello, Dad,' I said, walking into his arms. He gave me one of his hugs, enveloping me in the folds of his linen suit jacket. Even on the weekends, he wore shirts, jackets and trousers, minus the weekday tie. After I pulled away, I gave my mother a hug and a kiss, before they both looked towards Charlie.

'You must be Charlie,' said Dad. 'Come in.'

'It's a pleasure to meet you,' said Charlie, shaking Dad's hand. 'Although we have met before. Lanzarote, two thousand. I was there with my parents.'

We looked at my parents, who seemed like they were trying to remember, but clearly they had little recollection of Charlie, or perhaps the holiday at all.

'Oh, yes, right, of course,' said Mum unconvincingly.

I watched Charlie's face as we walked inside, and I could tell he was nervous. I found his vulnerability adorable, but I knew my father would only see a point of weakness. Dad came from money, a history of wealth and privilege, and he was a barrister. He was an expert at reading people and knowing how to destroy them if needed. We walked through into the large, newly fitted kitchen.

'Drink, Charlie?' said Dad, wandering off towards an elaborate drinks trolley.

'Charlie will have a whisky,' I said quickly.

'Oh, lovely,' said Mum. 'I'll have a martini!'

I knew Charlie didn't drink whisky, but it was all my father drank. It was how he judged men: schooling, career prospects and choice of alcohol.

'What do you want to drink, darling?' Mum asked me with a spirited New Year's Eve celebratory voice, but I declined because I was driving and wanted to keep my wits about me.

'Whisky man, eh?' Dad said to Charlie, a subtle look of distrust on his face.

'Yes! Love the stuff, can't get enough,' said Charlie, before he realised how that might sound and added quickly, 'not that I'm an alcoholic or anything like that. I just meant—'

'That he appreciates a good single malt,' I said, jumping in to save him.

'Good man,' said Dad, passing Charlie a tumbler full of whisky. No ice. *Never fucking ice!* 'Single malt. Ten years from the Scottish island of Islay. Bottoms up.'

'Bottoms up,' replied Charlie tentatively.

Dad took a sip of his whisky, and you could tell how much he loved it. His entire face melted with pleasure. I looked across at Charlie, who had downed his whole glass in one go. Dad didn't look impressed because you were supposed to sip it and savour the complexity of the flavours and the smoothness of it. Memories of being a girl and in trouble with my father shot through my mind. There was an awkward pause, while Charlie blushed red from either embarrassment or from the whisky, I couldn't tell.

'So, are we eating here or going out?' I said, breaking through the sudden layer of uncomfortableness in the room.

'I was thinking about ordering a takeaway. Is that okay, darling?' said Mum. 'I thought about cooking, but your father said he didn't want me in the kitchen the whole time.'

'No point in meeting Ashley's boyfriend, if you're stashed away in the kitchen like the hired help,' grumbled Dad.

'I think it's perfect,' I replied quickly, before my parents started taking potshots at each other. 'Where are the menus?'

Mum walked across to a cupboard and retrieved a pile of different takeaway menus. We had a choice of various foods from Indian, Chinese to pizza, or just old-fashioned fish and chips. In the end, we decided to go for an Indian, and we sat around the kitchen island, jotting down our order, until we were done, and then Mum rang it through.

'Ashley tells me you work in an office,' said Dad.

The witness cross-examination was under way.

'I do, yes,' replied Charlie.

'What sort of business is it?'

'It's a marketing and advertising company.'

'And is that what you want to do, Charlie? Marketing and advertising?'

'Well, no, not really.'

'Ashley says you got your degree in history,' said Mum, jumping in enthusiastically.

'I did.'

'Then why aren't you doing something with history?' said Dad pointedly.

'I might. I haven't really, you know, decided what I want to do long-term.'

'Then you need to think about it, Charlie, because let me tell you something I told Ashley. One problem with being young is you think you have all the time in the world, but you don't. If you don't have a plan, if you aren't ambitious, driven, focused, then you're going to be a failure. Don't be a failure, Charlie, because Ashley can't marry a failure.'

'Right, yes, of course,' mumbled Charlie uncomfortably.

It was painful listening to my father pull Charlie apart, and I recoiled in embarrassment at the mention of marriage, but I had to let it go because Charlie had to learn how to deal with him. Dad had the ability to turn most people into quivering wrecks, and poor Charlie didn't have the confidence to deal with it. Charlie hadn't grown up in the same world as my father, so he didn't know what it was to be like him. Men with nothing to fear because failure was never an option because no matter what mistakes they made they always had the safety net of privilege to fall back on. One of the things I had always loved about Charlie was that he was vulnerable. He didn't have the confidence of men like my father, but that gave me something to work with because he didn't have all the answers. Men like my father were solid, unbendable, but with Charlie, we felt like equals.

Charlie went off to use the toilet, and while he was gone, I had to say something.

'I know he's not what you want for me, Dad, but I really like him. He makes me happy.'

'Ashley,' said Dad, looking at me with his deep, dark eyes. Sometimes it was hard to tell whether he was my father or a barrister, and perhaps he never quite knew himself. 'Happiness is one thing and so many things can make you happy, but don't be fooled into thinking that happiness is what's most important in a relationship because it isn't. One day you'll wake up and realise you're too good for him, that he's held you back, and then you're going to feel bitter about it. A relationship can only last when the couple makes each other better, not when one of them drags the other one up. If you spend your life making him better, who is going to make you better?'

'How about me? I can make myself better!' I said, louder and more aggressively than I had intended. I heard a noise and, when I turned around, Charlie was standing there looking deeply uncomfortable, and then we heard the front doorbell ring, and our food had arrived.

No. 23

Charlie

You are definitely not going to die

'I'm dying,' mumbled Ash.

She was in bed covered in a mountain of blankets, her unwashed hair a mess, red-faced, and she looked terrible, but she definitely wasn't going to die. She just had the flu.

'You're not going to die, Ash.'

'I'm going to die in December, just before Christmas. It's so unfair.'

She had felt poorly at the beginning of the week and like a trooper had kept going, but it had gradually worsened and now she was in bed with the full-blown flu. Body aches, chills, congested to the point when no matter how much she blew, nothing significant came out, a temperature, and she had been in bed for the past three days. I had been supplying her with medicine, soup, and in return she occasionally told me she was dying and that I should inform her nearest and dearest.

It was bitterly cold outside, and from the bedroom window all I could see were bare trees and frost on the ground. People dashed past wrapped in thick winter coats while in Ash's room it was warm and smelled of Vicks. She was asleep and I was reading a book, my feet up on the bottom of her bed.

I enjoyed watching her sleep. The way she looked without make-up, without her hair being done, in her pyjamas, tucked up tight in bed. I loved it because she was letting me and only me into her private world. I remembered back at sixth form when I dreamed about her just knowing my name but now I was her person. I was the one man she let into her world, and she wasn't afraid to show me everything – the good, the bad and the very sick. I watched her sleeping, dreaming, and when she woke up dazed and disorientated, I stroked her hair and told her it was okay before she fell asleep again, mumbling incoherently. I got back to my book while the noise of Ash breathing deeply filled the room and, outside, the cold air whipped around the flat, but we were safe in our eucalyptus-and-menthol cocoon.

'I'm feeling a little better,' said Ash, waking up.

'Can I get you something?' I replied, looking at her in the bed. She smiled, then patted the bed for me to sit down next to her.

'Thank you for taking care of me and for not being completely disgusted with the amount of snotty tissues next to the bed.'

'I love the pile of snotty tissues.'

'Move in with me,' she said suddenly.

'What?'

'Move in with me, Charlie.'

'Are you sure you're okay?' I said, putting the back of my hand on her forehead and checking for a temperature.

'I'm being serious. Move in here with me.'

The thought had crossed my mind, too, but I was worried it was too soon. Things between us had been going so well, and I had even survived meeting her terrifying father. Why upset the applecart when it had been doing so well.

'Are you sure? You aren't just saying it because your brain has been addled by the flu?'

'I'm sure, Charlie. I'm addle-free. I want to live together.'

It felt almost impossible that I was going to live with Ash. From the moment I saw her at sixth form, the height of my desire then had been for her to just know my name. In Lanzarote, the idea of us sharing a simple kiss was beyond my wildest expectations, and now, we were going to live together in London. It was truly monumental like a life-long dream that had finally become a reality.

'Then yes!' I said, and for the first time in four days, I went to kiss her.

'I think I probably need to brush my teeth first,' said Ash with a smile.

'I don't care. I love you, stinky breath or not,' I said, and then I leaned in and kissed her, in the flat we would soon be sharing.

2008

No. 24

Ash

The restaurant you could never get reservations for

It was one of those restaurants you heard about on the grapevine. Overheard conversation on the Tube or in the kitchen at work while you made a cup of tea and caught up on all the latest gossip. They were featured in weekend supplements, were the talk of the town and everyone wanted to eat there. It might only last a few months until the bubble burst and a newer, trendier restaurant came along, but during those few months it was almost impossible to get a table, and yet I had managed to snag one. Admittedly, it was near the toilets and seemed to be in the way of just about everything, but as Charlie walked towards me, I felt quite thrilled about it. It was silly, but I felt as though I had finally arrived in London.

'This place is a bit trendy,' said Charlie after he had sat down. 'And it looks expensive.'

'Correct on both counts, but it doesn't matter because I have some news,' I said, brimming with excitement. 'I got a promotion. As of today, I'm officially an assistant editor!'

'That's brilliant, Ash,' Charlie replied, leaning across the table and kissing me.

It had been an incredible day at work. It had started off as just another normal day: coffee, emails, morning meeting, etcetera, until just before lunch, when I was called into Helen's office. Helen was the commissioning editor for women's fiction. I sat down and she explained that one of the current assistant editors had accepted a job at another publishing house, and I was being promoted. It was a big step up for me and the chance I had been waiting for ever since I had started working there.

'I finally get to build my own list of authors and I'll be working closely with Tim—'

'Tim?'

'Tim Pearson. He came across from another publishing house. He's brilliant, Charlie. Such an incredible eye for new talent.'

'You haven't mentioned him before.'

'He only started a few weeks ago. You'll probably get to meet him at some point. Luckily for him, he's married because all the girls in the office think he's very attractive.'

'And you don't?'

I detected something in his voice. It caught slightly before he spoke and, when I looked at him, he had an expression I hadn't seen before. His face was tense and there was a wrinkle above his eyes, and his mouth was ever so slightly pinched. He looked like he wanted to say something, but it was trapped inside of him, pushed down under the layers of his skin so no one would even know it was there. But I did.

'He's handsome, but not as handsome as you, obviously. Anyway, I've seen a photo of his wife and she's absolutely stunning. Tall, Swedish, with legs that go on forever.'

A waitress came over and offered us something to drink and I ordered a glass of Chardonnay and Charlie a beer. He still looked slightly off as the waitress walked away, skipping deftly between tables and then disappearing into the kitchen. I was hoping tonight was going to be a celebration of my success, but at that moment it was anything but, and I didn't know why.

'How was your day?' I said, changing subjects.

'Typically awful.'

'You need to look for something else. You need to find a job you love, Charlie.'

'Not everyone is as lucky as you,' he said, a bitterness in his tone that shocked me.

'What's that supposed to mean?'

'Nothing. I'm sorry. I just had a rough day.'

The waitress came back with our drinks and Charlie made a toast to me and my career, but my earlier excitement had been tinged with his annoyance and petty frustration.

It was strange because although I knew he didn't like his job, he had never seemed so resentful of my success before. It felt like the air had been let out of the balloon I had been carrying around with me all day. When the news had leaked at work, I'd had so many messages of congratulations and words of encouragement from colleagues. I had a quick coffee with Tim, and he said how happy he was for me and couldn't wait to get started. I had been walking on sunshine all day, and having dinner with Charlie was supposed to be the icing on the cake, but it was the opposite. The sunshine was now damp gloominess.

Charlie tried to make it up to me by asking questions and smiling at the right moments, but I knew that, underneath, something was going on. Whatever had happened at work had affected him, and he didn't want to talk to me about it. Instead, he pretended he was fine, shrugged it off as just another shit day at work, drank too much over dinner, and when we went to bed, he was asleep before me, and I sat up wondering what had happened to Charlie.

One of the things that had attracted me to Charlie was that he had a sort of naivety about him, as though the world hadn't affected him in the same way it had with others. He was open and had a raw honesty about him. He didn't expect anything from me, but he also had this other thing inside of him that scared me sometimes. I was aware he didn't think he was good enough for me, which was sweet at first, but then it gradually became this thing that slowly infiltrated different parts of our relationship. It was linked to his job, my career, money, my father, all of it enhancing this feeling he had that he was somehow not worthy of my love. Most of the time I didn't feel it, and I ignored it because it was the one negative of us and every relationship had its thing, right? I thought one day he would get a career of his own, and then it would go away, but thinking about how he had reacted to my promotion, it worried me. It also made me think about something my father had said the night he met Charlie: *A relationship can only last when the couple makes each other better, not when one of them drags the other one up.*

No. 25

Charlie

Sharing a bath in a country house

We were in Ash's car, heading away for a long weekend to a country estate. It was the back end of spring, the air was warm and all around us flowers and trees were full of life. I looked across at Ash, her hair blowing with the windows down, and a large pair of sunglasses tucked neatly on her nose. She looked more beautiful than ever. She had been working hard since her promotion, longer hours in the office and bringing work home at the weekends, and it felt like we both needed some time away.

Sometimes when you are living your day-to-day life, it is easy to get caught up in everything and to forget to enjoy the moment. So, two weeks ago, I suggested a weekend away and Ash had heard of this incredible hotel in Oxfordshire, an old stately home that was now a luxury hotel, and it would be the perfect place to escape London. It was expensive and would be a bit of a splurge, but with her job going well and us saving money by sharing a room, we decided to put it on a credit card and not worry about it.

I had prepared a road-trip playlist, and at that moment, Snow Patrol were 'Chasing Cars', and I reached across and held Ash's spare hand. The last six months since she had got her promotion had slipped by and I felt like something had changed between us. The early excitement of living together had been replaced with a sort of indifference. I wasn't even sure if it was indifference, but we had settled into a new rhythm, and it made me uncomfortable. Her career was rapidly growing and mine wasn't. I didn't know what it was I wanted to do, and so I stayed the same, shrunk down and stilted while Ash, buoyed by her promotion, had blossomed like a beautiful butterfly emerging from its cocoon with a real dash of certainty.

'Wow,' I said as we drove up the driveway to the hotel.

We had turned from a quiet country lane onto a long driveway marked with trees on either side at perfect intervals towards a sprawling country house. We drove through enormous gates into a spacious gravel forecourt, where Range Rovers sat like obedient dogs waiting for their owners. Ash pulled her Mini Cooper into a space, and we got out. The sun was shining on our faces, and it was impossible not to be happy at that moment.

'This is absolutely gorgeous,' said Ash, looking around.

'Yet not as gorgeous as you.'

'You old romantic. Come on, let's check in. I can't wait to see our room!'

I grabbed our suitcase from the boot, and we eagerly headed inside. The outside of the seventeenth-century stone house was incredible, and the inside didn't disappoint either. Lots of ornate wood panelling and so many original features it felt like we were on the set of a BBC historical drama. It felt wrong that the staff were dressed in contemporary clothes and not period costumes. We checked in and were shown to our room, a cosy bedroom with a wooden king-sized bed and attached en-suite bathroom with a roll-top bath. The walls were painted a moody grey that was offset with milky-white cornicing, and light green gingham soft furnishings. The view from the paned windows of the manicured gardens, and then the countryside beyond, was stunning.

'I could get used to this,' I said, falling on the bed. Ash lay next to me, her hand touching mine, and I held it gently. I turned and looked at her. 'I'm so glad we did this.'

'Me, too.'

The room smelled of lavender, and something else slightly spicy yet inviting that matched the earthy tones of the relaxed but elegantly designed space. We had come to unwind, but there was so much we had planned. Blenheim Palace was only a short drive away if we fancied a history hit, and there was a lovely old pub with a thatched roof within walking distance. The hotel offered tennis, croquet, a health spa, and if we didn't mind driving, Oxford wasn't far away, but at that moment, lying in bed with Ash, I just wanted to be with her.

'I think I'm going to take a bath,' said Ash, suddenly sitting up.

'It's a bit early for a bath, isn't it?'

'I don't know, is it?' said Ash with a suggestive smile.

We walked into the bathroom and looked down at the bathtub. It was much bigger than the tub at our flat and just about big enough for the both of us.

Ash turned the taps of the old white bathtub, and it slowly filled up. The hotel had left a variety of different bubble baths, and they all looked posh and were locally handmade, organic, and we put some in and then we undressed, which felt strange and a little risqué in the middle of the day, but it had been so long since we had broken our routine. We usually only ever had sex in our bed at the end of the day when we weren't already too tired. Lights out and music on so Edith didn't have to hear. Once the bath was three quarters full, we both slipped in.

'Oh, my God, that's hot!' said Ash with surprise.

'Fuck!' I said.

It was scalding hot, but we both eventually lay down, our wet bodies overlapping with legs across each other, her breasts halfway submerged under the water. I looked across at her and smiled.

'What?' she said.

'Nothing.'

'Tell me, Talbot.'

'I just had a thought,' I said, and then I paused for a moment. 'It's going to sound silly.'

'I love silly. It's my favourite thing in the entire world,' said Ash, and then she took a handful of bubbles and blew them across the bath at me.

'It's just… I had the thought that I was in a bath in a country house in Oxfordshire with you, and if I told my eighteen-year-old self that, he would never have believed me.'

'And what would eighteen-year-old Charlie have done with me in the tub?'

'Probably make a fool of himself in about five seconds flat.'

'And what are you going to do?' said Ash with a delicious smile.

She leaned forward and ran a hand up my leg under the water.

'I don't think I need to answer that question,' I said as her hand reached me.

No. 26

Ash

Big decisions in old rooms

The weekend was almost over, and it had come and gone far too quickly. Coming away had felt at first as though it was something we had forced ourselves into, and to be honest, I had lots going on at work and having a weekend away was the last thing on my mind, but I was also aware of this creeping sensation I had been having that Charlie and I were slowly pulling apart. At least I was from him.

Since we had begun living together, our relationship had unfolded in new and unexpected ways. I hadn't lived with someone before and neither had he, and I don't think either of us were prepared for the small, niggling annoyances that would seep into other parts of our relationship. Perhaps it was just the amount of space we were living in that was the problem. One small bedroom for two adults and a shared living space with Edith, and it had started to feel cramped when initially it had felt cosy. Edith had been lovely, so accommodating, and she and Charlie generally got on well, but the flat just wasn't intended for so many people. The frisson of excitement at the beginning of our relationship, like a flame that had sparked into a fire, had died down and there was definitely not a lot of heat left, but coming away had reminded us how good it could be with a little time and care away from London.

There was a luxurious old bar in the hotel, styled like something from the 1920s, and it made me feel as though I had travelled back in time. Lots of wood, leather, and it had a certain smell that reminded me of something from my childhood. I wanted to be dressed in a vintage frock with lots of sequins, and I felt like I should be holding a cigarette in one of those long holders. It was the last night of our stay, and we were reminiscing about the weekend. A glorious weekend of attempted croquet, countryside walks, pub lunches, afternoon sex and a visit to Blenheim Palace because history buff Charlie had always wanted to go.

'I was thinking,' I said.

I was drinking a negroni, and Charlie had taken to drinking red wine all weekend.

'A dangerous thing, thinking, but go on.'

'It seems to me that we've outgrown the flat.'

'What are you saying?'

'I think it's time we moved out and into our own place, and I know it will be expensive, Charlie, but we've saved money living together, and my parents have offered to help, too.'

It was something I had been thinking about all weekend. Getting our own flat felt like a big step. We would have to buy furniture, decor, and make decisions as a couple, but when faced with the reality that your relationship seemed to be stuck, bobbing about on the sea of life with little direction and the very real possibility that you might actually be lost, you needed something to change. Someone had to shoot a flare up into the sky, and I suppose I always knew that person would be me. I had some money, a gift from my grandmother that I had been keeping back for something like this, and my father had offered to pay the deposit on somewhere new when I was ready. I realised and appreciated how lucky we were to have their support in a city that was verging on impossibly expensive.

'Are you sure?' said Charlie, a smile on his face, his cheeks reddened by the wine.

'I am. You?'

'I mean, the money thing is a worry. I hate that it feels like it's all on you, and I'm just along for the ride.'

'Please don't worry about that. You'll be paying your fair share of the rent.'

I looked at Charlie and I didn't want him to feel like he wasn't providing enough for me, for us, but we needed to make the next step in our relationship. I had to make this work. After a moment, he smiled.

'Then I think it's a great idea, Ash. Our own place. It feels so grown-up!'

'It does. We'll get back to London and start looking right away!' I said excitedly, leaning forward and kissing Charlie, the perfect end to what had been a lovely weekend.

The prospect of moving out excited me and saddened me in equal measure because the Putney flat was my first home in London. Edith was my friend, and a great room-mate to boot, but it was time to move on. I felt the hands of time turning, and as Charlie and I left the bar and headed upstairs to our room, the promise of a night of passion ahead, I felt a genuine sense of loss for the person I had been when I had moved to London so full of optimism. I was still that person inside, but life had changed, and I was changing with it. We had to move on because standing still felt like going backwards, and I knew that might be the end of Charlie and me.

No. 27

Charlie

New flat fireworks

The flat was perfect and in a great location near a Tube station and, most importantly, in our price range. When we had made the decision to get our own place, we knew we would have to move further afield and finally, after a month of jetting around south London, adding locations to a spreadsheet, we decided on Streatham. It was close enough to everything we needed with good transport links to make our commutes reasonable and there were plenty of decent pubs, coffee shops, and Streatham Common on our doorstep. Our social life had suddenly become flat hunting, and so instead of the pub after work, we would dash from work on to trains to Streatham to view another flat that had 'literally just come on the market' and would be 'gone before the weekend'. We had seen flats that were disgusting, nothing like the descriptions, and a few flats we had loved but were too late and had lost out to rival couples. This flat, however, was exactly what we were looking for and we were the first ones to view it.

I was at work when our estate agent, a thin man in a sharp suit called Spike, rang and said he had a great flat that wasn't on the market yet, but we had to see it that night or risk losing it. I called Ash, and we both got there as fast as we could after work. It was a wet night; a constant all-day drizzle had turned into a downpour as we ran into the flat.

It was a substantial one-bed on the ground floor of a house just off the high street. It had bags of original features, including a lovely old fireplace in the living room, cornicing and wooden floors throughout. It needed a coat of paint, the kitchen wasn't in the best shape, but it was spacious and had a small private garden where we could barbecue with friends in the summer. After the Putney flat, it felt enormous, and it came unfurnished so we would have to get everything ourselves. It was perfect, and the prospect of it excited me. Perhaps after months of searching, we had found the ideal place to start our lives together.

'Well?' said Spike. 'What do you think?'

I looked at Ash, my face brimming with excitement, but she didn't look the same and I had no idea why. This was exactly what we had spent so long trying to find, and now we had I couldn't understand why she wouldn't be as jubilant as me.

'I love it,' I said to Spike. 'Ash?'

'It's lovely,' she said, a wide smile on her face, but I could tell that fluttering underneath the surface something else was going on that belied the look she had given Spike.

'Perfect! I'll get the paperwork sorted and we can get this done ASAP. I'll give you a few minutes to have a proper look around on your own. Get out the tape measure, imagine where the furniture will go!'

We smiled, and Spike left us alone. We were standing in the empty living room, our future surrounding us, and it felt enormous just for a living room. I was already imagining going to IKEA, buying furniture and spending a weekend putting it all together.

'I can't believe it. This is perfect,' I said.

'It is.'

'Ash,' I said, turning to her. I reached down and held her hands. 'What's going on?'

'What do you mean?'

'You don't look very excited, and I know something is on your mind because...' I stopped talking because I saw a tear slip out and down her face. I immediately felt afraid of what was to come. 'What is it?'

I was still holding her hands and I looked into those wonderful, too-green-to-be-real eyes. She was about to tell me something, and I hoped it wasn't going to destroy our world. She left a pause and the empty room around us seemed to make it quieter still.

'I'm pregnant, Charlie,' Ash said finally, and my heart leapt in my chest and then sank into my stomach. She was pregnant. How? We had always been so careful. I was suddenly hot, and I felt the beginnings of a sickness in my stomach. A build-up of fear. The future felt like it was suddenly and unexpectedly hurtling towards us at breakneck speed.

'What? I don't understand?'

'I'm pregnant, Charlie.'

'You're sure?'

'Yes.'

'Fuck.'

'I know.'

There was a sudden silence that seemed to stretch throughout the entire flat, and I stood and held her hands. She was having our baby, but we couldn't. We were only twenty-six, and we didn't have our life together in so many ways. We couldn't afford to have a baby and we were about to rent a one-bed flat for the next twelve months on the basis that it was just us. I had thought about having children one day, but that day was far in the future when we were married, I had a proper career, and we had a house. I needed to be ready and I just wasn't. All those dreams of the future and of us living so happily in that flat were suddenly gone, and it was just us standing in that empty room, her hands in mine, the weight of her words crushing me beneath them.

'Ready to sign some paperwork?' said Spike loudly, reappearing with an excitement that was jarring given our moods, his words like fireworks breaking through the dead of night.

No. 28

Ash

An inconvenient truth

It was a Saturday morning, and we were in a coffee shop sipping lattes while trying to decide the rest of our lives. It had been a few days since I had told Charlie I was pregnant, and we had signed the paperwork on the flat. It had been a tense time. I had cried a lot, Charlie had been supportive, and neither of us could understand how it had happened.

'I just don't know what to do,' I said to Charlie, the words sinking into the conversation, and then remaining in the air between us.

'Neither do I,' said Charlie before he took a sip of his coffee.

It was raining outside. Grey and leaden, the sky seemed to reflect our mood. I had obviously thought about having children and the answer was always the same: one day. I had always wanted a family of my own and had visions in my head of a happy family living in a large house somewhere in London. Busy, loud and full of love with people constantly coming and going. I suppose it was the middle-class dream, but like everyone else, I wanted it. The loving husband, brilliant kids and a house that had cost a fortune but was worth every penny. The plan in my head had been clear: work hard to become an editor, build up my list of authors so, when I had children, I would already have a fully-fledged career I could jump back into when I was ready.

The vision in my head was already too real, too fully formed, but we weren't ready for it yet. Charlie needed to sort his career out, I needed to progress in mine, and ideally we would get married and have our first house. All caveats to being great parents, I thought. The bottom line was that we weren't prepared, but I was pregnant with our baby, and the idea of not meeting this life we had created broke my heart. I wasn't sure I could do that either.

'Every time I think about getting an abortion, I start crying,' I said, batting away the tears that constantly threatened to make a dramatic and unwanted appearance on my face.

'I know.'

He didn't add 'Me, too', but I knew he meant it. I had caught him in moments staring off into space and I felt his sadness. I don't think he knew quite what to say and also I think deep down he knew the situation as much as me. This was my decision to make. He had a say, of course, but if I decided to keep our baby, there was nothing he could do about it.

'But then every time I think about keeping it, I have this overwhelming dread and I can't breathe because it's terrifying. We can't have a baby yet, Charlie. We're not ready.'

I looked at Charlie, and he smiled at me. A sad smile created without thinking. Muscle memory. Even when our brains didn't know what to do or say, our bodies did.

'What do you think?' I asked hopefully.

'Ash, I...'

'What?'

'I'm scared.'

'Me, too.'

We had agreed not to tell anyone until we had made a decision. We thought it was selfish to involve other people when it was our mess to clean up. That sounded too harsh because it wasn't a mess, it was our baby. A life was growing inside of me and whether we were ready or not, we had made it and terminating it before they even had a chance wasn't some-thing I could easily do. Keeping them would be challenging in so many ways, but we could do it. It was a sudden, and admittedly quite scary disruption in our plans, rather than a proper fucking disaster.

We drank our coffee without making a decision. As we zipped up our coats and walked into the rain back to our flat, we held hands, and I noticed Charlie's grip was tighter than usual. I turned to him and I couldn't tell if it was the rain or whether he was crying, but drops were running down his face. We kept walking back towards the flat that would soon no longer be our home. We were moving out in a week, but any excitement we felt about that was being tempered by the decision that was hanging over us.

I stopped suddenly in the rain and turned to Charlie. It was loud because of the traffic rushing past us and the rain that was falling on our faces.

'I'm sorry,' I yelled.

'What? Why?'

'Because I can't make a decision. I want to make one. It's just so fucking hard!' I yelled as a car sped by and splashed up water from a puddle that hit our shoes. 'I love you.'

'Love you, too,' he yelled back, and then we stood in the rain, and we kissed.

No. 29

Charlie

Packing clothes in black bin bags

The truth was the idea of being responsible for another life when I still didn't feel like I was doing a particularly good job with my own terrified me. It did things to me, twisted my mind in knots of confusion and terror, and made me feel things I hadn't felt before. When Ash and I stood in our new flat, I was overwhelmed with excitement at the prospect of the future. We were finally getting our own place, Ash's career was taking off, and I felt a renewed energy to sort out my own. Life felt like it was taking shape like a dough we had spent time kneading and kneading until it was a perfect, smooth ball, but then she told me she was pregnant, and the dough ball was suddenly pulled apart, stretched until it was almost broken into pieces. Neither of us were ready to be parents, but at the same time I felt this overwhelming love for Ash like a hard-wired biological need to protect her.

I wanted her to be okay, to be happy, but it also crystallised in me the idea that I wasn't ready to be a father. I had to sort my life out, feel worthy, and if I wasn't, I didn't know if I could do it. Being a dad might break me apart, and perhaps my relationship with Ash in the process.

It was the Friday before we were due to move into our new flat, and we still hadn't made a decision. Everything had happened so quickly, and we had to pay double rent to cover

Edith until she could get a new flatmate, but we couldn't risk losing the Streatham flat. Ash was at work, and I had taken the day off to get things ready. We had already gone to IKEA, ordered our furniture, and it was being delivered in the morning. Dad was coming to help put it all together, and Mum was coming along to help Ash with other bits and bobs. They had no idea she was pregnant, and it was going to be difficult having my parents with us all weekend without giving it away, but they had offered to help, and we couldn't say no.

I was alone in the flat packing clothes in black bin bags when my phone rang. It was warm, and the sun was shining through our bedroom window. I was going to miss some things about this place and I was definitely going to miss Putney. I would miss the view from our bedroom window of the rows of rooftops like something from *Mary Poppins*. It was also the first place Ash and I had shared together, and it would always hold a special place in my heart. I looked down at the number on my phone and saw Ash's name staring back at me.

'I was just thinking about you,' I said with a smile. 'Well us, actually.' There was a momentary pause, and that's when I heard the first sob. 'Ash? What's up? Are you okay?'

'I think I lost the baby,' she whispered.

Fuck.

'Where are you?'

'I'm in the toilets. I'm bleeding and I don't know what to do, Charlie. I'm scared.'

My heart sank, and I felt all at once an overwhelming feeling of loss, then a sharp coldness rattled my body, and I had to sit down on the bed to compose myself. Heartbreak, fear, and I hated myself for even thinking it, but a slight pang of relief.

'Do you need to go to the hospital?'

'Yes, probably, I'm not sure. It's so early, it's just...' She stopped and wept.

'Just stay there. I'll come and get you.'

'Okay,' she said quietly, her voice drenched in sorrow.

When we hung up, I sat for a moment and felt tears sting my eyes, but I quickly wiped them away with the back of my hand. I hated the thought of Ash sitting alone in the toilets at work crying because she had lost our baby. I quickly pulled myself together and got ready to leave. The flat was a mess, there were bags everywhere, and boxes still half filled, and we had much to do before the big move, but I left and headed towards Ash's work because the only thing that actually mattered, when it came down to it, was to protect her.

No. 30

Ash

The love heart in the tree

We had decorated the flat with a variety of decorations we had bought, made ourselves, and our small Christmas tree stood in front of the living room window, giving it a very festive feel. It was our first Christmas in our new home, and we had Charlie's parents coming for Christmas Day, along with Edith, whose parents had decided to spend Christmas in Portugal, and Matt, Charlie's old flatmate, who was working so hard he didn't have time to leave London, apparently.

It was ten o'clock in the morning and I was preparing the turkey, while Charlie was in charge of potatoes and vegetables. His parents were arriving at lunchtime and staying until the evening, while Edith and Matt were scheduled to arrive around two o'clock and stay until, well, knowing Matt, late into the evening or perhaps into Boxing Day. We were listening to Christmas music, working together in the kitchen, and the whole flat had a wonderfully joyful feel to it, which was suddenly broken by Charlie singing the Band Aid classic, 'Do They Know It's Christmas?' woefully out of tune.

'Do *you* know it's Christmas? Because if you did, you wouldn't be subjecting my ears to singing like that on Jesus' birthday,' I said, looking across at him with a playful smile.

'I'm a great singer. The voice of an angel, they proclaimed at my year six school play.'

I laughed. 'You did a school play?'

'I did,' said Charlie, peeling another potato, cutting it in half and then popping it in a large pan of salted water. '*Peter Pan* the musical. I was Peter.'

'How have I not heard about this before? Is there a video somewhere?'

'I'm afraid not, but the reviews were all top-notch. The voice of an angel! A future star of the stage and screen! The West End awaits!'

'You've got to be kidding me! You, a future star of the stage and screen?'

Charlie stopped peeling potatoes, looked at me, then said with a completely straight face, 'I was a child prodigy, Ash. Unfortunately, when my voice broke, my angelic tones were no more. My days of treading the boards were over before they had really begun.'

'Stop it, you're killing me,' I said, laughing.

'By year seven, I could barely get a part,' said Charlie, solemnly. 'And with choreography not being my strongest suit, they offered me the role of a donkey in *Aladdin*, which, given my previous run as Peter, I declined. I never performed again.'

I walked across, gave Charlie a hug and tried to stop myself from crying with laughter.

'You are joking, right?' I said, because it suddenly dawned on me that perhaps he was being serious. I looked at Charlie, he looked at me, before his face cracked.

'Of course! Have you heard me sing?' He laughed. 'Although I did once audition for a school play, and the drama teacher, Mr Gilbert, told me to stop and never sing again.'

'Ouch,' I said before we got back to preparing the food, Charlie still singing like a broken accordion, and me wondering how much a decent pair of earplugs would cost.

It had been a strange and challenging few months. After my miscarriage, we moved into the flat and life continued. The thing was, trying to make the decision whether to keep the baby or not was so difficult, but once they were gone, I wanted them more than anything in the world. I had thought I might be slightly relieved, but instead I was just terribly sad. I was in a bit of a daze afterwards, but after we moved into our flat, something changed between Charlie and me. We had been through something together that had altered the DNA of our relationship. We had felt a joint pain, suffered a loss and it had sealed us together.

'My parents will be here in two hours. I'm going to jump in the shower,' said Charlie.

'Make sure you wear the jumper I got for you.'

'Do I have to?'

'Yes, you do!'

'Fine,' huffed Charlie.

I had found us matching ugly Christmas jumpers from Marks and Spencer. They were a bit gaudy and silly, but it was Christmas. I had texted Charlie's mum and asked if they could do the same, but to keep it as a surprise for Charlie. I couldn't wait to see Charlie's face when he saw them. I had texted Edith and Matt, and they were both onboard, too.

It was a cold but clear day; the frosty blue-grey sky was flecked with clouds and there was a slight breeze in the air. The birds sang, and it was quiet outside. Children would be excitedly opening presents while parents made food and tried holding out until lunchtime until they started drinking. Charlie and I walked the short walk to Streatham Common and started along the pathway to the tree.

After the miscarriage, we had decided to do something to mark our baby's brief existence. So, we walked to Streatham Common and found an oak tree that looked as though it had been there for hundreds of years. We stood by the tree and thought about them, and then we carved a small love heart into the trunk. We didn't know if it would have been a boy or a girl, but we knew we would have loved them with all our hearts.

We stood in front of the tree, held hands and looked at the love heart. I couldn't help but cry, and Charlie gently squeezed my hand. We would have a baby one day, I was sure of that, but no matter what happened, how many children we had, I didn't want to forget this one.

'Merry Christmas,' I said.

'Merry Christmas,' said Charlie.

We stood by the tree in silence, each with our own thoughts, before we started the slow walk home to enjoy the rest of Christmas Day.

2009

No. 31

Charlie

The couple on the Tube

It was a clear, bright Saturday morning, we were on the tube heading to Portobello Road Market, and Ash had her head resting on my shoulder. It was one of those mornings when everything seemed to be right with the world. A perfect creamy latte at a lovely cafe, flaky, buttery croissants, and dappled sunshine. We would stroll around the eclectic market stalls for a few hours, perhaps buy something for the flat, and then go somewhere nice for lunch.

It was spring and life was taking hold again after the long, dark winter when we had talked about the baby we had lost. Our sadness seemed to die in the cold gloom of those days, and now we were only looking forward. We had turned the clocks forward by an hour, and there was a tantalising feeling of optimism and vibrancy in the air, at least with us. Across the Tube, another couple about the same age as us were in the middle of a heated argument. She had a face like thunder, and he was doing his best to ignore her by looking the other way.

'So what, you're not going to talk to me then?' said the girl across the Tube in a Geordie accent. You could tell he definitely didn't want to talk about whatever was going on. 'Typical! You act like a total bastard and expect me to take it, but I'm done taking it. Done!'

'Just shut up,' her boyfriend finally said. He turned to her. His eyes full of anger. 'Why can't you ever just let it go?'

'Because why should I?' she said, and suddenly the brashness and the annoyance turned to tears, and she was crying. A solid mass of emotion in double denim. 'You're always doing things, nasty things, and I know you kissed that girl at the club because Michelle told me—'

'I fucking didn't! That's the problem. You always believe that bitch over me!'

'Because she doesn't lie to me all the fucking time!' said the girl, her voice loud and harsh against the deafening silence of the carriage. Everyone was so uncomfortable, fervently pretending it wasn't happening while they played out their relationship drama in public.

She kept crying, and he started telling her to stop crying because she was 'always fucking crying' and she shouted at him and called him a 'bastard with a micro penis', which almost made me laugh but I managed to keep it inside. Luckily, at the next stop, they got off, and their arguing continued on the platform. As the doors closed and we pulled away, we could see them shouting at each other, pointing fingers, and it didn't look like it was going to end well. Ash sat up and looked at me, and I looked at her. We had never once argued like that, and I think we were both just thankful. She gave my hand a squeeze, and I did the same.

She rested her head on my shoulder, as the Tube continued on, rattling through dark tunnels towards Notting Hill. I knew that whatever happened, we would never be like that other couple, shouting at each other on the Tube, and airing our dirty laundry in public. Ash and I were in love, we were happy and nothing was going to change that. There were a few mumbled conversations about the arguing couple, and people shook their heads in disbelief until we finally got off at Notting Hill Gate and started walking towards the market.

'I'm glad we aren't like the couple on the Tube,' said Ash.

'Me, too.'

'I know that whatever happens with us—'

'Not that anything will happen with us.'

'Not that anything will happen with us,' she said with a smile. 'But if it did—'

'Which it won't.'

'Which it won't, but even if it did, I know we would never be like that.'

'Never. Not like that.'

She kissed me, and we walked into the market, each stall with so many things for sale, and the delicious aroma of street food that danced in the air like magic. It was packed with people, and amongst them all, Ash and I walked together, talking, enjoying the day without a care in the world and it felt like that would go on forever.

No. 32

Ash

Fancy dress argument

'I'm sorry, all right?' said Charlie, standing in our hallway, while I pulled on my ankle boots.

'I just don't get it, Charlie. Why would you throw it away like that?'

I looked at Charlie, who was standing there in his Peppa Pig costume. I was in my slutty nun outfit, and I hadn't planned on having an argument right before we left for Callie's fancy dress party, but then when I looked in the fridge for my leftover pizza and discovered Charlie had tossed it in the bin, I was a little upset.

'Because it had been in the fridge for days, Ash, and you hadn't eaten it.'

'So you thought, I know, I'll chuck it in the bin, so she has to leave the house starving. Brilliant, thanks,' I said, standing up, and having to pull my nun's habit down a little. The outfit was, unfortunately, veering more towards slutty than nun.

Callie from work was having a fancy dress party for her birthday, and we had been invited to her house in Dulwich. The birthday invitation itself had been hanging around on the fridge for a while, but for some reason at the last minute she had decided to make it a fancy dress party. Charlie and I had gone to different costume shops on different days, and I had returned as a slutty nun, which I hadn't loved, but it was better than some

123

of the other options, while Charlie had, for some reason, come back with Peppa Pig.

I walked into the bathroom and turned the light on. I needed to put on a bit of last-minute make-up, and Charlie followed behind me.

'I think you're being a bit unfair, Ash,' he said, loitering by the door.

'Excuse me?' I said, turning to face him.

'How was I to know you wanted it for dinner? I'm not a mind reader.'

'Please, Charlie. How many times have you left food in the fridge, and I've never tossed it in the bin without asking you. You know why? Because I'm not thoughtless.'

I looked at Charlie, decked out in full Peppa Pig costume, and it was hard to remain completely angry with him looking like that, but then he muttered something under his breath and started to walk away.

'What did you say?' I said, stopping him in his tracks.

'Nothing,' mumbled Charlie.

'No, go on, say it.'

'I said, what about when you've left your washing all over the bedroom floor for days on end? Is that you not being thoughtless?' said Charlie, and he knew this was an ongoing situation, and would rile me up. The washing debate had been raging for a while, along with the toothpaste conversation we kept having, and why, oh fucking why, couldn't he just put the television remote back in the drawer, instead of leaving it on the sofa where it would always, without fail, disappear down the gap between the cushions, and so I would be forced to constantly search for it? We had our things. Tiny cracks on the surface of our relationship.

'For fuck's sake, Charlie!' I said, louder than before. 'This isn't about the washing, or the amount of bread you constantly end up throwing in the bin. Just buy less fucking bread! It's about the pizza you threw away because you didn't consider me.'

'Oh, right, so let me guess, it isn't about the pizza, exactly, but what it represents,' said Charlie in the most condescending tone imaginable.

'Oh my God, I can't even look at you right now,' I said, furiously turning back to the mirror, before I added, 'And not even because of the stupid fucking Peppa Pig costume!'

'For your information,' retorted Charlie. 'It isn't Peppa Pig, it's Daddy Pig!'

Then he stormed off into the living room, while I stood in front of the bathroom mirror, trying to put on some lipstick, trying to stop the rage from taking over my entire body. I loved Charlie so much, but sometimes he could be such a thoughtless, irritating shit. Why would he throw the pizza away when I had specifically said I needed to eat something quickly before we left for the party? It was a warm night outside and we were getting the bus from Streatham to Dulwich, which Charlie also wasn't happy about. A sexy nun and Daddy Pig on the bus was definitely going to raise some eyebrows, but I didn't care.

I walked into the living room, where Charlie was sitting on the sofa, looking glum and slightly absurd.

'Ready?' I said, still annoyed.

'Ready,' said Charlie, standing up. 'Oh, and Ash.'

'Yes?' I said, my voice hardened with frustration.

'I love you.'

'What?'

'I said, I love you.'

I looked at Charlie in his Daddy Pig costume, standing in our living room, and he looked so sorrowful, and so ridiculous that I felt my frustration melt away. He took a step towards me, and I smiled at him.

'And maybe, I over-reacted a bit about the pizza. You know how I get when I'm hangry.'

'I do. And I'm sorry I threw it away.'

I took a step closer to him, and when I reached him, he put his arms around me.

'You know, I've always had a thing for sexy nuns.'

I laughed. 'Since when?'

'Since about thirty minutes ago when I first saw you in that costume,' said Charlie, and then he leaned in and kissed me.

'You know, if you play your cards right, I might let you take off my wimple when we get home!' I said, before we left for Callie's party, the fight over, and normal order was restored.

No. 33

Charlie

Standing by the side of the road in the rain

'I mean, could this be any worse?' said Ash from next to me, huddled together in our raincoats.

'There could be lightning then we couldn't stand under this tree for cover,' I replied, and she looked at me with a completely straight face, as the rain came down even harder.

We were on our way to Exeter for Ash's university reunion, when her car broke down on the A303 just past Wincanton. We were currently standing under a tree by the side of the road, trying not to get soaked. Ash had already called the RAC, and they said they should be there within the hour. Ash was also annoyed because we were late leaving, and her old university housemates, Anna and Cerys, were currently in a pub in Exeter waiting for us. I reached into my pocket and pulled out a Mars bar.

'Fancy sharing this?' I asked as a car flew by, kicking up some rain from the road and spraying it towards us. She looked at the Mars bar and then at me. I could see the disappointment on her face, but it cracked, and she smiled at me.

'Sure. Thank you.'

I opened the Mars bar, broke it in two halves, and then passed half to Ash, and then we stood by the side of the road, eating our Mars bars, watching the cars fly by. I knew Ash had been excited for this weekend, and it was an inopportune moment for her trusted Mini Cooper, which had always been so reliable, to break down. I just hoped it wasn't too serious and we would be on our way again soon. Anna and Cerys had both moved to different parts of the country after university with Anna now in Manchester, and Cerys back in her native Wales, and so they rarely all got together. I could feel Ash's frustration from next to me, and knew it was up to me to take her mind off it.

'You know the night we slept together at university?' I asked. She turned and looked at me with a quizzical expression.

'Of course. Why are you asking about that now?'

'Because we're heading to Exeter, and I just wondered how you felt when you were going back to uni the day after because I was fucking distraught.'

'Sorry.'

'No, it's okay. I understand why you had to do it, I do, but I've never really asked you how that day was for you.'

Ash took a bite of her Mars bar before she looked out towards the road, reaching her hand out from under the tree to feel the rain for a moment.

'It was really hard, Charlie. I felt like the worst person in the world for leaving you in bed that morning, and all the way back on the train, I went over and over it again and again in my mind. Was I doing the right thing? Should we at least keep in touch? Should we have exchanged emails. I honestly didn't know what to do, and I felt awful because it had been the best night of my life.'

'Me too,' I said, and we looked at each other in the rain, and then she leaned across and kissed me, before we both took a bite of our Mars bars.

'I actually wrote you a letter, but I didn't have the courage to post it,' said Ash after a minute.

'What? Really? What happened to the letter?'

'I put it in the bin, eventually, after countless walks to the post box.'

'What did it say?' I said, and I couldn't believe that there had been a letter.

'I don't remember. Probably just how sorry I was, and it's for the best, but I think I knew that despite everything, it was the right thing to do, which I think has been proven correct considering where we are now.'

'Standing by the side of the A303 in the rain?'

'You know what I mean, you idiot,' said Ash with a smile, leaning against me for a moment before she took the last bit of her Mars bar and put the whole thing in her mouth.

It was such a strange and crazy thing to imagine that six years before, Ash had sat on a train heading back to university after the night we had slept together. That day for me had been one of wildly conflicting emotions. On one hand, I had spent the night with the girl I had lusted after for years, but on the other, she had disappeared in the morning with just a note left behind. To think she had wrestled with the idea of us being together then, and how different our lives could have been if she had made a different decision, was a strange feeling. Was there an alternate reality where she had stayed, we'd had breakfast together, and promised to keep in touch, and if so, would we still have been standing under that tree on the side of the road waiting for the RAC man?

'I do know what you mean, and I'm so happy where we are now,' I replied.

'If you think I'm going to say, "What, standing by the side of the A303?" then you are sadly mistaken,' said Ash, and I laughed, as we saw the RAC van approaching through the rain.

No. 34

Ash

Waterloo

'And next up, we have Ash, Anna and Cerys, singing "Waterloo" by ABBA!' said the middle-aged man into the microphone, and we all stood up. I looked across at my old university mates, and I couldn't believe we were going to sing ABBA again after all these years. Admittedly, it was in quite a tired old pub in Streatham that was almost empty on a Friday evening, but I didn't care. This meant the world to me.

'Ready, girls?' I said.

'Ready,' they replied.

We walked out from behind the table and started towards the small stage in the corner of the pub, and that's when I saw Charlie, who had come walking into the pub at just the right moment. I told the girls to give me a minute.

'Sorry I'm late. Work stuff,' said Charlie.

'Actually you're just in time for our first number,' I said, giving him a kiss, before I quickly joined my friends on stage.

After I had met with Anna and Cerys in Exeter – after the break-down disaster, which although had delayed us by nearly three hours, wasn't all that bad in the end – we had agreed to get together again soon. A few months later and it was Anna's birthday, and we were in London together for the weekend. At university, karaoke was our thing. Anna was studying music and a brilliant singer, Cerys could dance like you wouldn't believe, and I enjoyed trying to keep up with them. We would seek out karaoke nights wherever we could, and ABBA were always our number one choice.

I joined Anna and Cerys on stage, we each grabbed a microphone, and then we stood waiting for the music to start. I looked across at Charlie, who had dashed there after work to see us perform. He had heard countless tales of us singing, but he had never actually seen us live. I smiled, and then pointed at him as the beginning of 'Waterloo' began. Gosh, I loved that song, and as soon as the guitar kicked on, we all got ready. We stood on stage in a single line, started dancing from side to side, and then we began singing. It immediately felt like old times again, and nostalgic clips of us performing at university shot through my mind. We danced, sang and, to me at least, we sounded just like we had all those years ago.

Eventually the song ended, and as soon as it was done, Charlie stood up and clapped, and he even did a couple of loud finger whistles. Unfortunately, he was the only one, but it was good enough for me.

'Oh my God!' I said to Anna and Cerys as we walked offstage. 'That was brilliant.'

'Let's get our names down for another one!' said Anna, who wandered off with Cerys to see the man in charge, while I walked across to Charlie who was standing at the bar.

'Well?' I said. 'What do you think?'

Charlie smiled at me.

'That was incredible, Ash. I wish I could have seen you performing at uni.'

I leaned in and kissed Charlie, and he kissed me back before I pulled away. 'Fancy doing a song with us? Maybe a Beatles number?'

'No, I'm good. I'm happy to just sit back and enjoy watching you,' said Charlie, and he looked at me with an expression that made me stop for a moment. He often told me he loved me, and he always made me feel special, but the way he was looking at me in that moment was different.

'What?' I asked.

'What?' he replied.

'What's that look for?'

'What look?'

'That one you just gave me. It was, I don't know, there was something beneath it.'

'I have no idea what you mean,' said Charlie with a delicious smile that definitely told me he wasn't telling me everything.

'Another ABBA song?' yelled Anna suddenly. '"Dancing Queen"?'

I looked across at Anna and Cerys, who were standing with the karaoke man, and I gave them the thumbs up.

'This isn't the end of the conversation, Talbot,' I said, walking away, and Charlie just smiled at me, before I joined Anna and Cerys onstage, wondering what my boyfriend was thinking about.

2010

No. 35

Charlie

A return to Teguise

The sun was hotter and stronger than I remembered as we walked from the hotel to the taxi that was waiting for us. Countless memories were ingrained in everything, and just lying by the pool, it was impossible not to get hurtled back in time, listening to the Beatles, and seeing Ash standing there. *I thought it was you.* I had booked us into the same hotel we had stayed at all those years ago, which, although updated, retained much of its original charm.

It was day three of our holiday in Lanzarote and it felt surreal to be back again. The place where my love for her had grown exponentially, and where we'd had our first moment. The beach where I had rubbed sun cream on her back and felt a deep longing for her that had never gone away. Lanzarote was the beginning for us, and now we were back.

'Teguise, please,' I said to the taxi driver, who didn't reply, and just started driving.

Ash was sitting next to me, holding my hand in a white cotton dress and flip-flops. Her legs were already the colour of caramel after just a few days of sunshine, while I was in shorts and a polo shirt, a cap keeping the sun from my face. The curse of being a redhead meant my pale skin would burn in moments in the hot sun without being slathered in factor-fifty sun cream.

'I remember Teguise. It's the town we went to on our last day. We had lunch by the square,' said Ash.

I turned to her and smiled. 'I was already madly in love with you by then.'

'I was with Scott and oblivious,' she said, and then she looked at me with a warm smile. 'Well, not completely.'

I couldn't turn back time, and even if I could, I wouldn't change a thing because we had ended up together. Maybe if we had kissed in Lanzarote, or I had confessed my love for her, we wouldn't be together now. I couldn't risk what we had now for some other dream with no idea of the ending. Everything we were now, every moment and piece of us, all of it was built by the experiences we'd shared.

'I was head over heels in love but far too shy to do anything about it. You were the best-looking girl at sixth form, dating the coolest boy, and I was a nobody.'

'You weren't a nobody, Charlie,' she said. A small frown wrinkled her forehead.

'And how did you see me?'

Ash looked across at me as we left the coast behind and started heading into the hills, as we had done all those years ago. There was something wonderful about reliving moments from the past. I suppose they were tinged with a sort of sweet sorrow. A sweetness because they had happened and a sorrow because they were gone.

'I thought you were funny, handsome, and if I hadn't been with Scott, I'm sure something would have happened between us.'

'Then I'm glad you were with Scott.'

'Why?'

'Because I'm here with you now and he isn't,' I said, and she smiled before she turned and looked out of the window of the taxi, her face framed by the glass.

Within thirty minutes we had arrived in Teguise. We got out of the taxi and strolled towards the same square we had visited on our last holiday. Whereas by the hotel some things had changed, in Teguise it was as if time had stood still. The ancient cobbled square full of tremendously white buildings with the bright green shutters was exactly as it had been, and the old church was as I remembered it. We had a quick walk around the market, but it was hot, and I was getting nervous. Small beads of sweat joined together and clung to my shirt.

We found the same table we had sat at before at the same restaurant and ordered a variety of tapas and two glasses of white wine. The scene was set. I waited until we had our food and wine before I began. I was so nervous, my heart raced in my chest, but I had rehearsed this a thousand times in my head and knew exactly what I was going to say.

'Ash.'

'Charlie,' she said before she took a sip of her wine.

She had no idea this moment was going to change her life.

'I love you so much, and I think from the moment I saw you in the sixth form refectory, I knew you were the girl for me. Then, of course, we had Lanzarote that changed everything, although I would never have imagined then that we would be back here at the same restaurant, and that we would be so happily in love. Ash,' I said, and then I reached into my pocket and brought out the ring box. I stood up and then got down on one knee beside her. Her face immediately changed, she covered her mouth with her hand in shock, and her eyes shimmered with moisture. 'There was a moment last year. You had just performed "Waterloo" at that karaoke night with Anna and Cerys, and you said that I had a look. Well, that was the moment I knew I was going to propose to you. Ashley Oliver, will you do me the greatest honour of becoming my wife?'

I looked up at Ash, as a single tear leaked out and slid down her face, at the smile that stretched her cheeks and the dimples it created. I loved her more in that moment than I ever had before. Then finally, as my knees were beginning to hurt pressed against the cobblestones, she spoke.

'Yes, of course, yes!'

I slid the ring on her finger, then we both stood up and kissed. I heard a few cheers from people nearby who had been watching, but the world seemed to disappear, and it was just us. Just Ash and me. My fiancée. The woman who would soon become my wife.

No. 36

Ash

A family picnic on Butser Hill

We stood looking out across the green fields and hedgerows of Hampshire and Sussex. Clusters of trees and church spires from nearby villages were dotted across the scene in front of us, and the chalky grey sky with heavy clouds held the promise of rain. It was about as quintessentially English as it was possible to be. We were at Butser Hill National Nature Reserve, a place that held fond memories for Charlie and his parents, and we had brought along a picnic, and Charlie had snuck in a bottle of fizz. His mum, Claire, stood next to me and then Charlie and his father, David. We had already walked a few miles to reach this spot.

'Now that's a view!' said David. 'Can't beat it. I could be anywhere in the world right now and I wouldn't have a better view than this.'

'But you've hardly travelled, Dad,' said Charlie. 'You can't really compare unless you've been somewhere else like, I don't know, the Grand Canyon or Machu Picchu.'

'Spoilsport,' replied David.

'Oh, you two,' said Claire with a smile.

'Should we eat?' I said.

'I'm starving!' said David. 'I wasn't allowed my usual bacon sandwich for breakfast—'

'Because the doctor said you needed to lose weight, and your blood pressure was high.'

'Rubbish. I'm as fit as a flea,' said David, jumping around like a boxer and throwing a few punches to show he definitely wasn't out of shape.

'All right, Frank Bruno. Calm down before you put your back out again,' said Claire.

'Fine, but I think that rabbit food you gave me for breakfast is going to kill me sooner than anything else.'

'You mean the extra-nutty muesli I got from Waitrose? I thought you liked it?'

'If I have that every morning, I'll go nuts!' said David, laughing, which turned into a bit of a wheeze, and then he had to sit down. He was only fifty-three but, according to Charlie, had lived a hard life and he had never eaten well or exercised. Hence the large stomach, and his recent dietary restrictions. Claire got out the picnic blanket, laid it out over the grass, and we took the backpack with the food and got it ready.

'What's that for?' said David.

He had spotted the bottle of Prosecco.

'Let's just eat,' said Charlie, trying his best to play it cool in front of his parents, but I didn't think he was fooling anyone. I looked at him, he looked at me and we both smiled.

We sat down, and Charlie spread the food out and filled our plastic cups with the Prosecco. It looked lovely, and I had quite an appetite from the walk. There was an uneasy air of excitement and confusion as we started eating because they knew something was going on.

It had been a whirlwind week since we had returned from Lanzarote. I was so happy, floating on air, showing off my ring at work and feeling like the luckiest girl in the world. I was genuinely shocked when Charlie proposed because I was usually good at picking up on things, and Charlie didn't get much past me, but when he got down on one knee, I was taken completely by surprise. Once he had popped the question, there was only one answer, and I couldn't wait to get married and start our life together as Mr and Mrs Talbot.

'So… we have some news,' said Charlie after a moment.

I looked at Claire and she had obviously figured it out because tears were already forming in her eyes. I am a crier and can weep at anything from rubbish television shows to heart-touching Christmas adverts, but Charlie's mum was worse. I looked at David and he looked perplexed, shoving a piece of pork pie in his mouth.

'We're engaged!' I said, bringing the ring from my pocket and putting it on my finger.

Claire immediately succumbed to her tears as she embraced me and then Charlie. David swallowed his pork pie, hugged me, and told me how happy he was, and that he still couldn't believe his son had snagged someone as perfect as me. I was soon crying, too, and we all stood on the hill looking out at England, at its green fields and at the birds that soared and flew down to eat from the ground below.

Butser Hill was a place of historical and scientific significance, an ancient chalk hill, and one of the highest points in Hampshire. They had a farm museum that explored prehistoric and Roman agricultural and building techniques, so you could see how humans lived thousands of years ago. We were a part of that history now, standing there within it, the chalk hill below us a reminder of all that had happened before, the layers of history and lives that had lived there, and it all seemed to wrap around us, making the moment even more special.

'To Charlie and Ash!' said David, raising his plastic cup of Prosecco in the air.

'Charlie and Ash!' said Claire.

'To us!' said Charlie and I, and we all raised our cups together.

I looked down at the ring on my finger, at the diamond that sparkled so brightly, and then at Charlie. I thought briefly about our wedding, the future, and then about the baby we had lost. I thought about the freedom I had felt during my gap year and how happy I had been then. I would never know freedom like that again to be out in the world with little or no responsibility. I thought about those moments and about how all of them had led me to that hill with Charlie and his family. It was overwhelming when you thought about life like that, and that every decision, every moment led us in new directions with the possibility of change. You stopped to tie your shoe, and you didn't walk into the road at the moment a car ran a red light. You said no when you should have said yes. You lost a baby when you could have gained a child. Every moment impacted the next and the next and you never really knew how it was going to turn out until the very end.

2011

No. 37

Charlie

At the mercy of the elements

We were in a busy pub in Southwark, and it was bustling and loud with office workers knocking back bottles of beer and colourful cocktails trying to rub away some of the pressure of work. I had an interview for a job that afternoon in the City and it had terrified the life out of me. My current office was just off the Marylebone Road, and it had space to it, felt easy-going, and there was a relaxed atmosphere in the office. The City was a different beast altogether. It was jagged, traditional and it had a severity about it that was jarring, and you knew you were somewhere important where big decisions were made. My current job had its pressures, but it felt comfortable. The job in the City was a big step up and it felt like it from the moment I walked in and was surrounded by men, who all spoke like they had been to public school. I only got the interview as a favour to Ash's father, who had rung an old university chum, and the next minute I had an interview for a job I was hopelessly unqualified for.

'How did it go?' said Ash excitedly.

'Terrible. I shouldn't have been there. I don't know why your dad got me the interview in the first place.'

'I think he was just trying to help,' said Ash, giving me a kiss on the cheek. 'Don't give up hope, you'll find something. Have you given any more thought to teaching?'

I looked at Ash, and I didn't know what to say. I constantly thought about going back to university and training to become a teacher. It would be a proper career in something I might actually love, but something always stopped me from taking that leap. I think it was the fear of failure. I had always said I would go into teaching at some point, but what if I wasn't any good or hated it? Then what? Plus the thought of going back into education terrified the life out of me. Teaching had always been the thing I would do one day, but what if I failed? There was also the fact that while I trained, I wouldn't be earning any money, and that would put even more financial strain on Ash, and potentially her family, which would only heighten the feeling I already had that I wasn't quite good enough for them.

A few of Ash's work colleagues were in the pub with us. Harriet and Callie, whom I had met before, and Tim, whom I had seen a few times, but not spent any real time with. Tim was tall, angular and you could tell he had strong bones beneath, no doubt passed down by generations of similarly tall, angular men. He was dressed in a smart suit and everything about him screamed ACCOMPLISHED! Dazzling eyes, a perfectly square jaw and a privately educated voice. Tim Pearson was exactly the sort of man I used to imagine Ash would marry, and it terrified the life out of me that they worked so closely together.

'You can tell me about it later,' said Ash, as Tim put a tray of drinks down on the table, closely followed by Harriet and Callie.

'A Pinot for Ash,' said Tim in his deep, posh voice. Apart from being tall, he obviously worked out. Muscles strained his jacket, rippling across his wide chest, enormous arms and, no doubt, stomach.

'A pale ale for the male,' he said to me, and the girls giggled.

'Cheers,' I said, catching his eye for a moment. Crystal blue and the whitest white.

'A Martini for Harriet and a Merlot for Callie. Is that it?'

'All present and correct,' said Harriet.

'Right, then I must use the WC,' said Tim, before he strode off across the pub.

What sort of person said WC instead of toilet? Loo perhaps, or even lavatory, but never WC. There was a moment's silence before Callie broke it.

'I saw his wife today. Unbelievable.'

'Isn't she?' said Harriet.

'It's no wonder, though. Tim's not exactly hard on the eye,' said Callie.

The girls laughed, including Ash.

'Oh, sorry, Charlie,' said Harriet.

'No, no, it's fine,' I said with a smile. 'He's a handsome man.'

I was tired, it hadn't been a good day, and I just wanted to go back to the flat. I was feeling low after the interview, and I wanted time alone with Ash, but I could tell she was in the mood to stay out. Tim came back from the WC and sat down next to me.

'So, how are the wedding plans going?' said Callie.

'Good,' said Ash, looking at me. 'We have a venue. The service and reception are going to be at the one location so it's nice and easy.'

'Wonderful,' said Harriet. 'I remember my wedding day. Best day of my life.'

I looked across at Ash, and she smiled at me. We were getting married in less than six weeks. She had done most of the wedding preparation, and her father had begrudgingly agreed to pay for it all. I was looking forward to it, but there was something in the back of my mind that was holding me back. My career had stalled, and I didn't have a plan or earn enough money, and I was starting to feel the pressure to be more successful. I needed to be the sort of man Ash's father might actually approve of. Despite being terrified at the interview today, being around that sort of money, I wanted it. I wanted to get the job because then perhaps Ash would be proud of me, and I could provide the sort of lifestyle she deserved, but the interview hadn't gone well, and I knew I hadn't got it.

There was a sudden laugh as Tim recounted a story from the office, an inside joke, and everyone laughed and so I laughed, too. Ash took a sip of her drink and she looked adorable, and once again I felt so proud, so utterly fortunate, that she was my fiancée. Harriet, Callie, Tim and Ash talked shop, and I listened, and felt the same acute pain I had felt for a long time that I was on the outside looking in, and not just with Ash and her work colleagues, but at my work, too. It felt as though all of London was in on the same joke and no one had bothered to tell me. So many people with proper careers they loved, all living their BEST LIFE! with a sort of forward motion, driving fearlessly towards a point in the distance, while I was lagging behind with little idea of where my point was. What was my destination? Perhaps I would never have one, and surely that meant I would always feel lost, drifting on a boat in the middle of the ocean at the mercy of the elements.

No. 38

Ash

Bus stop fish and chips

Big, fat drops of dirty London rain fell from the darkening charcoal sky, drenching everything in its way, as Charlie and I dashed for cover. As so often happened the rain wasn't forecast, and neither of us had an umbrella, so we covered our heads with our coats and Charlie protected the bag of chips. We found shelter at a nearby bus stop, which wasn't perfect, but would do until the rain eased up.

'Oh my God, where did that come from?' I said, sitting down on the small bench inside the shelter as rain lashed against the pavement.

'I don't know, but I hope it doesn't happen again next week.'

Charlie opened the bag of chips, and a waft of heat flooded out, tinged with the overwhelming smell of salt and vinegar. We each had a little wooden fork, and we tucked in.

'I can't believe this time next week we'll be married,' I said. 'Mr and Mrs Talbot.'

'It's going to be strange not being Ash Oliver any more.'

'You could always be one of those hyphenated people. Ash Oliver-Talbot.'

'Or Ash Talbot-Oliver?'

'You want me to be Charlie Talbot-Oliver?' said Charlie, a note of disgust in his voice.

'It's an option,' I said with a smile, already knowing I would be taking his name.

We both put chips into our mouths as the rain continued to get heavier, coming down in sheets. I felt the crunch and then the soft flesh of the potato and the sharp vinegar that cut through it. It was late July, and it shouldn't be raining like that, but this was England, and anything was possible. Luckily, our wedding plans were in place and there was a backup scenario in case of inclement weather, although the forecast was good.

The last six months had been hectic. Along with work and everything else, we had planned our perfect wedding, although to be honest, most of the heavy lifting fell on me. After an exhaustive search, I had found the wedding dress of my dreams, Charlie had the morning suits ready to go and we had the venue in Putney booked. The ceremony would be indoors along with the meal and then the afternoon cocktail party would be outside and there was a marquee for the evening. The setting was perfect, and I couldn't wait for our big day, but at that moment in the bus shelter eating our takeaway chips, it felt a million miles away.

'I can't wait to call you my wife,' said Charlie, looking across at me with a smile.

'Me, too. Although you realise being married is going to change things.'

'How so?'

'I'd like us to start looking at buying a house, and, you know, trying for a baby.'

'Oh, right,' said Charlie, and then there was a pause, and I detected something in his voice.

'What?'

'It's nothing.'

'Charlie, tell me,' I said, looking across at him, as we both ate chips and watched the rain falling. It was incredibly loud as it smacked against the bus stop roof, and cars drove past, kicking up rain that splashed the ground near our feet. 'Or I'll attack you with this very small wooden chip fork!'

Charlie smiled. 'It's just, I want to get my career sorted before we start a family, Ash.'

'Oh, right. Well, I didn't mean that we'd start trying right away.'

'Good. Maybe in a year or two,' said Charlie, and the uncertainty in his voice, and the fact that after all these years, he still hadn't sorted his career out, gave me cause for concern.

I didn't need to start a family right away, but I didn't want to put it off indefinitely either. Ever since the miscarriage, I had thought about the prospect of being pregnant again. It was as if having that baby inside of me, even for such a short period of time, had altered me. Before that I had contemplated it, and I knew that one day I wanted a family, but going through that had changed how my mind processed it, and how my body longed for it. I liked to think about the next five years of our life together. Buying a house somewhere in London, starting a family, and I would get one of those badges for the Tube that said 'Baby on Board'. We would paint the second bedroom and make it into the nursery, I would keep working, and Charlie might even consider becoming a stay-at-home dad or perhaps after the wedding, he would have a new-found determination to find a better job, and our timelines and schedules would align. I knew his slight reticence about having a baby was only down to money, and once that was sorted, everything would be fine.

'I am super excited about the honeymoon in Mexico,' I said after a moment. 'All that sun, sand, sea, and sex!'

'I'm mainly excited about the sex,' said Charlie. 'You know with my pale skin I'm no good in the sun, I'm terrified of the sea, and sand just seems to get in places it doesn't belong. Whereas sex is just brilliant!'

'Our sex life reviewed by Charlie. Five stars. Brilliant!' I said, and Charlie laughed.

We sat in the bus shelter and finished our chips until the rain subsided a little. It was only a five-minute dash to the Tube station, and we decided to make a run for it.

'Ready?' said Charlie.

'Ready,' I said, holding his hand.

I screamed a little as we ran out of the shelter and into the rain towards the Underground station. We ran, holding hands, dodging other pedestrians and splashing through puddles together. It felt like the word *together* was starting to mean something different. It was evolving, and we were evolving too, and I laughed as we ran, our feet getting wet, and I had never felt more alive and ready to face our future.

No. 39

Charlie

Waiting for her to come walking down the aisle

Waiting for Ash to come walking down the aisle, I had a feeling I had never had before. It wasn't merely nerves or even complete and utter joy, but something else that made my whole body shiver with a something I didn't quite know what to do with. I wasn't concerned about the prospect of her not showing up, or having a last-minute change of heart, but something deep within the complexities of my psyche told me I needed to be worried. It was probably the same logic that made me jealous of men like Tim because I had always known I wasn't good enough for Ash, and today felt like a defining moment in that ongoing mental struggle. The day she would exclaim to the world that in her eyes, at least, I was the man she had chosen to spend the rest of her life with. The feeling, I suddenly understood, was the realisation that after today, I had to be good enough for her.

I was standing next to Matt, my best man, and next to him were Gavin, Tom, and Sam. I was in my morning suit, black jacket, grey trousers, and I had gone with pink waistcoats and lemon-yellow ties. I looked out at the crowd of people all waiting for Ash, dressed up so smartly in their wedding day finest. Mum had on a new dress she had bought from Marks and Spencer and a large hat – 'Too bloody large if you ask me,' Dad had told me over the phone – and Dad was in his best suit, and they both looked full to the brim with emotion because their only son was getting married to the girl of their dreams.

I couldn't stop my hands from shaking and so I had them in the pockets of my suit jacket, shoved down and clenched tightly. Despite applying a lengthy spray of deodorant that morning, sweat was clinging to my shirt, and I felt like I might pass out because I was feeling light-headed and hot. I should have eaten more for breakfast, but I was too nervous and couldn't face it. I took a few deep breaths to compose myself.

The music started, which meant Ash was in the building. We had hired a string quartet, and they started playing the 'Canon in D'. The next moment the doors to the room opened and stood there was Ash in an exquisite wedding gown next to her father. As soon as I saw her, my whole body loosened up, and I stopped shaking as a few tears sprang unexpectedly to my eyes. She looked gorgeous in a classic white wedding dress, a long white train held by her maid of honour, Lilly, and her bridesmaids, Anna, Cerys and Edith, stretching out behind her as she clung to her father's arm. The string quartet continued, and she started walking slowly towards me, one foot carefully in front of the other.

It was an incredible moment as she approached me, and I thought of the girl I first saw at sixth form, and then the girl I slept with at university. I thought of her on the Underground in London when we met again; her waving her hands in the air to get my attention across the platform, and the night of our first date when I slept on her floor. I remembered us in Greenwich Park, looking out over London, and then going away to the hotel in Oxfordshire and sitting in that scalding-hot bath together. I thought of the sadness we felt the day she rang me from work to tell me she had lost our baby, and the night she had sung karaoke without a care in the world. I thought of every moment I had shared with her and how much I loved her, and as she got nearer, I wiped the tears from my face and smiled at her.

She stopped in front of me, I looked at Hugh and he shook my hand then took a step back, and finally it was just me and Ash. I reached across and pulled her veil up to reveal her beautiful face beneath, and when I saw it, my heart leapt in my chest.

'You came,' I whispered.

'Of course,' she replied, tears in her eyes, too.

The music stopped, and it was time for us to get married. Before I turned to face the officiant, I caught my father's eye for a split second and I saw tears. He rarely cried, wasn't prone to moments of emotional fragility, and I could count the number of times I had seen him cry on one hand: at his father's funeral, when he thought I wasn't looking at my university graduation, and today.

No. 40

Ash

A sweet moment of pure happiness

'Ashley Elizabeth Oliver, do you take Charles Ian Talbot to be your lawful wedded husband, to be loving, faithful, and loyal for the rest of your life?'

I looked at Charlie as we stood facing each other, my whole body filled with an all-consuming love. I was aware of the crowd of people watching us, but it felt as though it was just the two of us. I looked deep into his eyes, at his red hair, and I knew I would never love anyone else like that again for the rest of my life.

'I will.'

'And do you, Charles Ian Talbot, take Ashley Elizabeth Oliver to be your lawful wedded wife, to be loving, faithful, and loyal for the rest of your life?'

I looked across at Charlie, and he looked at me with nothing but love. It was sturdy, like a solid piece of furniture that had been passed down through generations. I knew no one else would ever look at me with the same degree of unadulterated love and certainty.

'I will,' said Charlie with the biggest smile.

There was a quietness in the room, a sweet moment of pure happiness, before we continued with the ceremony. We had both written our own vows, scribbled across the room from each other at the flat. Charlie would occasionally glance across at me, his notebook in his hand, and I would smile back at him, wondering what he was writing. I read my vows first, and then it was Charlie's turn. I settled myself as he unfolded the piece of paper he'd had in his suit pocket. He held the paper, his hands trembling slightly, and he looked at me for a moment and then began reading.

'There was once a girl I saw in sixth form. She was beautiful. Long, dark hair, the prettiest face I had ever seen, the greenest eyes, but she was too good for me. At seventeen, she was popular and cool, and I wasn't. I met a girl on holiday in Lanzarote. She was stunningly attractive, funny, smart, but vulnerable and soft, too. I wanted to tell her that I loved her, but I wasn't ready. I saw a girl in London while I was at university, equally beautiful but more grown-up. She had changed and so had I, but despite both of us realising there was something between us, the timing wasn't right. Years later, I met the girl again. We were both changed, our lives were different, and this time I knew I couldn't let her go without telling her how I felt. That she had altered my life by just existing and from the moment I saw her, I knew I didn't want to spend my life with anyone else. All these girls are standing in front of me today and all the boys are talking to her. Ash, I love you so much. You make cloudy days clear, wet days dry, and cold days warm. You are without doubt the sunshine of my life and I will love you forever.'

Charlie stopped, and I wiped the tears from my eyes, and then he folded up the piece of paper and put it back in his jacket pocket. One day, that piece of paper would be framed and on the wall of our bedroom. His words encased in glass for eternity. We exchanged rings, and then we were pronounced man and wife.

'You may now kiss the bride!'

Charlie and I kissed, our lips coming together in perhaps our sweetest ever kiss, full of love and relief because, after all the planning and waiting, we were finally married. A chorus of cheers and then claps swept around the room and it was done, but there was one thing left to enjoy. As we turned to face the crowd, a memory of something Charlie had once said to me was on my mind. Everyone stood, and then the music began, as we began our walk out. The string quartet started playing 'Hey Jude' as Charlie had once told me he wanted. He looked at me with a big smile.

'I can't believe you remembered.'

'I can't believe you don't think I would have,' I replied, and we walked out with 'Hey Jude' being played, and with everyone in the room singing along.

No. 41

Charlie

Sip every last drop

We ate a delicious three-course dinner with our closest friends and family, while speeches were given. Some were touching and funny, and some overly long, but with the best of intentions. It was an intense feeling getting married, an entire day to celebrate our love and I couldn't believe Ash had got the band to play 'Hey Jude' as we left the church. She had remembered my throwaway comment made years before, and it was perfect.

The evening reception was in full swing. We had the string quartet for the afternoon, but once the evening reception was under way, we had a DJ. Alcohol was flowing, all the stress leading up to the big day was over, and it felt like time to relax, let our hair down and revel in the fact we had everyone we loved in the same place at the same time.

We were in the marquee, people were getting drunk, and the dance floor was full of bodies in outfits that had started the day so perfectly, but we were now in the middle of the night and slightly more ragged. Ties were tossed aside, handbags and hats left on tables and high-heeled shoes discarded. Ash and I had fulfilled all our duties, said hello to everyone and now we were enjoying ourselves. Children ran across the dance floor, sliding on their knees and secretly eating food under tables.

I was at the bar with friends getting a drink and Ash was talking to a group of people from her work. She had been floating around all night, laughing, drinking and being the belle of the ball. I was looking out over the dance floor when one song ended and then a song came on that instantly changed the mood. It was 'Here Comes the Sun', Ash's parents' wedding dance song. Ash had mentioned it to me when we were trying to pick our own song because I had mentioned a few Beatles songs, but she had wanted to go with Take That, and so we had chosen 'How Deep Is Your Love'.

The dance floor cleared of all the younger single people, and then in a moment of magic, Ash appeared, and she beckoned me over. I saw Ash's parents start dancing together, and then my parents were up, too. I reached Ash and looked at her.

'This one's for you,' she said, holding out her hand.

I didn't say anything. I held her hand and then I felt her body in mine, her hands around me, and mine around her. It was dark outside now, and we danced together, moving around the dance floor, our eyes locked on each other. We spun around and I caught fleeting glimpses of my parents and her parents, and everyone had gathered around the dance floor to watch.

'I love you, Ashley Elizabeth Talbot.'

'Love you, too, Charles Ian Talbot.'

'I never liked Ian as a middle name. When we finally have kids, if we have a boy, he's going to have a brilliant middle name.'

'Like what?'

'I don't know, but not Ian. Maybe Elvis!'

'Oh God, no!' said Ash, laughing.

'How about John Paul George Ringo?'

'Okay, you aren't allowed to be in charge of names,' said Ash.

'Here Comes the Sun' came to an end and all the couples slowly pulled away, apart from Ash's parents, who were still together, slow dancing, her head on his shoulder. They were obviously sharing a moment, and I nodded to Ash and across at her parents. When she looked at them she smiled, and we walked off together before the DJ started playing 'Millennium' by Robbie Williams, and Lilly whisked Ash away to dance, and I headed back to the bar. The night was still young, and I wanted to take in every moment, sip every last drop of the day because I knew it was special, and something I would remember for the rest of my life.

No. 42

Ash

The best of my life

We were finally in bed, cuddled up together in our five-star hotel room in Chelsea. It had an enormous four-poster bed, a separate living room and the most incredible bathroom with a bathtub more than big enough for the both of us. We were going to be served a full English breakfast in bed in the morning, and I couldn't have been happier or more fulfilled. Our wedding day had been the best day of my life, and I was so full of love and gratitude, my heart felt fit to burst. It was almost one o'clock in the morning, and we were both so tired, cuddled up under the sheets, just staring at each other.

'We did it,' I said.

'We did, although your dad told me earlier that if I ever hurt you, he would hunt me down and rip me apart limb by limb, so that was nice.'

'You had better not hurt me then.'

'I don't think I could. I love you far too much.'

'I'm so tired,' I said, yawning.

'Me, too. We should probably have sex, though. It is our wedding night.'

'Sorry, but do we have to?'

'Of course not,' replied Charlie with a smile. 'I've had too much to drink, and to be honest, I'm exhausted.'

'Love you, husband.'

'Love you, wife.'

'Today was magical, wasn't it?'

'It was. Although a shame about your uncle Nigel.'

'Why? He's the one who started the conga.'

'But he wasn't wearing any trousers, Ash.'

I laughed. 'At least he was wearing underwear, which is more than can be said about the thing he did at cousin Ann-Marie's wedding in Glasgow.'

'Oh God, I don't think I want to know.'

'Let's just say,' I said, my eyes closing, 'that he wore a kilt the traditional way, and to be fair, you're asking for trouble playing the cancan at a Scottish wedding.'

'Eww.'

'Everyone was surprised how high he could kick his legs in the air,' I said, chuckling, and we lay in silence for a moment, both of us falling asleep.

'Thank you for "Hey Jude",' said Charlie, barely a whisper in the dark.

'You're welcome.'

I opened my eyes for a moment and looked at Charlie. This was just the beginning of our journey. I thought about the day and about my five-year plan. I was excited, tired, and when I closed my eyes my mind was full of the wonderful adventure that was ahead of us. I sank into the luxurious bed, a mixture of goose down and Egyptian cotton. The room had the finest of everything, and it smelled wonderful, too. It felt as though every single thing had been thought of and surely it was the best way to start married life.

The last thought I had before tiredness took me away was of Charlie as I walked up the aisle to get married. His red hair against the black of his suit jacket, the pink of his waistcoat and the huge smile on his face. In the background, the string quartet played the 'Canon in D', and I walked slowly towards him. I wouldn't ever forget that moment. It was ingrained in my soul. There are some days you would live over and over, and some you never want to experience again, but this was definitely a day I would live again as many times as I could.

2012

No. 43

Charlie

Pizza on the floor

The house was empty except for a few boxes we had moved over in Ash's car, and it felt enormous compared to our flat, and it was somehow all ours. Our first proper house together, and despite having jobs, university degrees and getting married, this felt like the most adult thing we had done by some distance.

Almost a year after our wedding, and with Ash's parents' help, we had cobbled enough money together to buy a two-bed house on the outskirts of Kingston upon Thames. It needed some cosmetic work and lots of TLC, but it had good bones and some nice original features. It was a mid-terraced Victorian house with a compact front room, a cosy dining room that led to a galley kitchen and then the family bathroom. Upstairs, it had a double bedroom at the front, and then a slightly smaller second bedroom at the rear of the house. The long, thin garden was completely overgrown and there was a small wooden shed at the bottom.

When we had been shown around the house by the estate agent, a Greek man in a grey suit, we had spoken about extending into the loft and adding a master bedroom with an en suite. We had talked about the possibility of extending the kitchen into the garden, and having that all-important kitchen–diner, and then Ash and I had spoken about taking up the carpets and refinishing the old wooden floors. But at that moment, sitting on the empty floor of the front room, with a large pizza box next to us, and a bottle of Prosecco, all of that felt like a million years away. This felt to us like the beginning of everything.

'I still can't believe this is our house,' I said.

We were both in weekend clothes of jogging bottoms and sweatshirts. It had been a busy day, and we were finally relaxing for the first time. We didn't have a television yet, or even a proper bed to sleep in, but we didn't care. We had a home.

'It feels completely surreal,' Ash replied, looking around the barren room.

'Although you do realise that we're now annoying London house owners, hated by all and sundry renters, and people like us just months ago.'

'I'm fine with that. We served our time.'

'And now we get to enjoy the fruits of our labour?'

'Something like that, and anyone who feels slightly bitter about it can just fuck off.'

'Hear, hear, more Prosecco, darling?' I said in my poshest voice, and Ash laughed.

We had only got the keys from the estate agent that morning, and we had spent most of the day at the flat tidying up, packing, and we had finally driven over with a few boxes before the big move tomorrow. Tonight felt like the calm before the storm, one last night to enjoy the simplicity of us in our new house before we would be assembling a whole life together.

'Do you want another slice of pizza?' I said, looking down at the box, and Ash said she could do one more. I picked up the largest slice and placed it on her paper plate before I swallowed a mouthful of the Prosecco. We hadn't bothered to bring cups, and so we were drinking it straight out of the bottle.

'So, tomorrow, we have to pick up the van at eight, go back to the flat, and load everything up,' said Ash.

'And you're sure we can do it all in one go?'

'How many times have I told you, Spatial Awareness Man, we don't have much stuff?'

'Correction, I don't have much stuff. You, Mrs Eighty Pairs Of Shoes—'

'Hey!' Ash replied, hitting my arm. 'And FYI, it's only sixty-seven pairs of shoes because I gave a load to that charity shop last week.'

'I apologise. Sixty-seven pairs of shoes, and how many coats?'

'I refuse to answer that,' said Ash, having a bite of her pizza. 'We should be fine, despite my shoe collection. My parents are meeting us here at two o'clock.'

'Oh, yes, your father is coming. I almost forgot.'

'Let's not forget that, without him, we wouldn't have been able to afford this house.'

'You don't have to worry about that. I'll never be able to forget.'

It wasn't that I wasn't grateful to Ash's parents for giving us the money for the deposit, it was that it reminded me yet again that I wasn't able to provide Ash the life I wished I could. I knew that most people our age didn't have fifty thousand pounds for a deposit, and those that did probably got it from a parent or an inheritance, but it felt like another occasion when her parents had jumped in to save us. Not that I wasn't thankful. I loved our house and without them, we would have been moving into a flat in a much less salubrious part of London, but I knew Hugh would never let me forget that he paid for a portion of our house.

'Just be nice, okay?' said Ash.

'I'll be the most charming man in south-west London moving into his first house,' I replied, and she retorted with a sarcastic smile.

We finished the pizza, bottle of Prosecco, and after we had brushed our teeth, I blew up the airbed we had brought along with sleeping bags and pillows, and we got into bed.

'What does one do when one doesn't have a television to watch and it's only nine o'clock?' said Ash with a cheeky grin.

'I imagine one probably has sex,' I replied, and she looked at me and then smiled. It was our first night in our new house, and we were in sleeping bags on a blow-up bed.

'Then you had better unzip your sleeping bag and get into mine.'

I quickly did as I was told and got into her sleeping bag. We had to unzip hers to give us slightly more room, and it was going to be a little tricky on the airbed that definitely wasn't, despite what Ash insisted, completely inflated, but this was going to be special. There was no better way to christen a new house than to have sex in it, and this was one time we definitely wouldn't forget.

No. 44

Ash

This wasn't supposed to happen to me

'I'm not coming out, Charlie!' I shouted from the security of our bedroom. 'Just tell everyone I've come down with something.'

I was sitting on the end of our bed, in a gorgeous, bought-for-the-occasion dress, and ready to go out, but all I wanted to do was get into my pyjamas. Perhaps Charlie could bring me a tub of ice cream, and we could watch a romantic comedy together that would make me feel better about the dreaded Big Three-O.

'Ash, it's okay,' said Charlie from the other side of the door, trying to placate me with a calming voice. 'It's just a number.'

'It's not just a number, Charlie! It means I'm officially old!'

'Thirty isn't old—'

'That's easy for you to say, you're only twenty-nine! You're practically a baby! Oh fuck, I'm one of those cradle-snatching cougars you hear about!'

I honestly didn't think turning thirty would be this traumatic, and indeed, leading up to the big day, I was bouncing on air and full of joy. We had finally moved into our forever home and were in the process of renovations. We had been to Farrow & Ball in Wimbledon and chosen the paint we wanted for the walls. We had been looking into someone to refinish the floors and restore them to their former glory. Charlie said we should just 'give it a bash ourselves', but despite Charlie's optimism, I wasn't prepared to 'give it a bash' and ruin our lovely wooden floors because he had watched a few episodes of *Changing Rooms* on the BBC. We had already spent an entire weekend in the garden cutting everything back, and it looked a hundred times better, and so much bigger. I was going from strength to strength at work and growing my list of authors every month. My life was just about perfect, and I really thought I would handle turning thirty with a bit of class, but while I was getting ready, something inside of me snapped.

'Ash, please unlock the door and let me in,' said Charlie ever so calmly.

'I can't.'

'Why not?'

'Because if I let you in, you'll try to convince me to go out.'

'How about you just let me in? That's it. That's all you have to do. One step at a time.'

I took a moment, and then I let Charlie into our bedroom. I got up, unlocked the door and then walked back and sat on the bed again. Charlie walked into the room, stood in front of me looking gorgeous in a pair of navy chinos and a pristine white shirt. He smiled at me.

'You look more beautiful than ever,' he said.

'You're just saying that to get me to go out.'

Charlie kneeled down in front of me, his hands on my legs.

'Ash, you have never looked more beautiful and sexier than you do now. Cross my heart and hope to die, stick a needle in my eye—'

'Stop it,' I said, finally cracking a smile.

'Honestly, if we don't go out, I will be more than happy to stay in and have lots of brilliant birthday sex.'

'You want to have sex with an old lady?'

'Lots and lots of sex until we both get so old we can only do the missionary position very slowly in case we get stuck and have to be surgically removed from each other.'

'So romantic.'

'I know, but seriously, Ash, right now, I just want to take you out to dinner for your birthday. There are currently eight people on their way to a restaurant in Chelsea, and if we don't get a move on, we're going to be late, and I've heard their starters are to die for.'

I looked at Charlie and I wanted him to understand that turning thirty meant something more to me than to him. He thought I was only worried about looking older, that things were getting a little plumper, sagging southwards, but it wasn't that, although I wasn't entirely happy about that either. Thirty was the age that made me realise I wanted a family more than anything, and soon because my biological clock was ticking, and it was getting faster and faster every year, and I could almost hear it roaring in my ears. My twenties seemed to have flown by, and I didn't want to wake up at forty and go, fuck, that's ten years I've wasted.

'This wasn't supposed to happen to me,' I said.

'What? Turning thirty?'

'Yes.'

'No offence, Ash, but I think it happens to all of us.' Charlie took my hands and held them softly in his. 'But you are the most beautiful, wonderful, and perfect thirty-year-old there has ever been, and not just in this bedroom, but in all the bedrooms in all the world.'

I didn't mean to start crying, but Charlie was being so nice, I couldn't stop myself.

'I'm sorry,' I said between sobs. 'But you're so lovely to me.'

'Lovely enough to get you out of the house and into a taxi?'

'I suppose so,' I said, taking a moment and then standing up. 'But I must warn you, I'm going to get incredibly drunk, and then tomorrow I'm going to regret it and have the most miserable hangover, and you're going to have to look after me, and I mean proper all day, getting me whatever I want from the shops, and cooking me whatever I desire at any point.'

'It's a deal.'

Charlie stood up, too, and then we kissed before we got ready for my thirtieth birthday meal with my nearest and dearest. I honestly didn't know what I would do without him. Charlie was my rock, my everything, and hopefully, one day the father of my children.

'Oh, and Charlie?' I said as we were about to walk out of the front door.

'Yes?'

'Remember when we talked about sexual fantasies after we read that article in *Cosmo*, and you said one of yours was going out with me and I wasn't wearing any knickers?'

'I do,' said Charlie, a sudden look of wonder on his face.

I looked at him, leaned in until I was inches from his face, and then I whispered, 'I'm not wearing any tonight.'

No. 45

Charlie

The one when we're sick

It was a cold, wet Tuesday morning, and we were both in bed with the same flu symptoms, and life felt pretty fucking awful. Ash had just returned to bed with two cups of Lemsip, pulling the duvet up to cover herself, blowing her nose on a tissue and then adding it to the pile of tissues on her nightstand that had been getting bigger and bigger every hour.

'I seriously don't think I've ever felt this sick before,' I said to Ash.

We were both miserable, and so it seemed like the perfect time to watch the entire series of *Friends*. We weren't sure it was possible, but that would depend on how long we were sick for. We had been home for two days and were midway through the second season.

'Next episode?' I said, holding the remote in my hand.

'Ready when you are,' said Ash, her voice sounding much like mine. Stuffy, quite rough, and definitely a little masculine. I pushed play on the remote and the next episode came on. It was 'The One with the Prom Video'.

'I love this episode,' I said, taking a sip of my Lemsip that was verging on being dangerously hot, but it felt so good at the same time. The hot lemony liquid slid down my throat, and then I coughed, Ash coughed, she sniffed, I sniffed, we both blew our noses, and then we added more snotty tissues to the pile.

The episode started in Chandler and Joey's apartment and, despite feeling wretched, we were both soon giggling. Ash laughed so hard it turned into a cough, and then she had to blow her nose again before we could continue.

'I remember when I first watched this episode,' said Ash. 'I was fourteen or fifteen, and *Friends* was my favourite show. It would have been in my bedroom on my old portable TV.'

'Sadly, I didn't have a portable TV and had to watch it in the front room, trying not to laugh at the sexy bits while my parents pretended someone hadn't just referenced a blow job,' I said, and then we looked across at each other and smiled. 'You know, we watched it only a few miles apart.'

'And here we are together—'

'As sick as dogs.'

'In our new home.'

Ash reached a hand across the bed and held mine. We kept watching until we came to the scene where Phoebe tells Ross that Rachel is his lobster.

'Oh my God, I remember this. The next day I told Lilly at school that one day I'd find my lobster. We were such losers back then.'

'And yet, here you are with your own lobster,' I said, and she looked across at me. 'I am your lobster, right?'

'You're my Ross.'

'I suppose that makes you my Rachel. I had such a crush on Jennifer Aniston.'

'I don't think you were the only one,' said Ash, who took a sip of her Lemsip, but then her glasses got steamed up from the heat, and she had to give them a wipe with the bed sheet.

The episode ended with the group of them at Monica's apartment, watching an old prom video. Rachel and Monica are going to their prom, but Rachel's date doesn't show up and Ross is aiming to be her stand-in. You can see how much Ross adores Rachel, and watching it, I couldn't help but be reminded of how I had felt for so long around Ash. In fact, when I thought about our relationship dynamics, they weren't that dissimilar to Ross and Rachel.

'It's weird to think of us watching that at fourteen, our whole lives ahead of us, and how everything has turned out,' I said as the credits rolled.

'What do you mean?' replied Ash, taking another sip of her Lemsip.

'Because at sixth form, I was Ross, and you were my Rachel, the cooler, beautiful girl that was way out of my league.'

Ash turned, looked at me, and said, 'Do you still see me like that?'

'Out of my league? The girl I didn't stand a chance with. Absolutely.'

'You shouldn't think of me like that. I have never thought of you as below me on the dating spectrum. You're my lobster, Charlie, because you're you.'

She looked at me, and a moment passed between us.

'I would kiss you now, but you've got a bit of snot hanging from your nose,' I said.

'And you still think I'm out of your league?' she said with a giggle.

'I mean, maybe not right now,' I said sarcastically, and then Ash blew her nose as the next episode began.

2013

No. 46

Ash

The telephone call

Some days you want to live over and over, but some you never want to experience again. It was like the day happened in slow motion. Everything was normal speed, but as soon as Charlie got off the phone, it changed in a flash and we both knew that life might never be the same again. Every moment, facial expression and second of indecision seemed to take forever. It was as if all of life had been squeezed into that moment, compressed until the pressure became too much, and was fit to burst.

It was a lazy Saturday afternoon, and we were at home, watching television and nibbling on snacks. We'd both had long weeks at work, it was grey and overcast, and so perfect for camping out on the sofa, and doing nothing. There had been tentative talk of ordering a takeaway, perhaps opening a bottle of wine and watching a film, but then it happened. Charlie's mobile phone rang. I barely looked across as he answered his phone until I heard his voice and immediately knew something terrible had happened.

'Is he all right?' said Charlie. He had stiffened up, and his voice cracked. 'You're on your way to the hospital now. Right. I'll be there as soon as I can. Okay. Love you. Bye, bye.'

Charlie hung up the phone and I looked at him. His face was ashen white, and he looked like he might cry or be sick, I wasn't sure which. He was almost too choked up to speak.

'What is it?'

'It's Dad. He's had a heart attack,' Charlie replied, and then he stood up. 'I have to go.'

He looked shaken and I put my hands on his shoulders and made him look at me.

'I'll drive. Just pack a few things in a bag. It's going to be all right, Charlie. We'll get there as soon as we can.'

Charlie looked at me, tears in his eyes, and he looked like he wanted to fall in a heap on the floor. Whatever the future held, I knew I had to keep him going, make him take care of the practical stuff and keep his mind off what had happened to his father.

We packed overnight bags, working in an uncomfortable silence, the tension of time that seemed so precious in those moments forcing us to hurry. Neither of us knew how serious it was, whether he would even be alive when we got there, or perhaps it was just a minor heart attack, and he would be home in a few days complaining about being forced to eat 'rabbit food'. We didn't know the seriousness of the situation, and that added another layer of stress as we packed up our stuff, throwing clothes into bags, until we stood at the front door.

'Ready?' I said.

'What if he doesn't make it, Ash? What if...'

I put my hand on his cheek and smiled a razor-thin smile full of hope. 'Let's just wait and see.'

I hugged him for a moment and felt the full weight of his body as it sank into me. We didn't say anything else, and then we left, and I started the drive. I let the radio play whatever was on. It was tuned to Radio 2, and a song by the Stereophonics came on that we loved. They sang about having a nice day, and just the thought of that felt impossible.

It was a surreal drive along the M3, the journey we had taken so many times over the years that felt so familiar, but something had changed. I could feel the fear emanating from Charlie. We both knew his father had never been the healthiest man, but like so many things in life, you didn't expect the worst to happen. His mum had always encouraged him to take better care of himself, eat healthier, exercise, but he was also only fifty-five and had so much more time left. He was a young man in so many ways, the life and soul of the party, but his father before him had died of a heart attack, and despite the warnings he still indulged too much, refused to exercise, and all of that information sat on my mind, and I'm sure Charlie's, too.

We sat in the car for a moment, and Charlie took a second to compose himself. We had finally arrived at the hospital and I had found a parking space. I looked across the car at Charlie, and I just wanted to protect him and make all the pain go away. I wished we were back at our house, where the biggest dilemma we faced was what film to watch, but that was a different life, an alternate reality that hadn't happened.

'Ready?' I said softly, and Charlie nodded.

I leaned across the car, and I hugged him, feeling his head buried in my shoulder. I think both of us were terrified to see his mother. At that moment, we didn't know what we were dealing with. Would today go down in our shared history as just one of those days that was a bit scary but ultimately okay, or would it change everything? I hugged him, and I prayed it wasn't the worst because I honestly didn't know what that would mean for us if it was.

No. 47

Charlie

Mum's the word

We dashed into the hospital and found Mum in the waiting room. I hated the thought of her being alone for so long and having to go through so much by herself. Her whole body was slumped forward in a sort of desperate sadness because the worst had happened.

'Mum,' I said, and she stood up, pools of tears in her eyes.

'Oh, Charlie,' she said when I hugged her. I felt her body in mine, and it felt so heavy, even though she was quite a small woman. It was like I could feel all the raw emotion inside of her. After a moment, I let her go, Ash hugged Mum too, and then we all sat down in a line.

'What happened?' I asked, desperate for information.

Mum looked at me, took a breath, and then said, 'It happened on the train—'

'The train? What were you doing on the train?'

'Going to Winchester for the day. Your father wanted to drive, but I said, let's go on the train for a change because we never go on the train. It was nice and ever so easy. Twenty minutes each way.'

'Okay, and what happened on the train?'

'We'd had a lovely day out, and we were coming back when it happened. He just slumped in his seat, Charlie, his whole face was red, and I knew something was wrong. I shouted for help, and luckily there was a junior doctor on the next carriage. He was returning home after a shift, and he quickly took care of your father. He did CPR, and I rang for an ambulance.'

'And where's Dad now?'

'Surgery, I think. They gave him some medicine in the ambulance, blood thinners, and then as soon as they got him here they took him away. I didn't even see him.'

'And when was the last time you heard something?' I said, feeling Ash's hand in mine.

'Half an hour ago. A doctor came out, a lovely woman, and said he needed a procedure. Something about blocked arteries. I had a hard time following, if I'm honest.'

'But did she seem positive?'

Mum looked at me, the lines and wrinkles on her pale face more pronounced than usual, and she looked suddenly older somehow.

'I don't know, Charlie. She said they were doing everything they could, and that's the best they can do, isn't it?'

'I suppose so, Mum,' I said, and then I looked at Ash, and I didn't know what to think. I slumped in my chair, Ash's hand was still in mine, and Mum was next to me,, staring off into space. She was probably in shock because I knew I was. Every moment since Mum had called had felt surreal. It was impossible to imagine a life without Dad, yet we were there in that hospital waiting room and it was one of the possible outcomes. While we sat, the last conversation I had with Dad jumped into my mind and refused to budge. Would it be the last conversation we ever had?

It had been on Wednesday night. Ash and I had just had dinner, she was upstairs taking a shower, and I had just finished tidying up when my phone rang.

'Hello, old man,' I said, walking from the kitchen into the living room and sitting down on the sofa. I switched on the television then scanned the channels to see what was on.

'Not so much of the old,' Dad replied.

'Fair enough. What's going on? Everything all right?'

'Yes, all good. I was just cleaning out the loft and I found a few of your old boxes.'

'Why are you cleaning out the loft? Surely the whole point of a loft is to store all the crap you don't actually need until one day you sell the house and you're forced to go into the loft and throw away all the crap you put up there for years to keep out of the way.'

'Your mother read an article about decluttering your life, and that true happiness comes from less stuff and more order. Apparently, it's all the rage. They even had a segment about it on *This Morning*. She's been a bit mental ever since. She got rid of my golf clubs last week without even asking me.'

'I didn't know you played golf, Dad.'

'I don't, but now even if I wanted to I couldn't because I don't have any clubs.'

'Right.'

'So, anyway, I found two boxes of your old stuff. There are photos, school reports, drawings, and other bits and pieces. I think, under the new regime, you either come and get it, or I have to burn it all at the allotment.'

'You have an allotment?'

'No, but Malcolm from across the road has one, and he's always burning things. Now that I think about it, there's a good chance he might be one of those pirate maniacs.'

'I think you mean pyromaniacs, Dad.'

'Do I? Okay. Look, I'll tell you what, I'll store the boxes in the shed for a few weeks.'

'Thanks, Dad.'

'No problem. Okay, I have to go, *The One Show* is about to start.'

'All right, Dad. We'll pop down soon so I can look at the boxes.'

'Mum's the word, though. If she finds boxes in the shed, she'll have my guts for garters.'

'Mum's the word,' I said, Dad laughed, and then we hung up.

The last words Dad had said to me were, 'she'll have my guts for garters', and just the thought of that brought tears to my eyes, but I quickly rubbed them away because I needed to be strong for Mum. I looked at her, she smiled a thin, uncertain smile at me, and I reached down and held her hand, and we sat there together, and waited for news.

No. 48

Ash

Positive vibes only

The waiting was the most difficult thing because within those unknown moments, all the worst-case scenarios raced through my mind. I held Charlie's hand, and next to him his poor mother sat in silence, probably imagining the worst, too. I didn't believe in God, but I prayed because I didn't know what else to do. I felt so utterly useless and, for some reason, praying to an arbitrary God felt better than doing nothing. What I wanted to do was ask questions, go online and research statistics about deaths, heart attacks, what they were doing to save his life, because to me not knowing anything was the worst thing of all. I wanted to feel like I was being useful, so I offered to get us all a cup of coffee while we waited for news.

'There's a Costa,' said Charlie's mum. 'But I'm not sure where it is, love.'

'It's okay, I'll find it,' I said, standing up.

I took their orders, gave Charlie a kiss on the cheek, and then I went off to find Costa Coffee, in the hope that some warm beverages might be something of a comfort. I walked along hallways, into and out of other waiting rooms, until I eventually found it. It was surprisingly busy, and I found myself in a queue of about half a dozen people. I stood behind a middle-aged man with dark hair and glasses, who turned, looked at me, and I smiled at him.

'Cancer,' he said suddenly.

'Sorry?' I replied, slightly taken aback.

'It's why I'm here. My wife has breast cancer.'

'Oh, shit, sorry.'

'They think she's going to be all right, though. Stage one. They caught it early.'

'That's good.'

'What about you?'

'Me?'

'What are you in for?'

'Oh, right, yes. Heart attack. My father-in-law.'

'How's he doing?'

'I'm not sure. They only brought him in a while ago. We're still waiting for news.'

The queue moved forward, and we slowly edged along with it.

'Fingers crossed. I hope everything works out.'

'Yes, for you, too, and your wife.'

'I'm sure it will be okay. It's good to be positive, I think. They say that people with a positive mental attitude recover faster. Maybe that works when you're waiting for news, too. Good vibes and all that.'

'I hope so,' I said, as we reached the front of the queue.

The man moved forward and placed his order, and then I waited and placed mine. Charlie wanted a flat white, Claire a cappuccino, and I was going to get a latte, and something to eat. I wasn't particularly hungry, but I thought I should get something because I had no idea how long we would be there for, so I grabbed a couple of flapjacks, and then I waited with the man. His drink came first, he smiled at me, wished me all the best and then wandered off back to his wife.

I eventually got our drinks and started the walk back. I wanted to think positively, and perhaps the man was right, and it might help. I had always believed a positive mindset was important in life, and that was something my father had given to me. It was always wrapped up in hard work and planning, but the message was always the same: be positive and positive things will follow. I had to believe that for Charlie's dad, too.

As I got back to them, I saw a doctor walk over, and so I hurried across.

'If you'd like to follow me,' said the doctor. She was late thirties, Southeast Asian maybe, glasses, and dark hair swept up into a bun. We followed her along a short hallway, and then into a smaller room. There was just a desk with a chair behind it, a computer and three chairs on the other side. 'Please, take a seat.'

On the wall was a photo of a beautiful beach fringed with palm trees. I wished I was there, I thought, and then I realised that was probably why it was on the wall in the first place.

'I think I'll stand, if it's all right with you,' said Charlie's mum.

'Me, too,' said Charlie.

I didn't speak but knew I was going to stand, too. I was still holding the coffees, in a tray, which now felt like a really bad prop in the scene, but I was grateful I had something to do.

'Right, okay then,' said the doctor, sitting on the edge of the desk, an obvious awareness of her actions and words. Her face wasn't giving much away, and I was holding on to my positive thinking. Only good vibes.

'Mrs Talbot, I'm afraid I have some bad news.'

The words didn't take long to sink into us. Bad news really only meant one thing. It wasn't going to be one of those 'close call' moments when it was so nearly a tragedy but ultimately nothing more than a wake-up call. It was suddenly like one of those moments on a television show when life seemed to go into an intense blur, and I knew the doctor was speaking, but I wasn't hearing any of her words. I was holding the coffee, while next to me Charlie and his mum were breaking down into tears as they got the news that David had died. I wanted to cry, too, but at that moment I couldn't because all I could think about was Charlie and his mum, and how much they were going to need me in the following days and weeks.

Charlie and his mum hugged, and then they slumped into the chairs, and the doctor was telling them exactly what had happened. I sat down, too, and I thought of the man I had met in the queue, and I hoped his wife was going to be all right. It was strange being in that hospital so full of sick people, and it was easy to forget about them once you left and were back in the real world, worried about getting home again because traffic would be awful, and work in the morning. But now Charlie's dad had died, we wouldn't be able to just leave and forget about it. His dad wouldn't be going home in a few days joking about his 'dicky ticker' and vowing to start taking care of himself. I looked at Charlie, at his face that was so sad, pale and full of tears, and I knew he was going to need me to be the positivity, and so I sat and held their coffee, and I didn't cry because I couldn't.

No. 49

Charlie

The funeral

I held Ash's hand on one side of me and Mum's on the other, and we stood together facing the church where Dad was going to be buried. The last few weeks had gone by in a surreal state of shock, slowly getting the practical things done, while all around us life continued on as it always did. Mum had a list, and we gradually worked our way through it, but it was done now, and we were there.

People dressed in black surrounded us, speaking in respectfully muted tones, looks of sorrow on their faces. Dad's family, his sister, his mother, who had already buried her husband years before, and a gaggle of distant relations I had never met, but they knew me from a wedding when I was 'knee-high to a grasshopper'. Friends of Dad, most I didn't know, but they were there, and I was grateful. Ash's hand was squeezed tightly into mine, and it was difficult to comprehend that just a few weeks ago life had felt so normal, so perfectly fine, and now I was burying my father. I wouldn't ever see him again or hear his embarrassingly loud laugh. It felt impossible, and yet it was true.

People started walking inside as the organ began to play, and it was time to go in. I gave Mum's hand a gentle squeeze, and she turned to look at me, her eyes glazed over with the same look of disbelief and of wretched despondency she'd had since Dad had died.

'Ready, Mum?'

She didn't say anything, and instead, she just nodded. I think she knew if she tried to speak, she would break down and, once the floodgates opened, it would be near impossible to close them again. I hadn't been inside a church for a long time, but there was something familiar about that particular church. It was the church nearest my old primary school, and we would go there for harvest festivals, Easter and Christmas. I wasn't religious, but my school was, and walking inside felt like taking a trip back to my childhood.

We walked to the front of the church and took our seats as the service began. I knew I had to give the eulogy, and when I had agreed to it, I thought I would be all right, but in that church that held so many memories, I didn't know if I could. Ash sat next to me, her hand still clasping mine with so much love. She had been wonderful since Dad had died. Mum and I were a mess afterwards and so Ash took charge of everything. She made phone calls, took care of paperwork and saved us from the frontline of dealing with the practicalities of death.

'Love you,' Ash whispered to me before I had to stand up and read out the eulogy. I had written so many drafts, and this was a sort of 'best of' version. I walked to the front of the church, turned to face everyone, and then I took out the piece of paper I had written the eulogy on. I slowly unfolded the paper, and then I began.

'It's hard to believe Dad is gone,' I started, my words echoing around the cavernous old building. 'Mainly because he was such a stubborn man, so full of life, it seemed like it would take something gargantuan to take him away from us. Growing up, he always seemed so strong, and it feels ironic that the man with the biggest heart, who would do anything for anyone, also had a weak one.' I stopped to take a breath and to compose myself. 'Dad always told me that no matter what happened in life, to follow my dreams, be true to myself, and to never give up. He always emphasised the last one because he worked so hard all his life to make sure I had all the opportunities he didn't. Never give up. Work hard to be the best version of yourself. Many people may have known Dad, and perhaps they just saw a man who worked in a factory. Married with a son, he was in many ways just an ordinary bloke, but there was more to him than that. He was smart, funny, sharp as a tack, and he could fix anything. I love you, Dad, and I'm going to miss you every day for the rest of my life.'

I sat down next to Ash, her hand in mine, and finally, after holding it in, I let myself cry. The rest of the service went by in a daze, but the thing I felt the entire time was Ash.

Outside, the sun shone brighter, as we all filtered out of the church, and people mumbled conversations about Dad, wished me all the best and said how sorry they were. We stood surrounded by moss-covered gravestones and wide oak trees, and all we did was speak about Dad and what he meant to us. There was a moment when I was having a conversation with one of my cousins and I looked across and saw Ash deep in conversation with her parents, who had come to show their support. Ash glanced at me, I looked across at her, she smiled at me, I smiled back, and in that moment, I knew I would be okay. Despite how heartbreakingly difficult it felt at that moment, life would go on, and I would be doing it with Ash.

We were back at my parents' house, and Mum and Ash were inside having tea, but I had snuck out to Dad's shed on my own. I opened the creaky old door and walked inside. Just the smell of it, and I was a boy again standing next to Dad. The shed was full of tools, gardening equipment, and at the very back of the shed, under a shelf, were two boxes. I walked across and, written across both boxes in felt-tip pen, it said, 'Charlie's Stuff'. Dad had kept them safe for me. I sat down next to the boxes, and I opened one. I knew that despite crying so much already, that I might cry again when I saw what was in the boxes, but I had to see. I looked inside and it was a real jumble of papers, old birthday cards, a couple of mixtapes, and there right on top was a photo. I picked it up and looked at it. It was me and Dad at the top of a hill somewhere, and it was obviously windy because both of our hair was sticking straight up and to the side. I was probably about eight or nine, Dad looked ever so young, had a moustache and was so much thinner. I smiled because the thought I had was the photo was placed on top because Dad had looked at it himself. He had probably held it just a few weeks ago, and he would have smiled, too.

No. 50

Ash

The need to feel alive

Since his father had died, Charlie had in many ways, stopped living himself. Life felt like it was drifting away from us, passing us in a daze when all we did was work, come home, eat, watch television, go to bed, and repeat. Nothing felt real or like it was going to change unless we did something different. It was like we were constantly hung-over, and perhaps we were. We needed a break from our life, and so I suggested a weekend in Brighton. We had been for the day once before, and we'd had the most wonderful time, and now we were staying for two nights. It was late summer, all the children were back at school, and I wanted to bring up the subject of starting a family again. Perhaps it would be the very antidote to the melancholy we had found ourselves in. A new life to replace an old one.

I had booked us into a bed and breakfast a street away from the beach, and the weather was glorious, which only added to the positivity of the weekend. We were strolling along the front, eating from a bag of chips, and we stopped and looked out at the sea. We had a dollop of mayonnaise in the bag, and I dunked a chip in it, then popped it in my mouth. It was delicious. There was something special about chips at the beach. They tasted better somehow.

'This is nice,' I said. 'Just what we needed.'

'Yeah, it's lovely,' replied Charlie, eating a chip himself, as a few seagulls lurked nearby, waiting for their moment to pounce.

'I think I could live by the beach.'

'Yeah? Thinking about a change?'

'Maybe one day,' I said, as we finished the last of the chips. 'Let's go on the beach. I want to do something.'

I put the chip box in a nearby bin, grabbed Charlie by the hand, and pulled him towards the beach. I was feeling impetuous and needed to do something slightly wild and out of character. We had become too safe, too reliant on familiar patterns, and the weight of Charlie's father's death constantly loomed over us. I wanted us to be fun again, to look forward with passion and excitement. We dashed down onto the pebbly beach, and I looked at Charlie.

'Okay, Talbot, undress,' I said, pulling my thin jumper up and over my head.

'What are you doing, Ash?' said Charlie, looking at me with the same stoic expression that had been etched into his face since the day his father had passed away.

'You and I are going in the sea!' I exclaimed, kicking my trainers off with a certain amount of wild abandon.

'What? But we don't have our stuff. Swim shorts, towels, we don't—'

'It doesn't matter, Charlie,' I said, bending over and pulling off my socks. 'Don't you see, we need to do something silly and reckless. We need to be spontaneous and have fun! It's been a fucking shit year, and I just want to do something different, something unlike us, and I think it's going in the sea in our underwear.'

I pulled my jeans off, and then I finally took off my T-shirt so I was standing there in my bra and knickers. I felt a little insecure because I definitely wasn't 'beach ready' but at that moment, I didn't care. Charlie was watching me, a look of incredulity on his face. The beach wasn't packed but it was busy and quite a few people were watching us. There were a few people in the sea, mainly children, but all were properly attired.

'I don't know about this, Ash.'

I walked towards Charlie until I was standing in front of him. 'Trust me.'

Then I pulled his sweatshirt off, helped him with his jeans, and then he had to sit down to take off his trainers and socks, until eventually we were both standing on Brighton beach in just our underwear.

'Ready?' I said, turning and looking at him.

'Not really.'

'Good, then it's time!' I said, grabbing his hand, and then I pulled him with me as I starting walking quickly towards the water. Despite the weather, and the fact we'd had a pretty decent summer, I knew the sea was going to be freezing. The English Channel was always bone-chillingly cold, no matter the time of the year. We walked slowly into the sea, our feet against the harshness of the rocks, and it was about as cold as I thought it might be.

'Jesus fucking—' said Charlie.

'Just keep going!' I said, holding his hand. 'We need this.'

We walked out into the sea in just our underwear, and after a minute we were deep enough to duck down, and Charlie was too scared and so I did what I had to do. I pulled him down with me as a wave crashed against us and we were soon both dripping wet, covered from head to toe in freezing cold English water. After the wave we both stood up, looked at each other, and we both started laughing.

'You're bonkers,' said Charlie.

'Perhaps, but doesn't it feel good? Doesn't it make you feel alive?'

Charlie looked at me, and the irony of what I said obviously wasn't lost on him. We had both been so focused on his father's death, that we had forgotten that we were still alive. We needed to live, to take the lesson from his father that we never knew how long we had, and so we had to embrace each day. Charlie looked at me, smiled, and then he splashed me with water.

'Oh, it's like that, is it?' I said, splashing him, and he tried to get away, but I jumped towards him, grabbed him, and then we were standing in the sea, holding each other, our skin covered in goosebumps, and I kissed him, tasting the salty water on our lips.

No. 51

Charlie

The scratch on the sideboard

Since we bought our house, we had done some of the work required, but there was still so much left to do. The garden was in good shape, and I had cleaned out the shed and turned it into a man cave, although mainly because Ash wouldn't go anywhere near it due to the number of spiders that had chosen to call it home. We had painted, had the wooden floors refinished and new carpet installed upstairs. We hadn't had the kitchen extension done, but we had a few quotes. It was a first step, but we needed more money before we could begin that project, likewise the loft extension. Apparently, all the hallway needed was a sideboard.

We were in IKEA, browsing the sideboards, and the conversation went like this: 'What about this one?' said Ash, standing next to a modern-looking white sideboard with short, angular legs.

'Yeah, it's all right.'

'What about this one? I like this one,' said Ash brightly, next to a dark grey traditional sideboard with brass knobs.

'Yeah, it's smart.'

'This one?' said Ash, next to an ultra-modern one in black.

'Nah. I think black is too dark.'

'Racist. Okay, that one?' said Ash, pointing to a light wooden one with white trim.

'Yeah, not bad, and I don't think you can be a sideboard racist, Ash.'

'That one?' she said, nodding towards a bright orange metal one.

'Too Dutch.'

'Xenophobic, too? IKEA really does bring out the worst in people.'

'I'm just realising the exact same thing.'

'Charlie?'

'Yes?'

'Are you just thinking about eating in the restaurant?'

'Yes,' I said because we had walked past the restaurant, I was hungry, and loved the Swedish meatballs.

'And, despite your many prejudices, do you really care what sideboard we get?'

'Ash, I trust your natural design instincts.'

'Then let's eat, and we can get the dark grey one on the way out.'

'Perfect,' I said, relieved to be done looking at sideboards, and happier to be heading towards the restaurant to indulge in a Swedish smorgasbord.

Once home the work began, and we unloaded the flat-packed boxes into the hallway. The first thing we did was unpack everything, and then we set about building it, and for this we had a tried-and-tested method. I would read out the directions and Ash would build the furniture. We had realised after our first few pieces of flat-packed furniture that Ash was much better at building than me, and I was better at under-standing and delivering the directions. I liked to think I was the brains behind the operation and Ash was the muscle, although obviously I never said that to her face.

'All done!' said Ash, looking at the sideboard that looked genuinely good in the hallway. We had painted the walls Farrow & Ball old white, which was a light green-grey colour, and the dark grey of the sideboard looked perfect against it. As usual,

Ash's sense of design was spot on. We stood back and admired the sideboard for a few minutes, taking in the new piece that completed the hallway. Aesthetically it was pleasing on the eye, but perhaps more importantly, we had somewhere to shove all the detritus that gathered near the front door.

After a minute, Ash left to make tea, and I said I would tidy up. I put the hammer in the toolbox, and I went to grab the screwdriver, and somehow I dropped it, fumbled it, tried to grab it, and then it fell against the top of the sideboard and made a scratch in it.

'Fuck!'

'What happened? Are you okay?' said Ash, suddenly appearing in the hallway.

'I dropped the screwdriver, and it scratched the top of the sideboard.'

Ash looked at me with a look she had given me before: unadulterated disbelief at my complete incompetence. Once, after a trip to Edinburgh, when Ash had bought a mug she had fallen in love with, and after the first time she had used it, I dropped it and smashed it to pieces. I had form.

'Really?' said Ash once she had inspected the sideboard.

'We can put something over the scratch. A plant pot or the bowl for the keys!'

'I know, but it's been in the house for less than an hour and it's already got a scratch.'

'I'm sorry.'

'I know you are, Charlie, but it's frustrating that everything we buy, you break.'

I was as annoyed as Ash, but I also knew it was just who I was. I had always been clumsy. Coordination and spatial awareness were not my forte. Jokes to lighten the mood, however, were much more my raison d'être.

'It's frustrating now but imagine if I die. You will see that scratch every day and it will remind you of me. The scratch will be a part of us, and it will make you happy.'

Ash looked at me, and then said in a tone that suggested she found none of this amusing: 'If you die, Charlie, and I see the scratch, all I will think is, it's time to buy a new sideboard.'

Then she walked back into the kitchen, leaving me and the now slightly flawed sideboard alone.

2014

No. 52

Ash

It's the hope that gets you in the end

Finally, after what felt like years, Charlie had applied for a job he was genuinely excited about, and after three positive interviews, we were waiting to find out if he had got the job. He had been stuck in a career-slump since university, and the problem he had faced for years was that he was never sure what he actually wanted to do. He had spoken often about teaching, but was never confident enough, it seemed, to pull the trigger. So, he had been stuck in the job he didn't love, unsure what to do, seemingly trapped by his own insecurities and fears. Then it happened. The perfect position had come up at a nearby university. It was an administration position but within the history department, which not only paid better than his current job and had more annual leave, but was within the realms of a subject he loved. He had made enquiries and if he worked there, the chance to study for his master's would be more affordable, and he had even started talking about studying for his PhD, and then perhaps one day becoming a lecturer. It was the perfect job for him, and it felt like, and I hated to even think it, but some sort of karma after the awful last year when we'd lost his father. Perhaps things were finally going to fall into place.

'Why haven't they called already?' said a nervous Charlie, his knee rapidly bouncing up and down. 'They said by end of day, and it's already four-fifty.'

'Just relax,' I replied, taking a sip of my tea. 'They will call.'

It was a Friday, and they had promised to call Charlie by five o'clock with news. Charlie, too nervous to go into work had taken the day off – actually he had called in sick – while I had taken the afternoon off to support him. It was the least I could do because this one event could change the course of our lives. I had told Charlie not to get ahead of himself, but it was difficult not to get excited because if he had a new job, a proper career with a clear long-term vision, then we could start trying for a family. It was hard not to daydream when the possibility of something so exciting was just around the corner.

Charlie took a sip of his tea. We were in the living room, unable to focus on anything but the phone call. We were both on our third cups of tea, a small plate of biscuits remained untouched. The room was silent, and then finally his mobile rang with a caller, and when he looked at his phone, it was them.

'Remember, just relax, and you know, whatever happens, we'll be okay,' I said with a smile, and he looked at me, nervousness and excitement jammed into every square inch of his face. He answered.

'Charlie Talbot,' he said into the phone, his voice bright and sharp.

I had been imagining this moment all day. I would be watching him, and slowly I would see his smile broaden, his eyes would light up and I would know he had got the job. It was down to the final two candidates. It was Charlie or a woman, and she hadn't studied history at university. Maths, apparently. After the phone call and the news that Charlie had got the job, we would go out for a slap-up meal, before home for congratulatory sex. After everything that had happened in the last year, this was going to be the start of something wonderful. A new page in our story, and we both wanted and needed it so badly.

I watched his face, but slowly the smile that was supposed to have been there, faded, and his whole face sort of collapsed, and his eyes lost their sparkle.

'Of course. I understand. Thank you for the opportunity. If anything else comes up... right, yes. You too. Okay. Thank you. Bye then. Bye,' said Charlie and that was it. He placed his mobile down on the coffee table, and he looked at me.

'I'm sorry,' I said, and I reached out to him, but he stood up quickly.

'It's okay, you know, it's fine,' said Charlie, and he walked off towards the kitchen.

'Charlie, it's okay to be sad about this,' I said, following him. 'Something else will come up. Maybe the university will have other positions, and—'

'I wanted this fucking job, Ash.'

'I know.'

'I thought I had it, too. I thought this was going to be the one.'

'I know,' I said, and I walked over to him. I put my arms around him, and I was sad too because I knew what this meant. We were putting off discussions about having a baby again. All the dreams and hopes I'd had all day were gone, and it seemed they were right: it's the hope that gets you in the end.

No. 53

Charlie

A lack of synchronicity

We were at Mum's house, which felt strange without Dad walking into the kitchen and asking why the kettle wasn't on, or in the garden mowing the lawn in one of his signature white vests. Memories were hiding around every corner, ready to jump out without warning and turn me into an emotional mess in seconds. Just the sight of a Bourbon biscuit and I was still struggling to keep myself together despite it being nearly a year since he passed away.

Ash and I had driven down for the weekend to visit Mum, and Ash was having dinner with her family later. Daniel was home and had brought his new girlfriend along. She was Scottish and, according to Ash, studying law, which obviously made Hugh incredibly happy. If only Ash had married a solicitor, then he would have been the proudest father in the entire world, but instead he had got me: a man with little direction, stuck in a low-paying job he despised that would eventually swallow him up.

I was in the kitchen having a cup of tea with Mum, while Ash was in the front room, on a call with Tim. They were working together on a new project, and apparently it needed them to be joined at the hip twenty-four-seven. She had mentioned the possibility of them going away for three days to a book fair in Germany. The two of them, in a foreign country, and presumably in adjoining hotel rooms. I didn't love the idea.

'So, Mum, how's things?' I said when she passed me my tea.

'You know. Keeping myself busy.'

'Doing what?'

Mum took a sip of her tea and then reached for a Rich Tea biscuit. 'My friend, Belinda. You remember Belinda?'

I thought for a moment. I literally had no idea who Belinda was. 'No, I don't think we've met, Mum.'

'Yes, you have. Belinda Hodgson? Married to Peter Hodgson. Tall, blond—'

'Who is tall and blond? Belinda or Peter?'

'Peter, of course. Belinda is a brunette. They have two kids, and one is at Oxford. A dog, too. A beagle. They have a caravan!' said Mum, as if the mention of the caravan would suddenly prompt me into remembering the woman I had never met.

'Sorry, Mum. Not ringing any bells.'

There was a sudden and ferocious laugh from the other room as though Ash was at a comedy club instead of Mum's front room. I hadn't heard Ash laugh like that in a long time, and certainly not at something I had said. I took a slightly concerned sip of my tea.

'Anyway, Belinda has started doing the park runs, and I've been going with her.'

'That's great, Mum. I didn't know you could run.'

'Oh, well, we haven't been able to run the whole thing yet, but we're getting better. Poor Belinda suffers horribly from shin splints, and I've never been much of an exercise person. I did a few aerobics classes back in the day, and I bought a yoga mat from Argos once, and that's about it. It's a chance to get outside, though, and have a good natter.'

'I think that's great, Mum.'

Another thunderous laugh from the other room. Was Tim really that funny? Yes, he was physically impressive, handsome, but was he could-sell-out-an-arena-on-a-comedy-tour hilarious? I had always thought being funny was my thing. I used to make Ash laugh all the time, although I couldn't remember the last time I had made her laugh like that.

'How's things with you and Ash?' said Mum, crunching on a second Rich Tea biscuit.

'Fine, yeah.'

'Still looking for another job?'

'Yes. I had the interview at the university, but since then nothing.'

'Luckily you're married to a go-getter like Ash then—'

'Who's a go-getter?' said Ash, suddenly walking into the kitchen.

'I was just saying that Charlie is lucky he married someone like you.'

'I wish Charlie appreciated me that much.'

She sat down at the table. Mum had made her a cup of tea, and she took a sip.

'I appreciate you,' I said defensively.

'You should,' said Mum. 'Ash's a real catch. Your father always said so.'

'Thank you,' said Ash, who smiled at Mum, and then gave me a look. 'Did you hear that, Charlie? A real catch.'

'Everything sorted out with Tim?' I asked.

'All good. Just discussing Germany.'

'Germany?' Mum chipped in.

'Tim and I are being flown to Germany for a book fair. It's a big deal in the publishing world, and a good chance to network with authors, agents, etcetera. Charlie doesn't like the fact I'm going with Tim.'

'Who's Tim?' asked Mum.

'Just a colleague,' said Ash.

'With a six-pack and biceps bigger than my legs,' I replied, hating myself for being so insecure, but it was hard when your wife spent most of her time with a man who was Brad Pitt gorgeous and also, apparently, a bit of a hoot.

'Sounds like someone is a little jealous,' Mum said after a moment.

'And needs to grow up,' added Ash, for good measure.

'Good for you, love! Chasing your dreams, and making them happen,' Mum said to Ash, and they knocked their teacups together in a show of unity. It seemed Mum was very much on Ash's side when it came to the matter of Tim Pearson. Girl Power reigned, which only made me long even more for my father.

We finished our tea, then Ash said she had to leave for dinner with her family. Before she left, Ash had an expression on her face I had seen with increasing regularity of late. She looked at me, her eyes with a sort of indifference, and I felt the gap between us that had been getting wider and wider. I knew she wanted to start trying for a baby, but I just wasn't ready yet, and her impatience had led to the tension between us. Now this trip with Tim had come up, our usual synchronicity was off. We had always been so close, and now, suddenly, we had never felt further apart, and I had no idea how to bridge that gap.

No. 54

Ash

A conversation in the shed

I opened the door to Charlie's dad's shed because I knew I would find Charlie inside. I walked in and he was sitting on a small wooden bench, staring into space.

'Do you mind if I come in?' I asked.

'Of course not,' he replied, patting the space on the bench next to him. I walked across and sat down, having a quick look around at the small shed. It had the same smell that reminded me of the shed we had growing up. Not that my father ever used it, of course, but we had a gardener, and he kept a variety of tools and gardening equipment in there. I remembered sneaking into the shed when I was little, and finding all manner of things, and being scared of the spiders that always seemed to be lurking in the corners. The shed was like its own little world, somewhere private, secret, yet in plain sight at the bottom of the garden.

'A penny for your thoughts,' I said after a moment of silence.

'Just thinking about Dad. I can't believe it's been a year since he died, Ash. He was so young, had so much to still live for, to experience, and I'm sad he's gone.'

'I know,' I said, resting my head on Charlie's shoulder.

Last night, I had a wonderful dinner with my family, and it felt like the first time we had all been together, and there was no drama or underlying tension between us. Daniel was down from Edinburgh with his girlfriend, Gemma, who was stunningly beautiful, lovely, and Daniel himself seemed so much more grown-up, and we actually had conversations where I stopped thinking of him as just my annoying little brother. My parents, who usually argued as though it were a sport, were relaxed and happy. My family, who had been an uncomfortable necessity for most of my life, were suddenly a joy. Unfortunately, it coincided with Charlie and me going through this horrible blip. But then when I thought of his father, and saw Charlie in his shed looking like a little boy who just missed his dad, I wanted to hold him and make all the pain go away. If only solving all our problems was as easy as a hug.

I decided, sitting in that shed with Charlie, to bring up Germany again. When I had first mentioned it to Charlie, he had performed his usual 'Man Pretending Not To Care But Clearly Jealous' routine, and it was becoming tedious. Since his father died, I had been giving Charlie quite a bit of leeway, but there was a point when I had to draw a line in the sand. We had to move on, re-focus ourselves, and sometimes Charlie needed a push.

'Charlie, about Germany,' I said, looking across at him. 'I need you to be okay with it.'

'I'm fine with it,' said Charlie with the look of a man who definitely wasn't fine with it.

'You realise there is absolutely nothing between me and Tim, don't you? He isn't even my type. Plus, he's happily married, and I'm happily married—'

'Are you?' said Charlie suddenly, taking me by surprise. There was a pensiveness in his voice, a melancholic tenderness that hit me and I didn't know what to say. Was I happily married? I had been happier, but saying I was actually unhappy seemed too big of a leap. Admitting that there was a space between us, a gap that needed filling was one thing, but declaring that the gap was actually more of a chasm, felt too monumental and something I don't think either of us were prepared for. Especially not in that shed.

'We've been better, Charlie, but I know we can be happy again.'

'I hope so,' said Charlie, and then we both took a moment to absorb what we had said.

We had both acknowledged for perhaps the first time that we were unhappy, and I felt a sadness envelop us in that shed. It was like every fibre of that wood that already held so many memories of Charlie and his father, years and years of love and shared moments ingrained within it, was cocooning us, and I felt all at once an overwhelming desire to hold onto Charlie because it had to get better. All those memories couldn't be for nothing. All of the moments of our lives that had led us to that particular place at that exact time, had to mean something. I rested my head back on his shoulder, and we sat and listened to the silence of his father's shed until my phone buzzed with a text, and when I looked down I saw a message from Tim.

Call me when you get home x

No. 55

Charlie

Work hard & be nice to people

I hadn't seen much of Edith since we moved out of the Putney flat, but Ash kept me updated on the major storylines of her life. Edith still worked in publishing and was married to Ollie who did something in television. They also lived in a gorgeous semi-detached house in Acton on one of those long, tree-lined avenues where Ash and I were standing and shivering because it was a bitterly cold evening. I was holding a bottle of wine, and Ash was next to me in a warm coat, although underneath she had on a stunning black dress.

The door opened, and Edith and Ollie appeared with smiles, telling us to come in quickly. They took our coats, and we all said hello in the stunning, and thankfully warm, hallway. Edith had changed over the years, and although she was still small with mousy brown hair, she dressed smarter and more sophisticated. When I first met her, she resembled a librarian, but now she looked grown-up, like the spectacled girl in a romantic comedy, who got a makeover and everyone suddenly realised how gorgeous she was all along. Ollie was tall with wavy light brown hair, glasses, and was dressed smartly in chinos, a white shirt and a thin navy jumper. He spoke as if he came from money, which, given the location and size of their house, seemed most likely.

'How are you? You look stunning,' Edith said to Ash.

'Thanks, you too, and this house, wow!' Ash replied.

'Let's open that bottle of wine, eh,' Ollie said to me, and we left the girls to catch up and I followed him into a beautiful, spacious kitchen.

'This is incredible,' I said, looking around at the vast space ahead of me. It had been extended and there was an enormous island with smart chairs, parquet floors and then room for a large dining table before the bifold doors that led to the garden. They had perfectly curated everything to create a gorgeous, open space that screamed style and money. A black and ivory Newgate clock with red hands sat on the wall next to a terrifyingly trendy print that declared WORK HARD & BE NICE TO PEOPLE. It was exactly the sort of thing Ash and I dreamed about doing to our own house when we could afford it. I suppose we just needed to work harder and be nicer to people.

'We didn't do it,' said Ollie, opening the bottle of wine. 'We viewed other properties we could have renovated, added value, but as soon as we saw this we knew we didn't want to spend a year in a building site. We have friends with horror stories about building work going on for six months longer than promised, thirty thousand over the estimate.'

Ollie passed me a glass of wine, and we both said cheers. Ollie held his wine glass loosely but confidently by the stem, and slowly swilled his wine around. He had the look of a seasoned sommelier, and probably knew things about acidity, clarity, and would describe our wine as having opening hints of fig and the merest suggestion of passion fruit, raspberry, with a subtle but complex aftertaste of burnt oak and buttery asparagus. Ollie took a sip of the wine, swilled it around his mouth for a moment, and finally swallowed it.

'Very fruit forward.'

'Definitely,' I replied because I had read the description on the wine bottle and 'fruit forward' was one of the things that had caught my attention.

'Edith tells me you work in marketing?' Ollie asked as we moved across to the island.

'Sort of. I work at a marketing company, but I work in administration.'

'Oh, right. Do you like it?'

'Not really, but it isn't forever. I'm still trying to figure out exactly what I want to do. What about you? I hear you work in television?'

Ollie smiled, then went into a fifteen-minute job description, and how much he loved it, and the sort of people he got to work with, and finally, when the girls walked in, he finished. Every single person in that gorgeous kitchen loved their jobs. They were all successful, ambitious, and it made me feel even more like a complete and utter failure.

'We made lamb,' Edith declared before she ushered us across to the dining table that looked like something from a Habitat catalogue. 'Well, Ollie made the lamb, the roast potatoes, the gravy from scratch, and the sourdough bread. I steamed the broccolini!'

'You make your own sourdough bread?' Ash asked Ollie.

'It's something I love to do. It's quite therapeutic,' replied Ollie.

'And delicious,' chipped in Edith. 'Although not good for the old waistline.'

The food looked incredible, and I had to admit, Ollie impressed me. Not only did he produce television shows I actually watched, but he made his own sourdough bread. It would be easy not to like him because he was smart, successful and seemingly the perfect husband, but he genuinely seemed like a nice bloke.

'So...' said Edith, as we started tucking into the food, reaching across and holding Ollie's hand as though they were about to make a joint statement on the news. 'There was another reason we asked you here tonight.' Edith looked at Ollie, and they smiled at each other before she said, 'I'm pregnant!'

The news hit us, and I immediately knew what Ash would be thinking. She had become obsessed with starting a family, and now one of her closest friends was pregnant.

'Oh gosh, that's wonderful news!' gushed Ash.

We all stood up, I shook Ollie by the hand, and gave Edith a kiss on the cheek, and then we sat down again and began eating while Edith explained she was about fifteen weeks pregnant, and that everything, fingers crossed, seemed to be going well apart from the terrible morning sickness that was just awful. They'd had a scan, and the baby seemed to be exactly as they should be, although they didn't want to find out the sex because it was nice to wait, wasn't it? I was sure Ash was happy for Edith, but I knew inside she was probably cursing the fact that her useless, failure of a husband wasn't ready to start trying yet. We ate dinner, which was incredible, and the conversation was pleasant, if not a little baby centric.

After dinner, Ollie and I washed up, while the girls went into the living room to talk. Ollie and I drank more wine, and I asked about becoming a father.

'Can't bloody wait,' said Ollie. 'I have two brothers, four nieces, three nephews, and I love them all to bits. What about you and Ash? Have you thought about it?'

The question I hated being asked. 'We've talked about it.'

'And?'

'One day, once we have our ducks in a row,' I replied, and luckily the girls reappeared, and the conversation was cut short, but all I could think about was how I wasn't ready to be a dad because I didn't feel good enough, wasn't good enough for Ash, and how could I be a father when I couldn't even support us at that moment? Ollie clearly earned good money, and so when Edith was ready to step away from work to be a mother, it wouldn't matter because he was a proper husband, who could support them financially, emotionally, and with delicious homemade sourdough bread.

No. 56

Ash

The C word

Our publishing company's annual Christmas party was at a swish Italian restaurant in Fitzrovia. Everyone was there, and we had delicious food, a free bar, and it was time to let our hair down after what had been a tough year. There had been much change with people coming and going, and Tim and I had worked so many hours, I couldn't even remember, but we had somehow got through it. We had gone to Germany for the book fair, which had been a resounding success. Tim was so great at networking and knew how to work a room. He excelled at so many things I didn't, and his natural charisma and charm had certainly given us an edge when it came to securing new authors. We were the dream team, but unfortunately, it seemed the better Tim and I did, the more it drove a wedge between me and Charlie, and as we came towards the end of the year, it was clear Charlie and I weren't in a healthy place.

'This one,' said Tim, pointing at me across the table. 'Absolute bloody legend.'

'Stop it,' I replied.

We had all had quite a few drinks, and the conversation was flowing along with the alcohol. I was at a long table with Tim, Harriet, Jane and Callie. We had all worked together for a number of years now and knew each other inside and out. Especially after a few drinks.

'She literally stalked this agent in Germany. They had one of the best debuts we had read in years, every publisher wanted it, so Ash spent a whole day attached to them. All day I was getting text updates. "She's in the toilets." "Getting coffee." Trust me, once she gets her claws into you, beware, she might never leave!' said Tim, and we all laughed.

'What about you? Talk about using your attributes. You literally had every girl at the book fair in your pocket,' I said, and I couldn't tell because of the light, but it looked like Tim was blushing. I took a sip of my wine, and I looked across at Tim, and he looked back at me, and we smiled at each other. We had become closer the last few months, but we had been working together for forty hours a week and sometimes longer, it was inevitable.

I was at the bar getting a drink when my phone buzzed with a call from Charlie. I was having such a good time, my head was fuzzy with alcohol, my stomach full of wonderful Italian food, and I didn't want to speak with Charlie because I knew he would only bring me down. We'd had an argument that morning, and I couldn't stand the thought of another one. So, I rejected his call and got back to the table.

That morning, I had been doing my best to get out of the house because I was already running late. I tried to say goodbye to Charlie, and he went into a thing about the Christmas party.

'What?' I asked.

'I just want to know what time you'll be home,' said Charlie, and I could tell by the look on his face, and the tone of his voice, that there were layers to this conversation.

'I don't know, Charlie, but I'm late, so—'

'But roughly what time?'

'I don't know… midnight?'

'So, late then.'

'It's a party, Charlie.'

'Do you want me to get you from the station?'

'I don't know. I'll text. Okay, I really have to—'

'Is Tim going?'

'What?'

'Tim. Is he going?'

'It's a work party, so yes, I imagine he is.'

'Right,' said Charlie pointedly.

'What does that mean?'

'It means nothing, Ash.'

'Well, with that nothing, I have to go,' I said, annoyed that Charlie and his ridiculous jealousy had delayed me another minute. I didn't even give him a kiss and went to leave.

'Bye then,' said Charlie petulantly, following me into the hallway.

'Bye,' I replied, grabbing my backpack. I turned to Charlie, but he looked annoyed, and I didn't have time to deal with him, and so I left, slamming the front door behind me.

My phone buzzed again. It wasn't a call this time, but a text from Charlie.

Screening your calls now?

Which only further irritated me. I drank my drink, and then I went to the bar to get another, where I was joined by Tim.

'How are you doing?' he asked.

'A little drunk, but determined to get more drunk,' I said, and I felt like having a rant and Tim was there, and would be nice enough to let me. 'What is it with men?'

'I, umm—'

'No, I'm talking, and you listen, okay? What is it with men that they think that just because you're married that they somehow own you and can get jealous because of their own lack of confidence? It isn't my fault he hates his fucking job and yet it feels like I'm being blamed for everything, and it isn't fair. He's being cunty, and yet he wants me to feel like I'm the cunt but I'm not. I am not the cunt in this relationship, Tim.'

I stopped and looked at Tim, and he looked at me. 'Having problems with Charlie?' he said after a moment.

'I just don't understand men, and I'm sorry I used the C word quite so liberally.'

Tim laughed. 'It's okay, it's a fantastic word, and just so you know, women are not any easier. Astrid thinks I'm emotionally unavailable and that I need to be "there for her", but I am when I'm not working so hard, and so sometimes, I need her to be more understanding of that.'

I looked at Tim, and he looked at me and we both laughed because it was Christmas and, sometimes, there was nothing else you could do.

'I think I'm a bit drunk,' I slurred, and Tim put his arm around me, and I fell into him. He was so big and strong, like a comfortable sofa.

'Me, too,' said Tim, and we stayed like that until the bartender was ready to get us another round of drinks.

2015

No. 57

Charlie

The beginning of something special

We were in a pub on one of the side streets near Covent Garden celebrating my good news because after four rounds of intense interviews, and a nervous three-day wait, I eventually got the call that the job was mine. The relief felt overwhelming because after so many years of procrastination and professional mediocrity, life was about to change.

After last year, when I felt my entire professional life since university had been a total failure, and the cracks that had started to appear in my relationship with Ash had begun to widen, I decided I had to do something. Searching for a new job wasn't so much something I did ad hoc, but it became a full-time job in itself. I spent hours and hours searching for and applying for new jobs, and when I saw this posting, it excited me. The role was for an office/project manager at a law firm based near Liverpool Street. The hours were long, the job had more stress, more moving parts, but also significantly higher pay and the chance to make a genuine career of it. It was something solid.

'To my incredibly talented husband and his new career in law!' said Ash, raising her glass of Pinot Grigio in the air.

'To me!' I said, raising my glass of pale ale and gently clinking it against hers. I looked across the table at Ash, who looked gorgeous in a yellow dress. 'I think this is going to be a brilliant year for us.'

'I hope so.'

'Not hope, Ash, it is. Positive thinking!'

'Who are you and what have you done with my husband?'

'I'm trying to be more dynamic. I know last year things were a little rubbish between us, and most of that was my fault, correction, all my fault, and I want to be better.'

Ash smiled, and then she reached a hand across the table and placed it softly over mine. 'I like the sound of that.'

'Me, too. Right, what should we order?'

We both looked down at our menus, and it all looked incredible. Sharing plates of chicken wings and a fancy British ploughman's, pan-fried sea bass, slow-cooked lamb and traditional fish and chips. The pub was warm, dimly lit, and sitting there with Ash, it truly felt like a fresh start, and maybe the beginning of something special.

'So, are you going to become a City man now, all power suits and big dick energy?' said Ash, as we strolled hand in hand along the streets of London towards the train station. We were meandering without a care in the world, our stomachs full, and I had a delicious taste in my mouth. I had ended the meal with a treacle and almond tart and a cappuccino.

'Give it six months, and I'll be drinking Scotch, and playing squash with Hugo.'

'Who's Hugo?'

'Boarding school, Oxford, married to Cressida, has a bolthole in the country.'

'Oh, right, that Hugo,' said Ash with a giggle. 'You know, I am so proud of you, Charlie.'

'Thanks. You, too.'

'Why are you proud of me?'

'Because you're incredible and believed in me when I didn't even believe in myself.'

'Well,' said Ash, stopping for a moment, turning and looking at me. 'I always knew you would get there in the end.'

Then she leaned in, we kissed, and I felt the love and the safety that Ash provided. She had made me better. Being a success in London felt impossible at times, like I was just a dot in a sea of people all striving to be richer, more successful, and it had without doubt overwhelmed me, but Ash hadn't let me give in. She had pushed me on with her boundless enthusiasm, and now, hopefully, I would reward that belief with some success. Ash and I continued on towards the train station and then home, our world and relationship that had felt on a slightly uneven keel for the past year, suddenly had some buoyancy to it.

No. 58

Ash

The need for a plan

I couldn't stop the tears that came quickly and ran down my face. I quickly wiped them way with the sleeve of my shirt, but more came afterwards. Charlie getting a new job was supposed to be the beginning of a new life for us. We had spoken at length about starting a family, and I was ready, had been ready for years in reality, but I had always been waiting on Charlie. Waiting for him to get a new job, feel ready, grow up, and I thought – so horribly wrong, apparently – that he would be ready soon and yet he wasn't. We had spoken and once again he had pleaded for more time, and I was starting to wonder whether it was all just a delaying tactic and whether he would ever be ready at all.

'Ash, I'm sorry,' said Charlie from next to me on the bed. 'I'm just not ready yet.'

'And when will you be ready, Charlie?' I asked, a spikiness in my voice, knowing I sounded angry but I was. I was tired of the excuses, of the need for him to 'get his ducks in a row' because maybe those fucking ducks would never be ready. Plus, I was on my period – to really hammer home the fact I definitely wasn't pregnant – and just really fucking pissed off. 'Because it seems to me that you keep putting it off with the hope that maybe one day I'll just stop asking.'

'That isn't fair, Ash. You know I want kids, too.'

'Do you?' I said, searching his face for the truth. Charlie wasn't good at hiding his feelings, and I was good at reading him.

'Of course. You know I do, I just—'

'I know. Need more time,' I said coldly, feeling my frustration and annoyance with him spreading through my body like a cold sweat.

We sat on the bed in silence, neither of us knowing where to take the conversation next because we had wandered into a cul-de-sac with no plan of how to escape. It had started out so positively, I thought, but had quickly dissolved into chaos and confusion. It was how I imagined politicians felt when they went into talks with politicians on the other side. Different parties with their own agendas, own needs and wants that didn't quite fit with yours. Two sides who both needed a victory to send a message that they had won, even though everyone knew a win for both was impossible. One of you had to give something up. We were at the point of mediation, and it seemed, neither of us were prepared to give up, or know how much to give up.

'How about this?' said Charlie finally. 'Give me a year, Ash. One year to get settled in my new job. A year to get myself ready, and then we can start trying for a baby. What do you say?'

A year. I was going to be thirty-three this year. If we started trying in a year, I would be thirty-four when I had my first child if we conceived straight away. Perhaps thirty-six with my second. It was older than I wanted to be, later than I had always planned, but it was something. I didn't want to wait a year, but if I was going to agree to his terms then I had to know it was definitely it. I wiped the last of the tears from my face, and looked at Charlie. I momentarily thought of the day at Brighton beach when we had jumped and frolicked in the sea. How had that been almost two years ago? Life felt like it was moving too quickly, and we didn't have time to wait. I had always been a big planner, needed the comfort of knowing what was on the horizon because that was how I thrived, or perhaps survived.

'I agree to a year, Charlie, but that's it, okay? No more excuses. No more messing about, and being ready six months later. If we agree to start trying in a year then I mean it, and you have to mean it as well. Do you promise?'

I looked at Charlie, and he smiled at me.

'I do,' he said, and with that the conversation was over. We had come to a decision and now I knew the plan, I could begin moving things into place. It was how I had always functioned and how I survived in a world where chaos and confusion liked to reign.

No. 59

Charlie

Meeting Rupert

I was meeting Ash at Edith and Ollie's house in Acton where we were going to meet their son, Rupert. I had worked late yet again, and I was on my way there. Ash had already texted twice and asked where I was, as I dashed into the Underground station. Working late had become something of a daily occurrence and I would put it down to the fact I was new and still learning the ropes, but most of the other employees and especially the lawyers seemed to work late, too. Law, it seemed, had no place for the nine-to-five, and most days I was in by eight and home whenever I was done. It was exhausting, but I loved the work, and after years of just getting by, I felt like I had finally taken a giant leap forward.

I walked quickly towards Edith and Ollie's house, memories of my last visit there were still fresh in my mind. Their beautiful home, delicious lamb, homemade sourdough bread, and talk of babies. Although this time, I actually had a job I could talk about. I was in a career rather than just an arbitrary job, and I wasn't exactly on the same level as Ollie, but I didn't have the same inferiority complex about money and status.

'Sorry I'm late,' I said when Ash opened the door. She didn't look best pleased.

'Where have you been? Rupert's already asleep.'

'Oh, shit, really?' I said, walking inside the hallway of Edith and Ollie's gorgeous home.

'It's why I texted you so many times,' said Ash as we walked along the hallway. 'He went down at six-thirty.'

'I couldn't just leave, Ash. I had things to—'

Ollie walked out from the kitchen to join us.

'Hello, mate,' said Ollie, offering me his hand to shake.

'Sorry I'm late. Work stuff,' I replied.

'No worries. Come through,' said Ollie, and despite his words and comforting smile, I could tell Ash was still annoyed with me.

I walked through into their cavernous kitchen, which had been incredible the last time I had been there, modern and clean, but was now filled with a plethora of baby detritus. An exhausted looking Edith was slumped in a chair, a pumping machine attached to her breast, and an elaborate car seat on the floor next to her.

'Hello, Charlie. Don't mind, do you? Rupert has quite the appetite,' said Edith.

'No, no, it's fine,' I said, walking across and sitting down as Ollie offered me a drink. I accepted a beer, and he had made some small plates of food, but we weren't eating a full meal because they didn't have the time, or probably the energy.

'Here you go, mate,' said Ollie, handing me a bottle of beer.

'Thanks,' I said, opening the beer and having a sip. It tasted so good after the day I'd had. 'So, how's parenthood?'

Ash was already deep in conversation with Edith about something Rupert related.

'Yes, all good,' said Ollie, who looked absolutely exhausted. 'A bit tiring, obviously. Although fair play to the little fella, he's a brilliant sleeper. It's just the nights when we're up three times at the moment. Edith usually does two and I'm up once, but then I lay there and can't fall back to sleep.'

'It sounds exhausting,' I replied.

'It is, but, you know, I'm so in love with Rupert. He's just incredible.'

'He really is,' reiterated Edith, who looked possibly more tired than Ollie, her breast squeezed into the pump.

I looked across at Ash, who had overheard our conversation, and she looked at me. I hadn't met Rupert, but I could imagine her holding him and falling in love, and it made me feel so guilty that I wasn't quite ready for all of this. I desperately wanted to be ready, and to give Ash everything she wanted, but as I sat in that kitchen, surrounding by love, family, and so much happiness and joy, all I could think was that it still terrified me. I wanted it, wanted to be like Ollie, who was a proper adult, a successful, accomplished man, but I didn't feel like that yet. I still had doubts about myself, about whether I was good enough for Ash, and good enough to be the father of her children. Doubts and insecurities that had been seeded in me long before all of this was barely a thought.

'I really am sorry,' I said to Ash, as we walked towards the Tube station on our way home.

'I know you are, Charlie.'

I reached down and held her hand in mine. It was warm and soft.

'So, how was Rupert?'

'Oh my gosh, Charlie. He was so adorable, and so tiny. He looked just like Ollie.'

'I mean, not exactly like Ollie, surely?'

'Same eyes, hair and nose. He did have Edith's chin though.'

'Strange. Still, I can't wait to meet him.'

'Yeah?' asked Ash with a smile. 'Feeling a little broody?'

I looked at Ash, who squeezed my hand and then I smiled at her, and we kept walking towards the Tube station, but I left her question unanswered.

No. 60

Ash

Life thru a lens

It was a Friday night, and I was home alone in the spare bedroom, sitting on the floor and looking around at the room we had purposely left empty until I was pregnant. The nursery. We had painted it the same colour as the rest of the house after we had moved in, but we had decided, once I was pregnant, we would decorate accordingly. As it was, it was unchanged, a blank canvas I was desperate to fill with our future baby's things.

Charlie had texted that he was going out with work, which had become something of a regularity the past few months. A part of me understood because he was trying to fit in at his new office, creating new relationships, but I missed him. He often worked late, came home exhausted, had a nibble of something to eat, we barely exchanged a few words, and then he went straight to bed. I felt like we didn't see each other any more, and that he was becoming little more than a lodger who was barely there, the only reminders that he still lived there the occasional mug or cereal bowl left on the side for me to wash up. I couldn't complain because I had pushed him to get a new job, but I hadn't foreseen the dramatic shift in his work-life balance tipping heavily against me.

I sat in the spare bedroom and imagined how different life would be if only we had a baby. If only we were a proper family instead of just two people trying to keep everything together

231

in a city where the pressure of work, life, and juggling the two seemed almost impossible. A baby would galvanise us, make our lives more meaningful, but at that moment, the lack of it seemed to be creating a gap between us once again. I had agreed to wait for a year, but I was becoming impatient as I was increasingly unsure what I was waiting for. Another year so Charlie could go out and get drunk with work. Another year he could avoid the responsibility of fatherhood. I hadn't always been sure what it was that Charlie needed before he could be ready, and as time went on, the feeling of uncertainty only increased.

I had a glass of wine, and I was listening to the Robbie Williams album *Life Thru A Lens*. I had loved that album when it came out, and had listened to it repeatedly for almost an entire year. Even now, whenever I heard 'Angels' it gave me goosebumps and transported me back in time. I was fifteen years old, thought Robbie Williams was the sexiest man alive, and that somehow we would end up together. I was convinced that one day we would meet, and it would be love at first sight. We still hadn't met, so I supposed there was still a chance.

My mobile started ringing, and I assumed it was Charlie, calling to tell me he was on his way home. A quick call from the train telling me what time he would be getting in.

'It's a late one,' I said before he had the chance to speak. 'I hope you aren't too drunk.'

'Sorry?' said a different but familiar voice.

'Shit, sorry, Tim. I thought it was Charlie.'

'Sorry to disappoint,' said Tim, laughing.

'No, it's fine. What's up?' I said, turning Robbie down, and then taking a sip of wine.

'I was just thinking about Monday.'

We had a publicity day with one of our more famous authors. A spot on *BBC Breakfast*, followed by two radio interviews and then a book signing at Foyles on Charing Cross Road.

'Not having the most exciting Friday night, then?'

'Umm,' said Tim, and I could sense that something was bothering him. His voice had an extra layer of something.

'Spill the beans, Pearson.'

'It's just... I shouldn't be burdening you with this, Ash, it's fine... I—'

'Timothy Pearson,' I said in my stern schoolteacher voice. 'We're mates. You can tell me anything, and trust me, it's not a burden.'

'I moved out of the house today.'

'Oh shit, sorry. I didn't realise things were that bad between you and Astrid.'

'They've just been getting worse and worse. We're broken, Ash, and I can't see a world where we get fixed. I think it's over.'

I knew Tim and his wife Astrid had problems. He touched on them briefly from time to time, but I had no idea it was so bad they were separated. Poor old Tim, or perhaps poor old Astrid, I didn't know. I only had his side of the story: her impatience with him, their differing parenting styles, her desire to move out of London, his desire to stay, and the lack of intimacy that had grown worse year on year.

'It's fine. It happens, right? People break up. The only thing I'm worried about right now is Liv. She's only six and doesn't know what's going on. I just want to protect her.'

'Of course you do. Is there anything I can do?'

'Right now, this late on a Friday night?' said Tim, and we both laughed.

'Not right now, you idiot, but whenever. I can help with Liv if you need a sitter. I can listen to you go on and on about it over drinks. Whatever you need, Tim, just say.'

There was a momentary pause, and then Tim said, 'Just having you in my life is enough, Ash.'

There was another pause, and I didn't know how I felt about it. It was a confusing pause. A silence that sat between us for a moment, a little awkwardly. I had never thought of Tim as anything else but a friend, a colleague, but I realised at that moment how close we had become. People joked at the office that he was my 'work husband', and we laughed, but that was when he had been happily married. When I had been more happily married. When Tim and I didn't have such personal conversations late on Friday nights. The pause lingered, holding within it all the confusion of London, of love, and then suddenly the front door opened and closed below me. Charlie was home.

No. 61

Charlie

Driving home for Christmas

We were in Ash's car, attempting to drive back to Southampton on Christmas Eve, but there had been a major pile-up on the M3, heading south, and the motorway was backed up all the way from Basingstoke. It was looking as though our usual drive of one and a half hours, was going to be more like three. At least we had some Christmas music on the radio, and I had five days off work, Ash had six, and we were going to spend Christmas with our families. We were staying with my mum, and visiting hers, but it was shaping up to be a brilliant festive period. Unfortunately, it had started with me running an hour late from work, which meant us leaving an hour later than planned, and then running into the world's biggest car park on the motorway. It wasn't ideal. I had already apologised multiple times, but it seemed Ash wasn't in a forgiving, Christmassy mood.

'What can I do to make it up to you?' I said across the car.

'Let me see,' said Ash, as Chris Rea sang, 'Driving Home for Christmas' on the radio. 'How about you invent a time machine, go back three hours, and leave work on time so we aren't stuck in this awful traffic?' said Ash sarcastically.

'Very funny. Can we please just try and enjoy ourselves this Christmas. I know things have been a little tense between us recently—'

'A little tense?' said Ash, before she laughed acerbically. 'That's an understatement.'

The traffic was currently ground to a halt, and we had no idea how much longer we were going to be stuck there. It was already past seven o'clock, and we were supposed to be at Ash's parents by eight o'clock for dinner and drinks. Ash's brother and his girlfriend were visiting from Scotland, and we were supposed to be popping in to see my mum first, but the plan had already changed and we were heading straight to Ash's parents' house. It was still unclear what time we would actually make it, and currently, in what sort of mood.

Ash had been openly annoyed at me for a while, and I knew why. She hated that I spent so many hours at work, going out with people from work, and she wanted to start a family as soon as possible. The rules of engagement were clear. I was hoping that with it being Christmas, such a poignant time of the year, and with both of us being off work and out of London that perhaps we could put everything behind us. I wanted to spend some time with Ash when we weren't arguing. I wanted to have sex with my wife because that had dried up too, and it mattered. It felt like that gap between us had widened since I had started at my new job, when the whole point of it, of me wanting to be better, was to make us closer.

'Look,' I said turning to Ash. 'I'm sorry, okay. I'm sorry that I work too much, go out too much, and that I'm not ready to be a dad yet. I'm sorry I'm not what you want, Ash, but it's Christmas and I love you, and I really want us to have some fun together. I want us to jump in the sea again like we did in Brighton and behave like teenagers. I want us to have brilliant, passionate sex again like we used to. I want to enjoy Christmas with my wife because I love Christmas, I fucking love you, and I want to be happy with you again because I feel like we haven't been happy in a while and I'm tired of not being happy. It's draining being miserable all the time, Ash. So, please, can we just stop being angry with each other and start being happy again? Chris Rea is singing one of the best Christmas songs ever, and it just feels wrong to be arguing when we're driving home for Christmas, doesn't it?'

I had said my piece, and I looked across the car at Ash, and she was smiling.

'You bloody idiot,' she said, and then she laughed a little. 'I don't think Chris Rea's Christmas classic has any bearing on whether we're happy or not, and for your information, Charlie, you are what I want.'

'Yeah?'

'Of course. Just perhaps a bit more of the old you who worked less and wasn't stressed all the time.'

'Well, it's Christmas, and we aren't working, so...?'

'So?'

'So, maybe, just for Christmas, we can be like the old us again. Relive the glory years!'

'Like a once famous rock 'n' roll band on one final, roll of the dice, desperation tour to get their careers back on track?' said Ash, as the traffic started moving ahead of us. 'Sorry, that was a little dark, wasn't it?'

'Perhaps. Although, you know, sometimes those last roll of the dice desperation tours actually work,' I replied, and suddenly we were off again, picking up speed, the traffic clearing, and Southampton and Christmas were getting closer.

2016

No. 62

Ash

Sex but not as we know it

It was late on a Wednesday night, Charlie and I were in bed under the sheets, and we were about to have sex. In years gone by, this would have been quite thrilling, and we would both have been looking forward to it, unable to keep our hands off each other, but now things were vastly different. This version of us – Ash and Charlie 2.0 – was not in a great place emotionally or physically, which led me to the question of why we were even bothering to have sex on a midweek night when clearly it wasn't going to be that good. In fact, it was probably going to be pretty awful, but we had to do it. Perhaps 'had' was a strong word, but we certainly needed to make the effort.

When things were really good between us and we had sex, there was always lots of kissing, long, smouldering looks, and plenty of foreplay, which you didn't want to end but couldn't help yourself because it was all too much. It was grabbing at each other's bodies, hands through hair, touch, feeling, raw emotion, and uncontrollable noises as we orgasmed in a crescendo of pleasure. Although the last time we'd had sex it had felt practical, perfunctory and devoid of the excitement and pleasure that had once been its hallmark. It was like the difference between a delicious six-course tasting menu at a Michelin-starred London restaurant and eating a fast-food burger on the night bus home. One was savoured, cherished, an experience, the other just to fulfil a need.

Neither of us were in the mood, didn't have high expectations for it, and I think we both just wanted to get it over and done with, which led me back to the question of why we were having sex on a gloomy Wednesday night in late March. The answer was that we had been watching television earlier, and Charlie had made the throw away comment that we hadn't yet had sex in 2016, and I don't know why but it struck a chord. I hadn't realised it had been that long. I also came to the realisation that it wasn't that far away from the year deadline when we were definitely going to start trying for a family. All of these micro facts had coalesced around my worry that if we didn't start getting our relationship back on track and soon, we might not have a relationship left to make a baby with. Hence why we were under the covers and naked.

'Ready?' I asked Charlie.

He looked at me, and I couldn't read his mind, but I knew he didn't want to do this, which was incredible because Charlie had always wanted to have sex in the past. He could never get enough, but that was before, and to be fair, he also looked quite tired.

'I am,' he replied.

I took off my T-shirt, removed my underwear, and Charlie did the same in silence. Everything felt slightly robotic and a bit emotionless. After we were both naked, he moved across the bed until he was next to me. The room was dark, but a thin sliver of creamy light had crept between the curtains and lay across us. Charlie leaned in and kissed me, his hand moving onto one of my breasts. He started slowly massaging my nipple and I closed my eyes, trying to feel something. I wanted to be in the mood. I wanted to want him like I had in the past, but it was hard to make those feelings magically appear. Luckily, Charlie seemed to have less of a problem getting ready than me, and he was soon on top of me, looking down at me. He leaned in and kissed me, and I wished he had shaved because he was quite scratchy, but I could live with that. I closed my eyes and kissed him back, feeling his penis pushed against me.

'Go down on me,' I said in the semi-darkness.

I didn't usually demand he do that, but I wanted to be ready and it was the only sure-fire way of making it happen. It was also something that Charlie had always been particularly good at. He moved down, and soon he was between my legs, and I began feeling it. I closed my eyes, and just focused everything I could on the feeling. It didn't take that long before I was ready, and I reached down and pulled Charlie up so he was on top of me again. Charlie was soon inside of me and moving faster and faster. I knew I wasn't going to orgasm, and so I made the right noises to help him along. Luckily, it didn't take him long, and after a few minutes, he orgasmed inside of me, and then quickly he pulled out and lay next to me, panting like an exhausted runner after a pretty decent 5k.

'That was great,' I said in the dark.

'Yeah, it really was,' replied Charlie.

I had always enjoyed the cuddling after sex because it meant something. Lying wrapped together in post-coital bliss had made me feel closer to Charlie, but now as he got up to use the toilet, I lay there on my own, and when he returned, we both sat on our phones, a foot or so away from each other, encased in the same duvet, but in reality still not that close. It would take more than just a quick midweek shag to make that happen, but at least we had made the effort. Perhaps all hope wasn't lost yet.

No. 63

Charlie

Dangerous men to know

I had turned my computer on and sat facing it, my inbox already full for the morning ahead. I had a meeting at nine o'clock, another at eleven, and then a full afternoon of overseeing a data migration. I had my coffee, a half-eaten morning bun, and I was getting in the right headspace for work when I noticed someone loitering near my desk. I looked up and that's when I saw Jez. Jeremy Grayson, or Jez as he preferred to be known, was sipping on a coffee, and looked like he was about to say something.

'Morning, mate,' he said in his deep, public-school voice. Jez, along with his partner in crime, Miles Spearing, were the self-styled 'work hard play hard' men of the office. Despite being trainee solicitors and practically living in the office, they still went out most weekends and usually had a Monday morning anecdote about some alcohol-fuelled high jinks that had happened over the course of another classic night out. They were the poster boys for the office when it came to overindulgence, but no one seemed to mind because they were good at their jobs, and both Jez and Miles had been to Oxford University and knew people in high places.

My phone pinged with a message from Ash: *Will you be home late again?*

I quickly replied: *Not sure.*

'Morning, Jez,' I replied. 'Can I help you with something?'

'No, mate. I was just walking by your desk, and I thought to myself. Jez, when was the last time Charlie boy came out for a big one? Then, I thought—'

'That you'd stand there until I asked what you were doing, and then you were going to tell me all about one of your legendary nights out that I simply had to come along on?' I replied, and Jez laughed. He was tall, good-looking in a public schoolboy way, and had an inordinate amount of confidence in himself, which I had always found a little jarring.

Another message from Ash. *Hoping we could have dinner together for a change.*

My heart sank. I already knew I would probably be home later than usual.

I replied: *Will do my best.*

'Yes, mate, something like that. Miles and I are going out in Shoreditch this Saturday if you fancy it. It's going to be massive. Miles found a speakeasy bar you need a bloody password to get in, incredible cocktails, and apparently, Saturday nights really go off. You should definitely come along.'

Ash: *I won't hold my breath then.*

Me: *I'll try Ash. Just a lot going on at the moment.*

When Jez said things like 'it's going to be massive' he really meant it. I had been on a few big nights out with them in the past, and it always ended up the same way: very drunk at a nightclub at two in the morning, with Jez and Miles telling me we were going to a strip club, and me having to bail on them before I ended up spending the best part of my wages trying not to get a lap dance. Jez and Miles had met at university and seemingly shared the same love of money, success and excess. If you wanted a proper hedonistic night out where you spent hundreds of pounds, were hung-over for days and wanted to get in trouble with your girlfriend or wife, they were the duo you turned to. It was why I hadn't been out with them in a while, and even if they were at the pub after work, I never went on with them to wherever they were going next. Once they had you, it was shots galore, and you weren't getting home until it was almost light outside. Jez and Miles were dangerous men to know.

Ash: *It would just be nice to see you once in a while.*

'I don't think so, Jez,' I said. 'But thanks anyway.'

'Well, if you change your mind, Charlie boy, you have my number.'

'I do, thanks,' I said, and then he smiled at me, walked off, and started talking to the pretty, new and straight-out-of-university girl we had recently hired, and I couldn't hear their conversation but knew exactly what Jez would be saying. She was definitely getting an invite to their big night out. I got back to my computer, trying to decide how to reply to Ash because I couldn't face another argument, and thinking that despite saying no to Jez, the thought of a night out actually sounded quite appealing given what was waiting for me at home.

No. 64

Ash

How had it come to this?

I glanced at the space next to me in bed; the sad, crumpled white sheet, and the pillow that hadn't been touched. Charlie had slept on the sofa, and I couldn't help but feel slightly heartbroken because it was the first time in all the years we had been married we had slept apart while under the same roof. I stretched up, and felt the sunshine come in through the window and hit the side of my face. It was a Saturday morning, and we had the whole day ahead of us. In years gone by, we would have strolled through a market, walked the South Bank with coffee, or had morning sex because we just had to do it. In the years gone by, when we were happy, there were countless things to do and memories to create, but we weren't happy any more. I felt the sudden urge to get away from London and Charlie. I needed a night back in Southampton to reset myself and perhaps us in the process.

I got up, had a shower and then packed myself an overnight bag. I made my way downstairs before I stood outside the door to the living room for a moment and took a breath. I almost didn't want to go in, but I had to tell him where I was going. I walked in and the room smelled stale, a few empty bottles of beer sat on the coffee table, the television remote was on the floor, alongside a few cushions from the sofa, and under a blanket lay Charlie. He was still asleep. He had one leg out of

246

the blanket, and I gave it a gentle kick. He stirred but didn't wake up and so I kicked him again.

'What's happening?' said Charlie, half sitting up.

'I'm going to my parents' for the night.'

He sat slightly more upright. 'What? Why?'

'I think we could both use some space, Charlie.'

He rubbed his eyes, and then stood up, swaying slightly, perhaps still drunk. 'Ash, you don't need to go to your parents'. Let me take a shower and we can get breakfast or something.'

'I need some space,' I said firmly, trying to keep my emotions in check. 'You slept on the sofa last night because you came home drunk again, and I can't take it any more.'

'Please, just stay and let's talk.'

'I'm going home. I need time to think.'

'About what?'

'About everything. I'm not fucking happy, Charlie!'

'Well, neither am I,' replied Charlie, slightly more aggressively.

'Then let's take a break. Hit the pause button for a day.'

Charlie sat down again, falling onto the sofa amongst the mess of blankets and cushions. I noticed his pile of clothes on the floor next to the sofa; a sock half rolled up.

'Fine,' he mumbled.

'I'll text you when I get there.'

'Okay.'

'Bye then.'

'Bye.'

I took one last look at Charlie, and then I left. I couldn't stand being in our house at that moment. The house where we had eaten pizza on the floor the night before we had moved in, when we had so much to look forward to, and I could never have imagined then that this was how things would go in the end. Was it the end? Was it only Charlie's readiness to be a father that had made us like this or was it something more?

Surely a stronger couple could get through something like that with their relationship still intact, and perhaps even stronger.

I closed our front door, hearing the familiar noise of the brass knocker hitting the wooden door. I walked to our front gate, opened it, closed it, and then walked across the road to my car. It was a bright day, and I got into my Mini Cooper, put my weekend bag on the back seat, before I started the car. I felt a few tears begin to settle in my eyes. My marriage was falling apart in front of my eyes, and it felt like nothing was going to save it. I thought for a second about going back inside because I was running away, and maybe we needed to spend the day hashing everything out over endless cups of tea until we had some sort of resolution, but I couldn't. I was exhausted and didn't have the mental capacity. I needed to get away for a night, spend time with my family, regroup and come back refreshed with new ideas, because I knew one thing for certain: we couldn't keep doing what we were doing because, if we did, it was only going to end one way and that was unbearable to even think about.

No. 65

Charlie

The night when everything fell apart

'She just fucking left,' I said, already feeling a little drunk, my voice harsher and angrier than I actually felt inside. I looked across the table at Jez and Miles. We had met at a pub in Spitalfields before heading into Shoreditch.

'Right, mate. Well, her loss is our gain. Ready for a big night?' said Jez.

I just wanted to get drunk. I finished the last inch of my beer, put it back on the table with a loud crack, and then I looked at them.

'I'm ready!'

'Then let's go!' said Jez with a look in his eye that, even in my slightly drunken state, felt a little terrifying. It was like when I was young and had agreed to go on a rollercoaster I knew was too big and too fast, but then once you were strapped in, there was no turning back whether you wanted to or not. It was best to just hold on tight and hope for the best.

After Ash left, the front door slamming shut behind her, I fell back to sleep, and then woke just before noon. I had a succinct text from Ash that she had arrived safely, but I felt awful and didn't reply. Why had she left like that? She was always the one who said we needed to talk, discuss our feelings, but once things got too much, she was the first to run away. I imagined her at home with her father, him with a glass of whisky, telling

249

her he had been right about me all along. Despite Hugh and me becoming somewhat closer over the years, I imagined him relishing the opportunity to drag my name through the mud. I needed a distraction, and that's when I remembered Jez's invitation for a big night out. I texted him and he sent me the details, and there I was, in the eye of the storm.

'Right,' said Jez. We were walking towards our next destination, a secret underground bar in Shoreditch. 'We're meeting Simon, Libbie and Zoe there. Libbie has the secret password to get in.'

'And they are?' I asked.

'Mates. Cool people. I think you'll really like Zoe,' replied Jez with a tantalising grin.

'Definitely Zoe,' added Miles. 'I think she's probably just your type.'

'I'm married. I don't have a type,' I said, and they just laughed, and we kept walking.

Once we got to the bar in Shoreditch, everything seemed to happen at a much faster pace. The whole night went into overdrive, drinks were bought, rounds and rounds of shots, and I was surrounded by young, attractive people in a bar that was like a speakeasy with lots of leather and sexy cocktails. I met Jez and Miles' friends, and they were much like them. Posh, rich and attractive. Zoe was, as they had said, just my type. Slim, brunette, with an infectious laugh, and she obviously worked out because she had an incredible body that fitted into a dress that left little to the imagination. We ordered cocktails, and I couldn't drink fast enough. I didn't have an endgame, I just wanted to get drunk and forget about everything else in my life, and especially Ash.

Later in the night, I found myself alone in a corner with Zoe, and she was standing so close to me, I felt her body knocking gently against mine, her hand slipped around my waist. We danced among a throng of people, all so close, and it was loud, and the drinks kept coming, and at some point in the evening,

Zoe and I ended up dancing closer and closer, her fit, young body wrapped into mine, her hands on me, her small, perfectly formed bottom pushed against and into me, and at some point we kissed, and I didn't stop her. I felt outside of myself, as though I was watching the entire night unfolding before me but with little control.

I had no idea what time it was when we left the bar, but the whole world seemed so different, and I felt caught up in it. Zoe's hand was in mine, and I let it stay there, and she had an Uber ordered and we got in. Just her and me, and she kissed me again, pulling my hand onto her breast. I wasn't out hunting for sex, but I had fallen into patterns of familiarity with Ash, and Zoe had stepped into my vision in the most unexpected way, and it broke everything that had come before it apart.

No. 66

Ash

When you know nothing will ever be the same again

The quietness was the worst thing. I hated the long silences that spread across the house like the stillness before a thunderstorm because, within them, I didn't know where we stood or what was to come next. We had spoken briefly on my return, and Charlie had been even more distant than before. He seemed angry with me and something else I couldn't quite put my finger on. We were two separate entities occupying the same space. We shared the occasional look, a cursory glance when we passed in the hallway, and a few mumbled questions about a cup of tea or what to eat for dinner, but all the joy seemed to have vanished from us. The magic that had brought us together was gone, and it left me wondering if perhaps it had just been a clever illusion all along. I didn't know what to say to him, he didn't know what to say to me, and so we didn't speak, and the silence stretched across the house, tearing us further apart.

'What do you want to watch?' I said.

It was Wednesday night, and we were in the living room.

'Don't mind. You choose.'

We both knew there was nothing on. I scrolled aimlessly through the channels until I came to an episode of *Would I Lie To You?*. I only trusted comedy at that moment because perhaps we might laugh together, and it might break the awful silence. After a moment, Charlie got up to use the toilet and almost immediately his phone buzzed with a text, the light from his phone shining against the dimness of the room. I gave it a cursory glance. *Jez*. Charlie had mentioned him before as something of a party animal at work and curiosity got the better of me. I picked up his phone before going to messages. I clicked on the message from *Jez*.

> Going out again this Saturday if you fancy a repeat. Zoe says hi!

Going out again this Saturday if you fancy a repeat. Zoe says hi. When had they gone out on a Saturday and who was Zoe? Charlie hadn't been out on a Saturday night in a long time, I thought, but then I stopped, and it came to me in a flash. When I had gone home for the weekend, he must have gone out with Jez and Zoe, whoever she was. I also noticed that there weren't any further messages from Jez, but that couldn't be true, could it? They must have exchanged messages at some point to arrange things, and so he must have deleted them. It was the only logical conclusion, and also if he had deleted them, why? After a few minutes, Charlie walked back into the room and sat down again.

'Did you go out on Saturday with Jez?' I said, looking across at him.

Immediately, his expression changed. Charlie had never been a good or convincing liar. He had something in him, a need to be truthful, and to explain himself fully. It was either an incredible superpower or a fatal flaw in his make-up.

'Umm… yeah,' he replied, his voice higher, his whole body tightened up, as he fidgeted in his seat. 'How do you know about that?'

'Who is Zoe?'

He looked at me, shock and confusion etched into his face like a rabbit cornered by a car, staring straight into the headlights, the fear rising up inside of him as he realised I knew something he didn't want me to know. 'Why are you asking me that?'

'Just answer the question, Charlie.'

'She, umm—' He wavered, his whole face suddenly red and, in that moment, I realised something had happened.

'What happened on Saturday?' I asked, a rising tension in the room.

At that moment, I didn't know how bad it was, or what it would mean for us, but I knew he had done something he felt guilty about. I could almost feel his guilt burning into me, melting against me, and then it wrapped around me, cocooning me within it. My heart began to beat faster, at the thought that Charlie might have made a terrible mistake.

I looked at him and he looked at me, and I could see him flailing. *Tell her the whole truth, a bit of it or nothing at all?* He knew he wasn't a good liar, and that eventually I would find out. The only question now was, how bad was it? Just a drunken snog? Maybe a bit more? Maybe the whole way and the beginning of an affair or, worse, an affair that had started months before, hundreds of deleted texts mapping out a complex series of lies and secret meetups.

'I'm sorry,' said Charlie eventually. 'I'm really, really sorry, Ash.'

This was when it hit me. I genuinely felt like someone had punched me in the heart, a smack so hard that, for a moment, I couldn't comprehend what had just happened. Charlie was so many things, and we had our issues, but I would never have imagined in a million years that he might cheat on me. I stood up suddenly, needing to move.

'What are you sorry for?' I said, my voice wavering between angry and heartbroken.

'I didn't mean for it to happen, Ash. It was just one night. I was so drunk, I—'

'What are you sorry for?'

'It won't ever happen again,' said Charlie, his voice drenched in fear and sadness. He stood up too and took a step towards me. 'Ash—'

'What are you sorry for?' I shouted. I didn't want to hear it, and yet I knew I had to know. This was one of those defining moments. A momentary silence descended on the room, and then it was instantly snapped.

'I slept with her,' said Charlie, and in that moment, I broke apart, and fell on the sofa, tears like fucking waterfalls gripped me, and I wanted to die.

No. 67

Charlie

The crushing end of the most wonderful thing

Ash was curled up in a ball on the sofa, crying, and I couldn't believe it had come to this. The pain was unbearable, but the guilt of what I had done was so much worse. I still couldn't believe I had done it because I hadn't intended to spend the night with Zoe, to have sex with her in that flat in Hackney, but I had and the guilt of it had torn me apart until I barely recognised the man staring back at me in the mirror. Even speaking to Ash had been impossible because I wanted to confess every time I opened my mouth. I deserved nothing from her, but the thought of losing her terrified me and so, although I knew what I had done was unforgivable, I needed her to give me another chance.

'I'm so sorry. I know what I did was terrible, but it meant nothing to me, and you mean everything, Ash. I was just so angry with you, and I lashed out. I was drunk, and I made a horrible decision, but I can't lose you. I love you so much, and I want us to be happy, to have children. I want all of that, and I promise, I will never do anything like this again. I swear, Ash, because you are all I want. You are everything.'

She finally stopped crying, and then she uncurled her body and lay on the sofa, her hands over her face. I kneeled on the floor next to her in silence.

'Ash, please say something. I'm so sorry. I'll do anything to make this right.'

In the morning, when I had awoken in Zoe's bed, the shame and guilt of what I had done hit me hard. A weight was suddenly on my chest, and it had been getting heavier by the day. I didn't blame Zoe for what we had done. I was the bastard husband, the piece of shit Ash's father had once tried to convince her I was, and he had been right all along. I longed to go back in time and make a different decision, a better choice. Ash finally sat up on the sofa.

'You have to go, Charlie.'

'What?'

'You have to leave.'

'But where? This is my home.'

'I don't care where you go. Stay with Zoe for all I care, but you aren't welcome here.'

She was speaking with a terrifying calmness. She had a stillness about her, like she was in complete control of the situation. At that moment, she reminded me of her father.

'Ash, please, I'm sorry. I just felt this inadequacy, have always felt like I wasn't good enough for you, and I just snapped, I—'

'Just because you have inadequacies, Charlie, it doesn't mean you get to pump them into another woman's fucking vagina!'

A quietness suddenly enveloped the room. The word vagina was said with such venom that it sucked all the oxygen and energy out of me until I could barely breathe.

'I know and I was a fucking idiot.' I looked at her and there was nothing in her face, in those eyes that I loved so much, but complete and utter hatred. 'Okay, fine, I'll go, but we need to talk. Maybe we can meet tomorrow. I could come here, and we could talk—'

'No,' said Ash sharply.

'But we have to talk about this. We have to—'

'No, we don't! There is nothing to say. I don't want to hear any more apologies or excuses, because that's all you can say. I don't want to hear any of that. We are done, Charlie. Our marriage is over. You slept with someone else and that is it!'

'No, Ash. We can fix this. It's us. You and me. We can get past this. We have our whole lives ahead of us. It was just one stupid mistake.'

'Maybe you can get past it, but I can't,' said Ash in the same frighteningly calm voice. 'Whatever we had is gone, and just so you know, Charlie, sometimes one mistake is all it takes. I want you to leave our house, and I don't want you to come back.'

I started pleading with her because I had to know there was a chance for us to get through this. She stood up and looked down at me in disgust.

'I'm going into the kitchen. Go upstairs, pack up your stuff, and go.'

I looked up at her. At Ash. My wife. The woman I had shared most of my adult life with. She had been my past and would have been my future, but we had wobbled for a moment, and now we had fallen, and it didn't feel like it was possible. There had to be a way out of this. We could speak to a relationship therapist, move away from London and start again somewhere new with no memories. Surely there had to be a possibility of a future together. Ash walked out and left me crying on the floor. The pain in my chest, in the very meat of my heart, was unbearable.

2017

No. 68

Ash

The scratch on the sideboard

The house had become a different place without Charlie. He hadn't lived there for months, but despite everything, ghosts of him still lived in the shadows. Memories of him still occupied the house, but I didn't want to sell it and start again because, despite everything, it was my home, and the thought of leaving it was unthinkable. I was in limbo, stuck, and unable to move in any one direction through fear I would topple over like someone playing Twister knowing one wrong move, one incorrect foot or hand placement, and the whole thing could come crashing down around me.

I had a glass of wine, and I was listening to my favourite Take That album, *Beautiful World*. I loved that album partly because every song was brilliant, but also because it was their comeback album. The excitement of my favourite band back together after a ten-year hiatus had been a little overwhelming, and it always made me think of renewal and that, even when everything seemed lost, there was always hope. All it took, sang Gary Barlow, was a bit of patience, and I was slowly coming to terms with that.

I was tidying the house, when I moved my handbag from the sideboard in the hallway and that's when I saw it. The scratch Charlie had made on the top the day we had put it together. He had joked at the time that if he died, the scratch would remind me of him, it would become a part of us, and I would cherish it forever. Charlie hadn't died, but he was gone, and the stupid bloody scratch reminded me of him, and I started to cry.

'Fuck you, Charlie,' I mumbled, and made a mental note to buy a new sideboard.

I turned up the volume of the music and danced around the house, tidying, cleaning, and trying to clear my mind, too. There's a song on the album called 'Like I Never Loved You At All', and it's about a couple that have broken up, and it asks the question: how did we fuck this up? It was a question I still couldn't properly answer. How did Charlie and I go from getting married, being so in love, planning a whole life together, to being separated? In moments when I stopped and asked myself that question, a proper answer still eluded me. The obvious answer was that Charlie had cheated, but I knew the actual answer probably traced back through the history of our relationship to a point long before his infidelity. I sat down, and my phone immediately buzzed with a call.

'Hello, you,' I said. 'What's going on?'

'What's going on,' said Edith. 'Is you and me this Saturday night. Dinner, drinks, and probably home before midnight, but you never know!'

I laughed. 'You don't have to do this just to cheer me up.'

'Oh, I'm not. I'm doing it because I need a night out. Ollie is away this weekend. He has a shoot in Glasgow, so it's my chance to have a girls' night out with you. I probably need this more than you, Ash. Do you know I haven't dressed up in years?'

'It hasn't been that long.'

'I'm not kidding. I live in frumpy mummy clothes covered in child detritus, my hair is perpetually up in a ponytail, and for one night, I would love to feel sexy again. At least as sexy as possible with a pair of boobs that look like deflated party balloons. Rupert is staying with my parents, so you can sleep over if you fancy it.'

'It will be like old times. A sleepover, and then a hung-over brunch in the morning.'

'The hung-over brunch was always my favourite bit.'

'Me, too. Eggs Benny and at least two strong flat whites.'

'Same for me. So, you're definitely in because I need to confirm with my parents? Apparently, they lead very busy lives these days and their calendar is full.'

I didn't need a moment to think about it. 'One hundred per cent.'

'And Ash?'

'Yes.'

'Love you.'

'Love you, too.'

We hung up, and I got back to my wine and Take That, while trying to forget all about Charlie and the scratch on the sideboard.

No. 69

Charlie

The party downstairs

My room was near the top of a large house in Brixton that felt a million miles away from my home with Ash. It was barely big enough for a double bed and a wardrobe, although I had heard the room in the eaves was smaller still. There were two bathrooms in the house, a shared kitchen and a living space. Each housemate had a plastic box in the kitchen to store their dry food, and everything that went into the fridge, whether it was labelled or not, was fair game, it seemed, because the first week here I bought some cheese to cheer myself up, and after a night out drinking it was all gone. It wasn't a shared house with much trust, but it was all I could afford.

The weeks and months following what happened with Ash were now a blur. I slept on Matt's sofa for a couple of weeks before I found this place. I begged and pleaded with Ash to give me another chance, a stay of execution, but she hadn't been willing to even speak to me. As far as she was concerned, we were done. I didn't blame her because what I had done was unforgivable, and so I had to take my punishment and hope that one day she might be prepared to give me another chance.

I was drinking my fifth can of beer of the evening, locked away in my room, while downstairs they seemed to be having a party. I could hear loud dance music with bass so deep I could feel it reverberating on my bedroom floor. They had mentioned that I should pop down, have a drink, but I wasn't in the mood. Plus, I was thirty-four and they were all in their mid-twenties. The girl who lived in the eaves looked nearer my age, but she was like a ghost appearing occasionally, a passing sight of her as she disappeared out of the front door or coming out of the bathroom.

The music continued to thump, and I heard a babble of voices below me, but I couldn't stand the thought of talking to strangers and meeting new people. I just wanted to go home and be with my wife, watching television on the sofa, my feet up with a cup of tea, cuddling before bed and then sex, lying in post-coital bliss, her body wrapped around mine, before falling asleep, happy and fulfilled. I had the perfect life, and I had thrown it away for a one-night stand. I hated myself, and so I drank to numb the pain. My days were all the same now, each slipped into the next. I woke up, went to work, hated it because it reminded me of what I had done, and then I usually grabbed some sort of fast food on the way home, and drank until I passed out. My life had disintegrated into one pathetic, pointless day followed by another because, without Ash, everything felt meaningless.

By midnight, when the music was still playing, I stumbled out of my room and downstairs. I walked into the kitchen where a group of strangers stood around talking, smoking, and I was sure someone was eating my crisps.

'Cigarette?' said a woman in a red shirt.

'Sure,' I said, taking one, and she lit it for me.

I hadn't had a cigarette in years, but it felt good. I started talking to the woman. Her name was Delia or Mehlia and she was Dutch, and before long I was dancing, and I didn't care that I had work in the morning. She passed me a shot of vodka, another cigarette, and we kissed, a sloppy snog in the garden before I ended up falling into bed at nearly three o'clock in the morning, disappointed, sad, and a body full of pain.

No. 70

Ash

An unexpected question

I was in a pub near our offices with a few work colleagues on a Tuesday evening. We had stayed late due to a sudden publication disaster and then, hungry, we had decamped to the nearest pub. Food, drinks, and conversations about authors, agents and the usual publishing topics were reeled off one after the other. Eventually, everyone headed off home to their partners and families until it was just me and Tim left standing.

'How's Liv doing?' I asked.

'She's okay, I think. She spends all week with Astrid, and she's with me on the weekend. It's not ideal, but it's the best we can manage at the moment.'

'Poor kid,' I said, and then, realising I might have sounded too judgy, and I didn't want to make Tim feel bad for something that was completely out of his control, I added fastidiously, 'but I'm sure you're both doing your best.'

'We are,' said Tim, forcing a smile. 'Anyway, how are things with you?'

'You don't want to hear about my terribly sad life.'

My life post–Charlie had gradually become smaller and smaller with each passing month. Apart from the occasional night out with Edith, it consisted solely of work and decorating the house. I worked as many hours as I could, and then I went home and spent the weekends on the house. I didn't want to

265

move, but I wanted to make it a completely different version of the home I had lived in with Charlie. I felt the need to wipe away all memories of him, and I was intent on overhauling everything. Without Charlie's income, my parents had kindly offered to help with the mortgage, and so I was focusing on the house and work, and that was it for the time being. I was giving myself time to heal.

'That's where you're wrong,' said Tim. 'Because I do want to hear about your terribly sad life because it probably isn't as sad as mine.'

'You think your life is worse than mine?'

'Undoubtedly.'

I laughed and then looked across at Tim, who looked incredibly handsome in his work suit, his hair immaculately styled, as always, and his face clean-shaven. He had fabulous skin and must have had a daily skin regime that far outweighed mine.

'Let me see,' I said, picking up my glass and having a sip of wine. 'I spend about fifty hours a week at work, and probably another ten working at home. I spend every weekend working on my house, watching reality shows in my spare time because they require zero mental capacity, and I have no social life. You think your life is as desperately sad as that?'

'Let me see. I spend about fifty hours a week at work with you, and probably another ten working at home. I spend another ten hours at the gym because I can't stand the prospect of being home alone. I eat sad meals for one, have no social life, and then I spend all weekend trying to connect with my daughter, and fit an entire week of love into two days and hope she doesn't end up hating me for it.'

'Fine, you win,' I said with a giggle.

'My life is infinitely more depressing than yours. I do have a question for you, though.'

'Sounds intriguing.'

He took a moment before he asked me. 'When do you think you will be ready to start dating again?'

'Oh my gosh, dating,' I said when I had stopped laughing. 'Let me see. Well, I haven't shaved my legs in nearly a month, so that would need to change, and the thought of meeting someone new, going on dates, and heaven forbid, kissing a stranger, all sound utterly terrifying. So, in answer to your question, not anytime soon. What about you?'

'Me? I feel about as ready as you.'

'But surely someone as handsome as you doesn't have to try too hard to get a date.'

'You'd be surprised. Anyway, it isn't about dating anyone, it's about dating someone.'

I looked at him, and he looked bashful, which was unlike him. Someone? He knew someone he wanted to date. I wondered who it was. I had heard rumours that Maggie, in publicity, had her eyes on Tim, and she seemed like the sort of girl Tim might go for. Tall, blonde, and sporty.

'So, there is someone?' I asked, noticing Tim blushing.

'There is someone I like, but I don't know if she would want to date me.'

'I can't imagine anyone not wanting to date you,' I said casually, leaning back in my chair and taking another sip of wine.

'Really?'

'I think most of the single girls at work would date you in a heartbeat, and perhaps even some of the married ones!'

A pause. A beat.

'And what about you?' said Tim, and suddenly he was looking at me with an expression on his face that told me he was being serious.

'Me? Umm, well... I... don't know. Me? Are you being serious because if this is a joke, Tim, it isn't a very funny one?'

'I'm being serious, Ash. I've always thought you were gorgeous, we get on, and maybe it's just me, but I've always felt like we had a connection.'

He looked at me and smiled, and now it was my turn to blush wildly. I didn't know what to think. Tim and I were great friends, and he was the most handsome man I knew, but could I see him like that? I didn't know. Maybe. I looked at him and smiled a terribly self-effacing smile and continued to glow from the extreme heat that seemed to have suddenly gripped my entire body. Me and Tim. Was it a possibility?

No. 71

Charlie

Everything hanging in the balance

I was meeting Ash at the Boaters Inn on the banks of the Thames, and I felt an air of optimism as I walked towards it. A text had arrived out of the blue that morning, causing a tangle of improbable thoughts to sit in my mind and refuse to budge. Perhaps she was ready to talk about the possibility of us again. It had been almost eight months, and with the luxury of time, perhaps she realised she still had feelings for me. All I had was hope because my life at that point was staring grimly into the abyss. I was drinking too much, smoking again, and due to my performance at work, my job was hanging precariously in the balance.

I walked towards the pub and saw Ash sitting outside at a table facing the river. She had changed her hair colour, it was lighter, almost blonde, and she'd had it cut shorter with layers. She was wearing a flowery dress, white pumps, a denim jacket over the top, and she looked more beautiful than ever. My heart skipped a beat. I walked across and sat down.

'Hi,' I said.

'Hello, Charlie.'

We hadn't spoken a word to each other in months.

'Love the hair. You always said you wanted to try being blonde. Are you having more fun yet?'

She smiled. 'Not yet, but it's new, so...'

She stopped and paused. I couldn't read the room and didn't know what she was thinking. What were the meeting headlines?

'Do you want a drink?' I asked quickly because I needed one to settle my nerves.

'I'm fine, thanks.'

'Right, back in a minute,' I said, getting up and walking inside to the bar. It felt surreal to be back in Kingston upon Thames with Ash. The place we had called home for so long, and where we had created so many wonderful memories. My heart was beating quickly, nerves fluttered in my stomach, and I felt sweat gathering under my armpits. I got a pint of pale ale and headed back to the table. 'I'm so glad you wanted to meet, Ash, I have so much I—'

'I want to buy you out of the house,' she said, stopping me dead in my tracks.

'Sorry, what?'

'The house, Charlie. It makes sense. I'm sure you could use the money, and it seems silly if you aren't living there and I'm paying the mortgage. I think it's best for both of us.'

I felt a sudden despair grip me. This was it. The end. She didn't want to meet because she missed me and wanted to get back together, she wanted to move on. My heart hurt, my mind was fuzzy, and I felt like I might be sick. I took a long pull of my pint, and then put my glass back down on the table with a louder than expected crack.

'So this is it then? The end.'

'It's been over since that day, Charlie. This is just me being practical. Think what you could do with the money. I've had the house appraised, and it's worth more than I thought.'

'It's not about the money,' I said, my voice suddenly higher, more aggressive. 'I thought maybe today was going to be about us.'

'There is no us, Charlie,' said Ash very deliberately, and then she looked off towards the water for a moment. Two boats went by, four rowers in each, gliding effortlessly across the water, lush green plants across the other side draped into the river like curtains. It was an idyllic scene, which seemed to mirror how absolutely fucking awful it was at our table. Eventually, she looked back towards me. 'There's something else.'

I looked at her. I knew she wasn't trying to hurt me, it wasn't in her nature, but she was, and I deserved it. All this was my fault, and whether she bought me out of the house or not, it wouldn't take away any of the pain.

'What's that?'

'I'm seeing someone.'

A stab to my heart. I felt momentarily winded.

'Oh.'

'It's Tim.'

A pain suddenly exploded in my chest, and then into my head. She was dating handsome, posh, successful and perfect fucking Tim. I always knew they had something. An anger came over me like a sudden weight had fallen on me, and I couldn't move it. A veil of jealousy and rage overtook my mind, and I didn't know what I was capable of at that moment. I wanted to destroy something, smash up my life and hers, too.

'I fucking knew it!' I said, my voice full of spite.

'Knew what?'

'That you liked him. You always denied it, but I fucking knew. God, I'm so fucking stupid. Of course you're dating him.'

'It isn't like that. It just happened, and anyway, it's none of your business. I only told you in case you found out from someone else. I was trying to be courteous.'

'Courteous would be not fucking Tim just to get back at me because I know that's what you're doing, Ash, and it's fucking pathetic!'

'Oh, grow up,' said Ash, standing up. 'Just let me know about the house.'

She went to leave, and I stood up.

'I still fucking love you!' I shouted. People looked across at us. People trying to enjoy a drink, some food and the ambience of the river. Parents with children nearby, looking on with judgemental faces, desperately trying to cover their poor children's ears.

Ash took one last look at me, and then kept walking. I just wanted to get drunk. It was the only thing I could think about at that moment. I wanted to get out of my mind, so I didn't have to think about them together. Tim was exactly the sort of man that had dogged my life with doubt and self-loathing. He was just another Scott Laird, only this time he had taken the girl from me, and it was unbearable, but not because it was Tim, or even that she seemed completely over me, but because it was all my fault.

No. 72

Ash

The end of something and the beginning of something else

We were in my living room, on the sofa, and Tim had come over for dinner, to watch a film and spend the night. We were taking things slowly, and tonight was the first night we were going to spend together. Despite being unsure about the idea of dating Tim, we had gone out on a few dates, and it seemed he was right. We had something, and it was nice being with someone I already felt comfortable with. Our relationship had grown so organically, it felt like we had already been dating for so much longer than just a month.

'He was so angry, Tim, and he looked awful. I barely recognised the man I married,' I said, a glass of wine held loosely in my hand.

'I'm sorry. I know the break-up was his fault, but losing you, this house, it probably destroyed him.'

'I actually felt bad for him.'

'Because you're a lovely person, with a big heart.'

'I think the word is gullible.'

Tim put his glass of wine down, turned to me, and without a word, he kissed me. It still felt strange that he was my boyfriend. I couldn't quite get over how handsome he was and that his body was so different from Charlie's. Charlie was slim and had little muscle or definition, but Tim was the polar opposite. Taller than Charlie, he had washboard abs, large, muscular arms, and even his legs were perfectly formed. He also waxed, so his body was mostly hairless. It was a real wake-up call to my own hair removal routine that had, I admit, become quite lax. He was a complete contrast to Charlie, but the thing was, I didn't care. I knew Tim was handsome, but that was just superficial and meant nothing when we were alone. What really mattered to me was him, and how he made me feel about myself. The fact it came in such a gorgeous package was just garnishing.

I had the momentary thought that maybe we should discard the film, a high-concept romantic comedy, and head straight upstairs to the bedroom, but then we heard a noise outside. Someone was in the front garden. Then we heard a loud hammering on the front door.

'Ash!' Charlie shouted. 'Ash!'

He rang the doorbell repeatedly. He was obviously drunk, and my heart sank in my chest because this was the last thing I wanted to deal with.

'Do you want me to go?' said Tim, standing up.

'No, no, it's okay, I'll go.'

The last thing I wanted was for Charlie to see Tim because I couldn't stand the thought of them arguing on my doorstep. Hopefully, if I asked him to leave, he would go quietly without causing a scene. I walked to the front door, where Charlie was still ringing and knocking incessantly, and I opened the door. Charlie was clearly drunk, and he looked awful. He stood, swaying gently from side to side, his face was bloated, his eyes a distant relation to the eyes of the man I had fallen in love with. He looked, for want of a better word, broken.

'Ash,' slurred Charlie. 'You can't—'

'You're drunk, Charlie. Please, just go home.'

'I don't have a home. This is my home. You… you're—'

I thought he was going to start crying.

'Just go home, sleep it off, and I'll call you in the morning,' I said, hoping he would go, but then from behind me, Tim appeared, and immediately I saw Charlie's expression change.

'What the fuck is he doing in my house?' said Charlie, lunging forward and into the house, his feet on the mat in the hallway. He was hammered. I could always tell when he was that drunk because it was like there was a glitch in his matrix. His walk would stutter, stop, sway, and then continue on wildly fast, as if he had robotic legs. He had that same walk as he stumbled into my house. His eyes were glazed over like a stranger had possessed him and today that stranger was a pissed, jealous ex-husband knobhead looking for trouble.

'Charlie, please just go!' I shouted at him, but it was too late.

'You cunt!' barked Charlie, going towards Tim. 'She's my fucking wife!'

Charlie lurched forward and tried to punch Tim, but he easily stepped aside, and Charlie fell, hitting the wooden floor with an almighty bang.

'I think you need to leave,' said Tim, picking up Charlie with ease, and taking him outside. Charlie was thrashing around, kicking and screaming like a toddler, shouting that he loved me, I was his wife, and I couldn't help but cry. I hated what Charlie had done to me, but I could see how heart-broken he was. I knew then that I had to call his mother in the morning because he needed help. Maybe I was gullible, but I had loved him and couldn't bear the thought of his life falling apart. After a few minutes, Tim came back inside, closed the door, and he hugged me tight. 'It's all right, Ash, he's gone now.'

I buried myself deep in Tim's shoulder and wept. I wasn't entirely sure what I was crying for, but I knew it felt like the end of something. An entire chapter of my life was gone, and it was time to start looking forward to whatever was next, because unlike Charlie, I wasn't going to wallow in the past and long for something that was already gone.

No. 73

Charlie

Back on solid ground

I was standing on Mum's doorstep, a duffel bag at my feet, nerves in the pit of my stomach, and I don't think I had ever felt worse. My life that had been teetering on the brink for months had finally crumbled. I had made an absolute fool of myself at Ash's house and then I had lost my job soon after. I didn't even complain when my manager asked me into her office and told me she had to let me go. She had every right to fire me given my lack of application and my continued lateness. I apologised profusely, and she said she would write me a good letter of recommendation, but that I needed to get myself together. She obviously saw what was happening to me, and so I decided to come home. Ash was right. I needed help, and there was no one more qualified to get me back on the straight and narrow than my mother. I also craved the security and simplicity of Southampton. I had to get back on some sort of steady ground again before I could even begin to start moving forward.

The door opened, and Mum stood there smiling, her wonderfully warm, knowing eyes peeling away the layers of my sadness, and I burst into tears. She ushered me inside the house, dropping my bag at the foot of the stairs, before she took me in her arms and just hugged me. We stayed like that for a few minutes before we went into the living room, sat on the sofa with cups of strong tea and I told her everything.

'I'm such a mess. I've ruined my relationship with Ash and lost my job.'

'Oh, Charlie,' said Mum, her eyes that knew me so well looking at me with nothing but love. 'Do you know how proud your dad was of you? Wherever we went, he would forever be telling people about his son that had been to university, lived in London, and had a swish job. He loved that you had achieved so much more than him.'

'I don't think he would be proud of me now, Mum. I had everything, and I threw it away.'

'Listen,' said Mum, a concrete hardness to her voice. 'You made a mistake. We all make mistakes, but it's how you react that matters. You know, right after we bought this house, your dad got made redundant. We were terrified, but what did your dad do? He didn't feel sorry for himself, he didn't give up. The next day, he went out, knocking on doors, until he found himself a new job. It took him less than two weeks because he knew the only way to make the situation better was to work even harder. Face life head on.'

'But I'm not Dad, Mum. I don't know if I'm that strong.'

'Look at me,' said Mum, putting her cup of tea down on the coffee table. 'You're going to stay here with me, and we are going to figure this out together. First, you're going to sell your share of the house to Ash because you need the money, then you're going to decide what sort of life you want. Okay?'

I looked at Mum. She had been through a lot in her life. She had lost one of her siblings when she was only seven in a car crash. She had lost her father, her husband, and she had worked hard to scrape the money together to help put me through university. She was a tough woman, and there was no way she was going to let me fail because I was all she had left.

'Okay,' I replied, and Mum smiled at me.

'Good boy. Now, go put your stuff in your bedroom, and I'll make us something to eat.'

We both stood up and, before she left the room, I stopped her. 'Mum.'

'Yes?'

'Thank you,' I said, and then I hugged her and gave her a kiss on the cheek.

She touched her hand to my cheek, smiled, and then walked off towards the kitchen while I took my bag upstairs to my old bedroom. It had completely changed since I left home for university. She used it as a guest room now, and so it had generic decor instead of all my old posters, and my duvet with the football on. Now it resembled a standard bed-and-breakfast room with a bowl of potpourri on top of the dresser.

I unpacked my things and lay down on the bed. I put my arms behind my head and stared up at the ceiling I had stared at so often as a boy. I was thirty-five years old, and I felt like I had already lived a whole life. I needed to start all over again, construct a brand-new existence from scratch, and it would start with a phone call to Ash in the morning. I had to sell her my share of the house because I needed the money, and then I had to figure out exactly what I wanted to do with the rest of my life, because I knew one thing for certain: I couldn't let Dad down. He was a fighter, and I had to be the same.

2018

No. 74

Ash

Holding hands tightly

Tim and I were sitting on a Central Line Tube heading towards
Notting Hill Gate and then Portobello Road Market. Tim was
sitting on one side of his daughter, Liv, and I was on the other.
It was her first time going to the market, and she was genuinely
excited in that way that only children can be. I could see the
buzz of adrenaline on her face as we rode the Tube, her eyes
wide with wonder. She was eight years old, her parents officially
divorced but on good terms, and was growing into quite the
young lady. After a bit of a shaky start to our relationship, we
had gradually become friends, and my burgeoning relationship
with Tim seemed to be going from strength to strength, too.
He lived in his two-bed flat in Balham and I had my house, so
although we spent a great deal of time together, we still had the
luxury of our own spaces when we needed a breather. We were
both coming out of tough break-ups, loaded with baggage, and
knew we had to take our time.

'Are you excited about the market?' I said to Liv once we
were off the Tube and walking with hundreds of other people
towards Portobello Road.

'Very! I have ten pounds Mummy gave me.'

'That's a lot of money.'

She was holding Tim's hand tightly.

'It's going to be very busy, so you must hold one of our hands
all the time,' said Tim.

'Yes, Daddy, I know,' Liv replied with a sort of tired acknowledgement.

Liv explained how she had been on school trips to the National Gallery, the British Museum, HMS *Belfast*, and she had held her friend Ava's hand all day and hadn't got lost once. Tim was a surprisingly tentative father, which felt in contradiction to the Tim I knew, who always came across full of confidence and bluster. Perhaps it was a nervousness born out of the fact he only had her at weekends, wanted everything to be perfect and felt the need to cram an entire week of love into just forty-eight hours. For my side, I loved spending time with Liv, although it only hardened my desire for children of my own.

Liv was the most adorable girl. She had stunning blonde hair and large, perfectly blue eyes that sparkled like crystals. When she smiled, she got delightful dimples in her pale cheeks, and she had the most infectious laugh. I was beginning to love her and could see myself being a part of her life, but she still wasn't mine. I knew I wanted my own child, and having Liv, too, was like an added blessing. I already imagined Liv being the protective older sister, but I knew I was getting ahead of myself. My need for a baby seemed to almost outweigh my feelings for Tim. Our relationship was solid, and Tim was exactly what I needed after the breakdown of my marriage, but despite my feelings for him, I still found myself thinking about Charlie from time to time, and wondering how he was. I could never quite let him go in the way I wanted to.

We finally reached the market, and it was busier than I remembered. It seemed like all of London had come to Portobello Road. It was gloriously sunny, and perfect for a stroll around the market before lunch somewhere child-friendly for Liv, who only enjoyed hamburgers or pizza, although she wasn't picky about dessert and would accept anything that contained large amounts of sugar. Tim popped into a newsagent to grab a couple of drinks, and so it was just Liv and me, and she reached her hand into mine.

'Daddy said I had to hold someone's hand the whole time,' she said, a note of sarcasm in her voice.

'That's right,' I replied, feeling a warm glow inside of me.

I loved the feeling of her hand in mind, and how it made me feel. We had only known each other for six months, and I was gradually becoming something of a fixture in her life. It gave me something I had known I had wanted for so long, but it also gave me the feeling of what might have been with Charlie. If he had been ready to have children, our relationship wouldn't have suffered, and we would probably still be together. I would have had my own child with him, instead of the adopted family I now had with Tim. So, despite the glow of happiness, feeling the glorious sunshine on my face with Liv's soft little hand in mine, there was a part of me that knew I should have had this with Charlie, and despite doing my best to think positively about the future, it was also hard not to feel the pain of failure.

No. 75

Charlie

The end of us

I was meeting Ash at her solicitor's, and we were going to go over the terms of the contract. I had agreed to sell her my share of the house, and I would have been happy to just have her send me a cheque, but her father had insisted we do everything by the book – of course. He wanted to make sure that once I had my money, I would be gone from her life for good. Luckily, Ash had persuaded him not to attend the actual meeting because she knew it would be a complete fucking disaster. So, it was a damp Friday morning, that I found myself loitering outside a cafe in Southampton, sipping on a coffee, and waiting for Ash. The solicitors were next door, but I had arrived early, nervously drinking a flat white in preparation for seeing her again for the first time in what felt like forever.

I was in a considerably better place than the last time I had seen her. I looked better, had lost a bit of weight, and I felt something like my old self again. I had also been accepted on a teacher training PGCE course in London. My life would be changing once again, and I was ready to say goodbye to Ash.

'Oh, hi,' said Ash suddenly.

I was momentarily taken by surprise, as she had appeared around a corner as if by magic, and then she was standing in front of me in a long brown coat, and leather ankle boots. She looked, as always, perfect. She had her hair tied back, a pair of earrings hanging from her gorgeous ears, her slender neck – the neck I had kissed hundreds of times over the years – disappearing into a grey jumper. I missed having her in my life. Her presence, her laugh, and just being able to look at her and wonder how anyone could be that beautiful.

'How are you?' she said when it was clear I wasn't going to say anything.

'Umm, yeah, good. You?'

'No complaints,' said Ash with a razor-thin smile.

I hated everything about that moment. The painful awkwardness like we were strangers and not two people who had once been everything to each other. I had rubbed sun cream on her back in Lanzarote, made her soup when she was sick, and rubbed her sore feet on the sofa after a long day at work. We'd had sex more times than I could remember. All of those memories hadn't been erased, and yet it was like they had never happened.

'This is strange,' I said after a pause.

'Yes, it is. Thanks for being so understanding about the house.'

'No, no, it's fine, honestly,' I replied, searching her face for something that said the old Ash was still in there. Was she just holding it all in, playing the part of the stoic ex-wife, or was that just who she was now? 'I'm just glad we can get it all sorted out.'

'Yes, me too. Time to move on.'

'Onwards and upwards!' I said with an almost tasteless level of excitement that seemed to be at odds with the mood of the moment. 'Sorry.'

'It's fine,' said Ash with a tight smile, and then we stood in silence, and I finished the last dregs of my coffee. I thought for a moment about telling her about my teaching year – perhaps she would be impressed, I had thought on my way there – but it suddenly felt inappropriate and inconsequential. She wouldn't care and why should she? We were two separate people now. A once loving couple that had fallen out of love, and now it was all about crossing the I's and dotting the T's with the least amount of fuss.

'How's things with you and T—'

'We should probably go in. Our appointment is at eleven,' said Ash sharply.

We both looked down at our watches at the same time.

'Right, yes,' I replied, and we shuffled uncomfortably towards the solicitor's office to finalise the end of us. One day we might get divorced, but would we even need to see each other for that? It could probably all be done online nowadays or perhaps via post. Perhaps years from now we might see each other across a room. Two people who used to know each other, had once lain on the sofa together, curled into each other, watching a film, safe in the knowledge that they were with the right person, their only person. I might see her across that crowded room, and perhaps we might smile in acknowledgment or even wave and that would be it.

We walked into her solicitor's office, I let Ash go in ahead of me, and then the door closed behind me with a sharp snap.

No. 76

Ash

Where was the mess?

I had this idea when I was a teenager. I suppose it was less of
an idea and more of an image of the sort of person I wanted to
become. I imagined myself at ages twenty and thirty, although
I hadn't thought far enough ahead to think of myself at forty
because that felt as ancient and incomprehensible as becoming
a National Lottery millionaire when I was fifteen.

At twenty, I saw myself at university, a social butterfly,
trendy, smart and with a gorgeous boyfriend. I imagined he
played rugby or rowed and studied something solid like engin-
eering. At thirty, I imagined myself with a career in publishing,
working with world-renowned authors, living in the hustle and
bustle of London in a beautiful house on one of those gorgeous
tree-lined streets you saw in magazines. I would be married to a
successful man, and we would have a couple of children. When
I was younger, it all seemed like a distant dream, but now I was
in my mid-thirties, and the dream remained somewhere inside
of me, and it was so much closer. I had the career, to some
extent the house, but the rest remained in the balance, and it
was the rest that was on my mind.

Tim and I were eating dinner at his flat in Balham, a delicious
spaghetti alle vongole he had whipped up. Tim's flat was a
beautiful two-bed on the ground-floor of a lovely old Victorian
house that reminded me of a model home because it didn't look

like an actual human being lived there. It was so perfectly neat and tidy, and much like Tim himself, it was all a bit too good to be true. I had to ask myself: where was the mess?

'We should talk about tomorrow,' said Tim.

'Do we have to? I'm really enjoying dinner,' I replied, twisting spaghetti onto my fork.

'This is a big one,' said Tim, still in his Charles Tyrwhitt work shirt and trousers. I don't think he owned any lazing-around-the-house clothes. He had piles of gym attire, work suits, and then business casual for the weekends, but everything was high-end and smart. 'If we can get this over the line, Ash, it will be huge. Imagine us publishing Sally Hawkesbury!'

'Let's not get too excited, it's only a meeting. She's published her last five books with the same publisher, there's no guarantee she will go with us. If anything, she's using us as leverage to get a better deal.'

'Perhaps, but we have to make this work. Whatever it takes. Do you know she's one of the top five bestselling authors in the world today?'

'I am aware.'

'If we can get her onboard, it will give the company a huge lift. Not to mention giving us leverage for a pay rise,' said Tim with a smile before he took a sip of his wine.

I smiled back and continued eating. There was a significant difference between me and Tim when it came to work. I had wanted to work in publishing because I loved reading, adored the world of literature and I got genuine pleasure from helping authors achieve their dreams. For me, it was more about lifestyle than money. I was happier helping an interesting debut author navigate the complex world of publishing and garnering some mild success with a book I genuinely believed in, while Tim wanted to snag big-name authors and make money.

He had spoken passionately about starting his own publishing house one day. He said publishing was evolving and he wanted to be at the forefront of the digital revolution. He, of course, wanted me to join him, but I wasn't interested and loved my current job. They offered decent benefits, maternity leave, and that was something I wanted to explore, and soon. Tim was laser-focused on starting his own business, and I was more invested in starting a family.

'Tim, you know I want children, right?' I said, as we loaded the dishwasher. I wanted to chat about the topic we hadn't yet broached with any sort of satisfactory conclusion.

He was rinsing a plate in the sink. 'I know.'

'Do you think it's something you might want as well? I've always wanted a family of my own, and unfortunately I'm not getting any younger.'

'But that just isn't true. I swear you look younger every day,' said Tim, passing me the plate, and then rinsing another.

'That's lovely, but I'm being serious. I'm thirty-five, and whatever eggs I have left aren't going to stay around forever. As much as I don't want to pressure you, we are fighting a losing battle with my biological clock.'

Tim looked at me, put the plate down, and then took me in his arms.

'I'm just not ready right now. You know I'm focused on work, and potentially starting my own publishing house. I just don't know where we fit a child into that jigsaw puzzle.'

'But it's important to me.'

'I know, and we'll talk about it again soon. Promise.'

He smiled, leaned in and then he kissed me, his hands reaching around me and onto my bottom, and it seemed all thoughts of loading the dishwasher were over with. We stumbled, kissing frantically, towards the sofa, where we fell down, and I knew we were going to have sex, but all I could think about was the last time I had brought up the subject, he had said exactly the same thing. But what if he didn't want to have a child with me? Could I go my whole life and not have children of my own? The vision I'd had since I was a teenager always included children. It was one of the constant things in my life: career, husband, house and babies. If Tim wasn't on board with it, perhaps he wasn't the one for me, but if that was true, it raised a plethora of questions that would need answering sooner rather than later.

No. 77

Charlie

The familiar smell of school

The school was a thirty-minute bus ride from my shared house in Twickenham, and arriving on that first day, I had never felt more nervous. It was the first school experience module of my teaching year, and after all the emotional turmoil of the past few years, I was finally going into a school to learn how to be a teacher. I stood outside for a moment and took a deep breath. Although I had thought about becoming a teacher for years, it had always been just this intangible thing, and I was about to face the reality of it for the first time. As I took a second deep breath, my hands clammy with nervous sweat, a group of schoolboys pushed past me, almost knocking me over, my backpack falling on the floor.

'Watch where you're going!' I instinctively said, reaching down to pick up my bag.

'Yeah, all right, sir,' one of them retorted, and they all laughed and carried on.

Many of the boys walking into school were bigger than me, and even some of the girls. I was amazed by the sheer size of the school itself, and I felt a fear and an apprehensiveness, but after a moment I pulled myself together, and walked into the reception.

I explained who I was, and whom I was there to meet, took a seat while I waited, looking around at the place I would call home for the next few months. The familiar smell of school hit me, and although I hadn't been inside a school for twenty years, the smell of it was somehow ingrained in my brain and it transported me back to my own teenage years. It was actually quite a pleasant reception area with corporate-looking red chairs, a light wooden coffee table and a selection of leafy green plants. It resembled a bright, modern office rather than the school I had attended that was all ancient wood flooring, stone grey walls and strictly no decor of any kind through fear it might actually detract from the serious business of learning. I waited for five minutes before I was greeted by Mrs Stourton, a neat woman in her forties, who had been teaching secondary history for over fifteen years.

'I'm Alison Stourton,' she said with a friendly smile and a firm handshake. 'But everyone calls me Ally.'

'Charlie. Charlie Talbot,' I replied, nerves caught in my throat.

'Right, Charlie Talbot, follow me, and let's get started, shall we?'

I smiled and followed her through into the staffroom where something funny happened to me that I couldn't explain. I felt at home in that room with its slightly crap furniture and suddenly most of my nerves subsided. Working in the high-pressure corporate world for so long, I had never felt like I belonged there. The people, the atmosphere and the constant struggle to survive, day in day out, in a career I didn't love had left me with scars, but walking into that school staffroom, and seeing the sort of people I would be working alongside, I knew that I had found my tribe. Like-minded souls who looked tired, broken down by the pressures of the job and no doubt the pupils, but I felt an immediate camaraderie with them that I had never felt before.

Mrs Stourton – or Ally as she asked me to call her when not around the pupils – got us both a cup of tea, and we sat down on an old green sofa that had definitely seen better days.

'So, Charlie, without wishing to put you off, why the hell do you want to become a teacher?'

We both laughed, but I could see there was a seriousness in her expression that told me she wasn't entirely joking. I had heard all the negative things about teaching and read about teachers leaving the profession in droves, but it was hard to put into words what it meant to me. It felt somehow intertwined with Ash, who had encouraged me to go into teaching, and to a lesser extent my father, who had always told me to follow my dreams. It was also the only career I could think of where I could use my degree, my love of history, and it was a link back to that part of my brain that had been neglected for so long.

'I'm passionate about history, and I was tired of doing jobs that gave me no sense of purpose. Teaching was always something I considered, and I'm not getting any younger,' I said, taking a sip of my tea. 'So, here I am.'

'I'm not going to lie to you, Charlie, it's tough. Stressful, long hours, demanding parents, and sometimes the kids can be challenging, but if you love it, and are passionate about history, you might just make it,' said Ally standing up suddenly. 'Ready then?'

'As I'll ever be,' I replied, and then I followed Ally to her classroom to begin my career as a teacher.

2019

No. 78

Ash

How many of the best still wanted children?

'I can't believe you're leaving London,' I said to Edith. 'I vividly remember when we met. You said you would never live anywhere else but London. What's the Samuel Johnson quote? If a man is tired of London, he is tired of life.'

'One, I am a woman and not tired of London, and two, you should see the new house, Ash, it's so beautiful.'

'But Godalming feels like a hundred miles away. Isn't it in the middle of nowhere?'

'You can be at Waterloo in under an hour.'

'That's not bad.'

'My commute won't change much, but the house, Ash... and the garden is enormous! I can't wait to have you and Tim over for summer barbecues.'

Edith and I were in an Italian restaurant in Kensington, and she was delivering her news in person. She had texted me a few weeks ago to say that everything had been finalised, and they were officially moving out of London. Her, Ollie and their son, Rupert. Edith had also mentioned that they were trying for a second baby. Her life was blossoming and moving to a large four-bed house in the country with an enormous garden, while mine felt like a car that was stalled on a steep hill, struggling to go forward, knowing reverse wasn't an option, hoping the whole fucking thing didn't just break down and get stuck forever.

'I don't know about me and Tim,' I said, looking across the table at Edith, my whole body full of doubt and insecurity. 'I don't think he wants to have a baby, and, well, I do.'

'Oh, Ash. Are you sure?'

'He won't commit to it and keeps pushing the conversation down the track. I pitch the idea, and he keeps batting it away.'

'Oh,' said Edith, as our arancini starters arrived. 'That doesn't sound promising.'

'And I love his daughter, Liv. She's wonderful, but she isn't mine.'

'He doesn't understand your need to have a baby of your own?'

'I don't know if it's that he doesn't understand, but more he's focused on his career and nothing else matters.'

'Including you?' said Edith, taking a bite of her arancini. 'Oh my God, this is incredible!'

I took a quick bite of the arancini, and she was right. 'That is amazing,' I said, before I added: 'I don't know if that includes me or not. At the moment, I'm definitely veering towards not.'

'Well, if he doesn't realise how bloody wonderful you are, and doesn't appreciate you enough, then bugger him. You deserve the best.'

'Thank you. I really am going to miss you.'

'I'm not dying, Ash, I'm just moving to the country.'

'Then why does it feel the same?'

Edith laughed, and we tucked into our arancini, before our main courses arrived. Edith had gone for the aubergine parmigiana, and I had gone with the lamb. They were both superb, and I finished off my wine, while Edith stuck to sparkling water. She was due her period any day, but hopefully, she said, it wouldn't come. She was on the brink of having two children to my none. Edith said I deserved the best, but how many of the best were still single at thirty-five in London, and how many of the ones who were left wanted children? I didn't have the time it took to forge a new relationship from scratch. It had taken

Charlie and me years to really get to know each other to the point where I could look at him and know what he was thinking without a word exchanged. I barely had that with Tim yet, and I had known him for years, before we even got together. If I met someone new, it might take a year or two before we were even ready to start talking about the possibility of children. I would be in my late thirties, the last flickering embers of my youth, and I just didn't know if I had the time.

Edith and I stood outside the restaurant and said goodbye. We hugged, and I wished her all the best. She and I were the same age, but she was exactly the image I had of myself as an adult. Edith had the career, a handsome husband, the house and also the children. Everything I wanted she had, but I wasn't jealous of her because I wanted only good things for her. The hard part was coming to terms with the idea that I might not have all those things myself. Having it all seemed practically impossible, and despite being so happy in so many parts of my life, I would probably have to settle on having some of it, but not all.

No. 79

Charlie

Favourite television show?

My hands were covered with a thin layer of sweat, my heart was racing, and I felt the fear grip me tighter as I stood outside the pub, debating the moral implications of doing a runner. I hadn't been this nervous since my first day teaching, but this was for a different reason entirely. One of the women on my course, Vanessa, had asked me out. At first, I didn't know what to say because I wasn't in the right headspace for a date, but eventually I agreed because it was the first time I had ever been asked out, and maybe, whether I was ready or not, I needed to get back on the horse.

I eventually walked into the pub, and saw Vanessa was already sitting down, two pints on the table in front of her. I gingerly walked across, and when she saw me, she stood up.

'All right, Charlie,' she said in her thick Stoke accent.

'Hi. Hello.'

When I reached her, I gave her a quick peck on the cheek before sitting across from her. She slid the second pint across towards me.

'I wasn't sure what you wanted, so I got you the same as me,' she said with a smile.

'Perfect, thanks,' I said, taking a long pull of my pint before I looked back towards her. I honestly didn't know what to say. I hadn't been on a date since my first with Ash and that wasn't a date in the truest sense of the word because we had already kissed the day before. Technically, this was the first proper date of my life, and I was frozen in fear like a child during the school pantomime gripped by stage fright and unable to remember any of their lines. Luckily for me, Vanessa didn't have the same problem.

'It's so weird, isn't it? Dating, I mean. Cause, I knew I liked you from the start of the course, but I didn't want to, you know, seem too eager.'

'If it helps, I had no idea.'

'I suppose. Let's just have a drink and see what happens, yeah?'

'Right, yes, let's see,' I mumbled, searching my brain for the smallest kernel of a conversational titbit, but literally nothing came to me. It was clear Vanessa had made an effort. She was in a tight-fitting, low-cut black top that seemed to almost gift-wrap her reasonably large breasts. She had clearly spent time doing her hair that was razor straight, and she was wearing quite a lot of make-up. She was quite pretty, if not really my type. She was also only twenty-seven, so quite a bit younger than me, and I felt it.

'Favourite television show?' said Vanessa suddenly.

'Umm, of all time?'

'Yeah, I'll go first. *This Morning*. I could literally watch it forever.'

'*This Morning*, the daytime magazine show, is your all-time favourite television show?'

'Yeah, love it, and next is probably *Love Island*, *Gogglebox*, and then maybe *A Place in the Sun*. I've always wanted to get a flat or something in Spain. One day. You never know!'

'So, you like reality shows?'

'Love them! I literally spend all my time when I'm not working, watching reality shows, or if I'm hung-over, I'll watch *This Morning*. It just makes you feel better, doesn't it?'

'I suppose so,' I said, having another pull of my pint until it was almost gone. 'Another drink?'

'Yeah, same again,' said Vanessa with a big, warm smile.

I went to the bar and stood there for a moment, trying to collect my thoughts. It was clear Vanessa and I weren't suited for each other. She was lovely, obviously fun, but just not the sort of girl for me. To be honest, going on a date with Vanessa just reminded me how far I was from being over Ash. I still had such deep feelings for her and didn't know when I would be ready to date again, to even think about someone else in the same way I thought about her, but I knew as I stood at the bar, got our drinks, then walked back to the table, I wasn't ready yet. I needed to focus on my career and then maybe I might think about the prospect of love. Also, perhaps with someone whose favourite television show wasn't *This Morning*. Call me old-fashioned, but I preferred well-written sitcoms or gritty psychological thrillers.

'Favourite film?' said Vanessa when I sat down again.

'Umm...'

'I'll go. First, *Legally Blonde*. I'm literally obsessed. Then either *Van Wilder* with Ryan Reynolds because he's so hot or *Scary Movie*. Oh my God, have you seen it? It's so funny.'

'I haven't.'

'It's literally the funniest film ever!'

I hadn't seen *Scary Movie*, but I had my doubts over her claim it was the funniest film ever. I also believed we were each entitled to our own opinions when it came to favourite television shows, music, and films because Matt had watched *Neighbours* religiously when we lived together, and I was still rather fond of him. Despite quickly realising that Vanessa definitely wasn't The One, I liked her. She was funny, quirky and, above all, optimistic. I could tell she was genuinely looking for her soulmate, and when we said good night, I told her that. I thanked her for asking me out, and said that one day she would find her perfect partner. She smiled and then asked if I still fancied a quick snog in the pub car park, which I felt like I had to decline before I headed off home.

No. 80

Ash

Everything but the baby

'I just don't think you understand,' I said, a frustration caught in my voice because it felt like we had started this conversation days ago and were going around in painfully repetitive circles. I looked at Tim on the other end of his sofa. It was a gorgeous light grey Chesterfield from Habitat with lemon cord cushions. 'And I think we should break up.'

'Wait,' said Tim, sitting up and looking more concerned. The situation was suddenly critical. 'Break up? Ash, we can figure this out. We can't break up over this.'

'And that's why we have to – because you just don't understand how important this is to me. I've always wanted children of my own, and you don't. It's fine, I understand, you already have Liv. I'm not angry with you, Tim. I'm not anything except sad.'

Tim moved closer to me on the sofa. He looked slightly desperate, like he might cry, which would be a first and actually made me a little nervous. Tim was solidly masculine and the prospect of seeing him break down didn't bear thinking about.

The conversation had started three hours earlier. I had told him I wanted children, that we couldn't keep putting it off, and then we had retreated to our usual corners with Tim trying to placate me, telling me he needed more time and me telling him that I needed an answer. We kept going until we arrived at this point when I realised we had reached the end of the road.

'Fine, if you want children so badly, we can have one,' said Tim bluntly.

I looked at him because I couldn't believe what he was saying. 'You'd do that for me?'

'If it means keeping you.'

'But do you want to be a father again? Do you want the sleepless nights, the dirty nappies, and the responsibility of raising another human being?'

'I want you,' he replied with a conciliatory smile, holding my hands gently in his.

'But that's not enough. I'm sorry, Tim, but I want to have a baby with someone who really wants one, too. I love you. I love us—'

'Then don't break up with me. Stay. We can figure this out.'

'No,' I said, standing up. 'We won't figure this out. I need to be with someone who wants what I want, and that isn't you, Tim. It isn't your fault, and it isn't mine. It's just the way it is.'

'You're going to throw all of this away just because you want a baby? We could have everything. The money, the perfect house, and as many holidays abroad as you want. I'm offering you everything, Ash.'

'Except the one thing I actually need,' I said, feeling tears begin to fill my eyes as the realisation of what was happening took hold. 'I have to go. I'm sorry.'

'I love you,' said Tim desperately, holding on to my hand.

'I love you, too,' I said, before I released my hand from his and walked out of his flat for the last time.

Tim was right, he could offer me everything, and we had a wonderful life together, but my whole body craved a baby, and I wanted to experience that with someone who wanted it just as much as me. I needed to be with someone who wanted parenthood, and I didn't know if I would find that man, but I couldn't stay with someone who definitely didn't want it.

I left Tim's flat, wiping the tears from my eyes, before I started the walk towards the Tube station. I would go home and be alone once again. Alone in the house I had bought with Charlie, where we were supposed to have raised a family together. How had my life ended up like this? I always had a plan, always knew what sort of life I wanted, and I believed if I rigidly followed the plan, played it by the book, everything would fall into place. Perhaps it was time to throw away the plan and try something new. As I walked towards home, I felt a weight begin to shift off of me, but it was replaced by an unsettling feeling of not knowing what was next. The push and pull of life, of certainty and uncertainty, and the clamour to somehow be happy amongst it all.

No. 81

Charlie

The butt-dial

I had my first proper teaching job at a secondary school in Clapham, and despite the overwhelming fear I felt every morning as my classroom filled up with sulky, angst-ridden teenagers, I was ready for the next chapter of my life. With the money from my share of the house, and my salary, I rented a one-bed flat in Clapham, and living alone for the first time was something of a relief after multiple shared houses.

The flat was at the top of a lovely old house a stone's throw from Clapham Common, and there was a young professional couple below me and a retired couple below them. The house had been kept in wonderful condition, and the shared garden was well taken care of. I often saw the older couple out there weeding and taking care of the plants. After the last few years when my life seemed to have been hurtling towards destruction, I was finally settled, and everything felt calm. I didn't know what the future held, but I had a career, somewhere nice to live, and from where I was after my break-up with Ash, I felt lucky to be back on track again. Dad would have been proud of me.

It was a Monday morning, a few weeks into the start of term, and I was getting ready to leave the flat and head off to work. One of the nicest things about living alone was that everything in the flat belonged to me, so any plates left in the sink or dirty laundry on the floor was mine, and so it would always be as clean as I made it. I didn't have to worry about someone stealing my food, or as often happened in my last house, someone waking me up at two o'clock in the morning with an impromptu party. I was entering a new phase of my life when all I craved was peace and quiet.

I grabbed my leather satchel, put on my brown Oxford shoes, grabbed my green Joules padded coat, and was about to head out of the door when my mobile rang. I glanced down at the caller, and that's when I froze. It was Ash. We hadn't spoken in forever. I wondered why she was calling so early on a Monday morning. Good news? Bad news? I sat on my sofa, tried to compose myself, and then I answered.

'Ash?' I said as brightly as I could, but she didn't reply and instead all I heard was noise. Was she walking somewhere? Was that traffic? 'Hello? Ash?' I said, a little louder, but still nothing but background noise, and then it occurred to me that she must have dialled my number by mistake. My heart sank in my chest because, for a moment, the smallest of seconds, I thought she wanted to speak to me. I longed to hear her voice again. I was about to hang up when I heard something new.

'Oh shit, sorry, I don't know what happened,' said Ash suddenly.

'Ash. Hi, hello, you okay?'

'Yes, sorry. I must have butt-dialled you by mistake. I'm just on my way into the office.'

It was wonderful hearing her voice again. It sounded different somehow, but also the same voice I knew and loved.

'I was just on my way out, too. Heading to school.'

'Oh, right. Finally a teacher?'

'Yes. Secondary history at a school in Clapham.'

'That's great, Charlie. I'm happy for you.'

'Thank you.'

There was a pause. It felt strange that Ash and I were connected again. That the universe had somehow put us together once more. The silence stretched and I knew I had to fill it.

'How are you?' I said.

'You don't have to do this.'

'I'm just interested in how you are, that's all,' I said, and it was the truth. I always wanted to know how she was, even when she wasn't my business. 'Scout's honour.'

'I'm fine, and you weren't in the scouts,' she said, and we both laughed, and it released some of the tension, but I could tell from her voice that something had happened. I didn't know what it was, something professional or personal, but she was holding something back from me. I knew her voice, every octave, note and beat of it.

'I'm glad you're fine. It's good to hear your voice again.'

She paused, probably not sure what to say. It was awkward.

'I'm about to get on the train, Charlie.'

'Oh, right, okay.'

'Sorry for the butt-dial.'

'No, it's fine, really.'

'Better go then.'

'Okay then.'

'Bye.'

'Bye.'

Then she hung up, and I sat on my sofa in the small open-plan living room/kitchen of my flat, and I took a moment to compose myself. She still had such an effect on me. I felt it deeply and quickly ingrained in every part of my body like a tattoo. I stood up, ready to leave and head off to school. I had a new job, a new life, but Ash was still calling for me. The girl I first saw in sixth form, standing in the refectory, still did something profound to me and perhaps always would.

No. 82

Ash

I really had no idea

I reached my desk, sat down on my swivel chair, and switched my computer on. I couldn't believe I had butt-dialled Charlie on my way into work. How awkward was that? Fuck, even thinking about it again, I felt myself blushing. It was strange, undeniably awkward because I hadn't meant to call him, but once we had settled, it felt nice, comforting to hear his voice again. It still did something to me, affected me in ways I didn't fully understand.

I took a sip of my coffee and sat back in my chair, mentally preparing myself for the day ahead. I started my day as I usually did, going through my emails, catching up on the latest news in the publishing world, but I was quickly called into a meeting with Henrietta, the head of fiction. I was in the meeting with Sasha Cohen, editorial assistant to Henrietta, Guy Branson, international rights director, and Sharon Morgan, digital communications director. This was obviously serious, and the air in the office was thick with tension.

'Please come in, take a seat,' said Henrietta quickly.

We all sat down. I took a sip of my coffee in preparation for whatever the news was.

'This morning, I spoke with Tim Pearson, and he resigned with immediate effect,' said Henrietta, and I was in shock. Tim and I had just broken up, but he hadn't mentioned anything about resigning. I didn't know what to say. We might have ended our romantic relationship, but we were still a bloody good team at work. Henrietta immediately looked across at me. 'You and Tim are together, Ash. Did he say anything to you?'

'No, I really had no idea. He never said anything about leaving.'

'This will affect you the most as you worked so closely together,' said Henrietta sharply. 'Did anyone else have an inkling?'

Everyone shook their heads and mumbled that it was news to them. It seemed Tim had taken us all by surprise and blindsided even me. He had spoken about starting his own digital-first publishing house, but I didn't think he was ready to go. Perhaps he wasn't but breaking up with me had given him a push. Henrietta told us we were going to have to pick up the slack until we could replace him. Eventually, everyone left the room, wandering off to their own corners of the office, but Henrietta asked me to stay behind for a quick chat.

'You really had no idea?' she said to me, perched on the corner of her table in a neat grey suit, a baby-blue blouse beneath, and a takeaway coffee in her hand. 'He never said anything about moving on?'

'He had spoken about starting his own publishing house one day, but it always felt like something in the distant future. I definitely didn't think it would be this soon, if that's what he's done.'

'Right, well, sorry, but you'll have to pick up most of the slack, I'm afraid, Ash.'

'Of course, and just so you know, Tim and I are no longer dating.'

'Oh, right. Okay. Sorry—'

'No, it's fine. I just wanted you to know.'

'Well, expect lots of messages today. His email and phone have already been disabled, and I have pointed everything towards you.' I smiled at Henrietta because she had always been kind to me. 'Thank you, and Ash, if you need anything…'

'I know where you are,' I replied, and she smiled back at me, gave me a quick tap on the shoulder, and left the room in a hurry, probably to another emergency meeting about my ex-boyfriend and his disappearing act.

Tim had left us all in the lurch, and I wanted to ring him and find out what the hell was going on, but I knew I couldn't. I had to let it go and move on. He had made his decision, and like with Charlie, he had left me to pick up the pieces. Two of the most important men in my life had desperately disappointed me, and I was beginning to wonder if, perhaps, it was something to do with me. Did I only attract men destined to one day disappoint me?

No. 83

Charlie

Time to move on

I had taken the train to Southampton for the weekend, the same trip I had done so many times over the years. When I was with Ash, she would drive us in her Mini Cooper, but now I was single, I had turned once again to the train. I actually enjoyed the train because it gave me time to think, and today my mind drifted towards Ash. Whenever I returned to Southampton, it was impossible not to think about her because it was where my love for her had started. Since the butt-dial, she had been on my mind, but I also couldn't stop thinking about the fact she was still with Tim. Apart from my date with Vanessa, which hadn't exactly been a resounding success, my chances of any sort of romance felt unlikely – especially when I was still madly in love with my ex-wife.

'Mum, I'm home,' I said, dumping my bag at the foot of the stairs and walking into her hallway. The house was quiet, which was unusual because she knew I was coming, and so I expected her to be on guard with a cup of tea at the ready. 'Mum?' I walked past an empty front room, and then into the kitchen but she wasn't there either. 'Mum?' I said, a bit louder, but then I looked outside into the garden, and saw her, sitting in a deckchair and enjoying the sunshine. It had been raining for most of the week, but today there had been a break and a few beams of sunshine were cracking through the clouds. I walked outside and joined her.

'Hi, Mum,' I said. There was a small wooden table next to her with a tall glass of water on it, and she was reading a book and wearing a large floppy hat.

'Charlie,' said Mum, looking up at me. 'How are you?'

I leant down and gave her a kiss on the cheek.

'I'm good, Mum,' I said, grabbing a deckchair from the shed and sitting down next to her. She marked the page in the book she was reading, placed it on her lap, and then we had a quick catch-up. She asked me how I was, and I told her I was enjoying teaching, my flat was perfect, and I hadn't been so happy in a long time. It was also half-term, which was another fantastic addition to my life. I had been used to working all year with just a few weeks off for holidays and bank holidays, but suddenly having a week off every six weeks, two weeks every twelve, plus summer holidays, had given me so much free time.

'And what about Ash? Have you spoken to her at all?' asked Mum.

'Not really. She butt-dialled me a little while ago, but that was it.'

'Butt-dialled?'

'You know, when you accidentally dial someone's number by mistake.'

'And that's called butt-dialling, is it?'

'Yes, Mum. And what's happening with you?' I said, changing the subject.

'Actually, Charlie, I have a bit of news.'

'Oh yes, I'm interested. Go on.'

Mum looked at me with an expression of excitement, trepidation and something else I couldn't quite put my finger on, but whatever the news was, it was important. I sat back in my chair, feeling the warm sun on my face.

'A while ago I joined face books. I wasn't bothered, but Gail from next door said it was good for keeping in touch. Anyway, I was on face books, and I got a friend request from Alan—'

'Who's Alan?'

'Alan McIntosh. He was my first and only boyfriend at school before your father.'

'It sounds like Alan online-stalked you.'

'Don't be silly, he was head boy. Anyway, Alan and I got to talking on face books, and then we spoke on the phone.'

'Are you trying to tell me that you and Alan are dating, Mum?'

'This is the thing. Alan emigrated to Australia twenty-five years ago, but he got divorced from his wife. She moved back to England, Hull, I think, and Alan is still in Australia.'

'Mum. What exactly are you saying?'

'Alan invited me over to stay with him in Australia. He's doing well for himself. He's got a beautiful house in Sydney. You can see the harbour bridge from his kitchen window, and he's a surfer, Charlie! He's going to pay for the airfare and everything.'

'You're going to Australia to visit your ex-boyfriend from school – Alan?'

'That's right,' said Mum with a smile.

I didn't know what to say. This was the woman who had been crushed when Dad died, but that was six years ago now and she had every right to move on and be happy. She deserved a slice of good luck after what had happened with Dad, and maybe Alan from Sydney was just that. It worried me, though, because I didn't know Alan, and Australia was so far away. What if it all went wrong, and she had to come home quickly? What if she needed me? What if Alan was a weirdo or a con artist? I couldn't exactly jump on a plane and get to her within a few hours. All my anxieties rushed through my head, but also the thought that, after all this time, and despite being heartbroken, she was bravely picking up the pieces of her life and moving on.

'I'm really happy for you, Mum,' I said, and she smiled at me.

We sat in our chairs, enjoying the sunshine on our faces, and I couldn't help but think about how brave Mum was. She clearly had no idea how to pronounce Facebook, but she was prepared to travel across the world for a shot at love, and given my situation and difficulties in that department, I wished I had her courage. I was going out with Sam later, a chance to relive our glory years in Southampton, and perhaps it was time I started the process of moving on from Ash. I couldn't keep living in the past when it was clear she had moved on, and if Mum could pick herself up after losing Dad, then surely it was time I did the same.

No. 84

Ash

You need to think more positively, darlings

'You're what?' I said incredulously.

'Getting married again,' said Dad with an almost too calm voice that was actually a little unsettling, while standing proudly next to Mum.

Daniel was home from Edinburgh for the weekend with his now fiancée, Gemma. I adored her wonderful Scottish brogue and could listen to her all day. Daniel was an engineer now, and they lived in a gorgeous period flat in the centre of Edinburgh. I had been meaning to get up and visit them, but I had been so busy with work.

'Next summer, in Italy,' said Mum. 'It's always been a dream of mine. A warm Mediterranean wedding with lots of local food in a vineyard!'

'We just want to reaffirm our vows and commitment to each other,' chipped in Dad.

'Well, congratulations, I suppose,' I said, leaning in and giving my parents a kiss each. Daniel and Gemma did the same, and then Dad went off to get a bottle of champagne to celebrate. I couldn't believe my parents, who had spent most of my life seemingly locked in a constant battle, were renewing their wedding vows. When Dad rang me during the week and asked me to come home because they had news, I hadn't expected this.

'I can't believe it,' said Daniel when we were sitting down, glasses of champagne in hand. 'On the way down, I already told Gemma it was probably going to be something bad.'

'I imagined something bad, too,' I replied.

'Charming!' said Mum. 'You need to think more positively, darlings.'

Dad walked across with a flute of champagne and sat on the corner of Mum's chair and put his arm around her. I had to admit, they did look genuinely happy and in love. Two words I never normally associated with my parents.

'We're happier now than we've ever been,' said Dad.

'Definitely better in the bedroom!' said Mum, and Daniel put two fingers in his mouth as though he was going to vomit, and I couldn't help but laugh.

'How's life in Edinburgh?' I said a short while later. Mum and Dad were in the kitchen sorting out sandwiches, and I was in the living room with Daniel and Gemma.

'Life is great,' said Daniel. He was so tall now, and lean. He obviously took care of himself, and Gemma looked in good shape, too. I knew that apart from being a solicitor, she was also obsessively into fitness. She had a YouTube channel with thousands of followers. 'Work's going well, and this one keeps me on my toes.'

'Someone has to,' said Gemma. 'You know, when I met your wee brother, he had never been inside a gym. He didn't even know what a squat jump was or a burpee! Now I have him training with me, and he's even signed up for his first half-marathon.'

'Impressive,' I replied, not being much of a fitness person myself. I had tried going to the gym once, but after a couple of sessions with a personal trainer, and not being able to move for days afterwards, I promised myself never again. Now I stuck to a bit of yoga, and I walked everywhere.

'So, when are you going to pop up and visit us?' said Daniel. 'We have the spare room.'

'Soon. Definitely this year. I've just been so busy with work, and—'

'These London people, always so busy,' said Daniel. 'You know I'm an engineer, right? And Gemma is a solicitor with a thriving YouTube channel. We're all busy, Ash.'

'Yes, I am aware you're a super-important engineer, little brother.'

'I'm just saying. There's more to life than work,' said Daniel, and I knew he was right. It was just a question of finding out what the 'more' was.

I had a relaxed dinner with my family before I got ready for my big night out. I was heading into town with my childhood best friend, Lilly. She still lived nearby, and was married with two children, and had a career working for an insurance company. I hadn't seen her in a while, and so it was the perfect chance for us to catch up and relive our teenage years. Just the thought of it made me slightly giddy with excitement, but the nearer it got to leaving, I had to ask myself: was it possible to relive your teenage years in your thirties? Would Scott Laird still be there? Would we dance until two o'clock in the morning, or more likely be in bed before midnight feeling rather middle-aged and past it? But then again, if my parents could get married again, surely there was hope for me yet.

No. 85

Charlie

Just like the good old days

It was one of those moments that felt surreal and took me back to a specific moment in time. I was seventeen years old, and out in town for one of the first times I could remember. I saw Scott Laird's band play, and I saw Ash that night, too. I was back in that same pub with Sam, and it felt like the nineties all over again. Unfortunately, Gavin couldn't make it down from Guildford, where he currently lived with his partner, Alice.

'This is a bit weird, isn't it?' I said to Sam as we stood outside in the pub garden, watching all the students drinking their pints, smoking their hand-rolled cigarettes, and behaving just like us twenty years ago.

'Just a bit. I remember when you threw up in that corner of the pub garden.' Sam pointed towards the far corner of the garden and laughed.

'That wasn't me, mate.' I had a pretty awful memory, but I knew I hadn't thrown up in that particular pub garden.

'You sure? Because I vividly remember someone throwing up in that corner.'

'Yes,' I said, as the entire night came back to me in a flash. 'It was you, you idiot. It was the night you kissed that girl who looked vaguely like Cat Deeley.'

'You mean the girl who looked exactly like Cat Deeley?'

'You got a bit carried away, claimed you could down an entire pint to impress said girl, who looked a bit like Cat Deeley, and then you threw up in that corner.'

'Oh, yeah,' said Sam, laughing. 'We were such idiots back then, weren't we?'

'We were. Another pint?' I said, showing him my empty glass.

'Please.'

I walked back inside the pub, past a room where a student band were playing the Suede song 'Beautiful Ones' to a small crowd of people, and then up a short flight of stairs. The pub was busy, and I made my way towards the bar, using my elbows to squeeze myself between a couple of people. It didn't feel exactly like it had twenty years before, and obviously I was one of the older people in that pub, but I felt a flash of nostalgia. If only I could feel that level of freedom, of youthful excitement, once again because that was what we were searching for, wasn't it? It wasn't just going back to the same places, repeating the same nights out, but actually trying to recapture an essence of how we felt.

'Oh my God! I don't believe it,' said a voice suddenly, and that was when I turned my head and saw her standing there, just like that night from all those years ago. Talk about déjà vu.

'Ash! What are you doing here?'

'I'm back for the weekend, and out with Lilly.'

'That's incredible. I'm back for the weekend and out with Sam.'

We looked at each other, and then just laughed. I mean, what were the chances?

We got our drinks and found a quiet spot in the corner of the pub. So many times over the years, from Lanzarote to London, I had found myself unexpectedly with Ash. She always seemed to appear when I needed her the most. I wasn't a spiritual man, didn't believe in star signs, reading tea leaves, and yet there was something that kept bringing us together. It was becoming harder to ignore and put down to pure coincidence.

'What brought you to this old student dump?' I said once we were settled.

'Nostalgia, mainly. We thought it would be fun to relive our teenage years one more time.'

'I imagine Scott Laird must be on his way then,' I said, and she laughed.

'Oh God, I hope not!' she said with the smile that always made my heart skip a beat. She was still the most beautiful girl in that room. She was the most beautiful girl in every room.

'How are you? How's things with Tim?' I said, trying to force out the word 'Tim' without the jealousy appearing on my face. I was a new man, a more mature me. I wanted her to be happy, even if it meant with him.

'We broke up, actually.'

'Oh, wow, sorry, I—'

'It's okay, you don't need to pretend to be sad about it.'

'Good, because I'm really not,' I said with a laugh that was perhaps verging on being a little too smug, before I added: 'I just didn't think he was good enough for you, that's all.'

'And who would be, Charlie?'

'Now that I come to think of it, absolutely no one.'

Ash looked at me and smiled, but I couldn't read her expression. After a moment, she said we should probably find our friends and give them their drinks, but it was clear we were going to spend the rest of the night together. Me, Sam, Ash and Lilly, just like it was 1999 all over again.

No. 86

Ash

Reliving another teenage moment

'I think I'm a little drunk,' I said to Charlie as we stood in the middle of town, waving our friends off in their shared Uber. It was just past midnight, and we hadn't quite managed to relive our teenage years because the idea of going to a nightclub seemed absolutely awful, and we were all tipsy and ready to go home. The desire in our minds to be teenagers again wasn't, unfortunately, matched by our bodies.

'I think you are. Let me get you home.'

'I'm fine,' I said, and then, despite standing still, I almost stumbled over.

'Okay, you are definitely not fine. I'll order an Uber back to yours.'

'Back to mine, eh? Saucy!' I said, and despite my drunken state, even I realised what I was saying and the ramifications of it.

The thing was, spending the evening with Charlie had been lovely. He was like the old Charlie again. The Charlie from Lanzarote, and the Charlie I had started dating in London. He was funny, charming, and there was a lightness about him and a confidence that he had somehow lost over the years we were together. I forgot at that moment about all the bad things, the fact he had cheated on me, and I enjoyed his company again. He made me feel good about myself, and no one had ever looked

319

at me the way he did. We knew how to be together, and there was something truly comforting in that. I could be myself with Charlie in a way I had never been able to be with anyone else.

'Let's get you home safe and sound,' said Charlie, and I felt myself blushing slightly, but then he added, 'then we'll take care of the sauce.' And, despite myself, I couldn't stop laughing.

We jumped into the back of an Uber and headed to my parents' house, sitting so close our legs were touching, and gradually during the fifteen-minute journey, we got closer and closer until we were staring longingly into each other's eyes. I couldn't believe it, but I wanted to kiss him. I would never have imagined I would feel that desperate longing for him once again. I had hated him so much for cheating with that girl and blowing up our life in the process, but that was a long time ago and so much had happened since. The feeling was overwhelming, and it rose up inside of me and I could tell he felt the same.

We arrived at my parents' house, got out, and stood outside for a moment, holding hands without even thinking, under a full moon that lit up our faces. It was crazy, and maybe it was just being back in Southampton, Mum and Dad getting married again, bumping into him so randomly, being a little drunk, or that it was Charlie, but I knew I wanted to spend the night with him. It wasn't even a decision, it just was. I leaned forward and kissed him, our lips coming together, and there was something magical in that moment that transported me back to all the wonderful kisses we had shared over the years. It truly felt like coming home.

'So, are you coming in?' I said when we pulled away, scouring my handbag for the front door key, and he looked at me like he couldn't quite believe it. It was the same look he had on his face when I turned up in Lanzarote and saw him at the pool. The same look when I had surprised him at his student house in north London. Like he couldn't believe he was that lucky, which I had always thought was ironic because it was exactly how I felt about him, too.

'As long as you're sure. I know we're both a little drunk, and—'

'I'm sure,' I said, leaning forward and kissing him again. 'Just be quiet because my parents are here, and my brother and his fiancée.'

'Daniel is engaged?'

'He is. Right, I'll go in first and make sure the coast is clear.'

I crept into my old house to make sure it was quiet, and we had no chance of being caught before I snuck Charlie into my old bedroom. It felt a little dangerous, a touch risky, and I didn't know how I or he would feel in the morning, but I knew I wanted to do it. Charlie and me, in my old bedroom, felt like an opportunity I couldn't turn down. We'd had so many moments in the course of our relationship, and this felt like another pivotal one.

No. 87

Charlie

You need to leave out of the window

I was on my side, facing the window. I heard the noise of traffic, birds singing and the gentle hum of a radio playing downstairs. I slowly opened my eyes as the soft light of a new day seeped through the thin curtains of Ash's bedroom, and then I heard feet on the landing, the creaking of an old floorboard, and I turned over and saw Ash next to me. She had her eyes open and was looking at me. I had thought I would never see her like that again.

'Morning,' I whispered.

'Morning,' she whispered back.

'Doubt she's awake yet,' I heard Ash's father outside her bedroom door. 'Didn't hear her come home last night.' Just hearing his voice sent a shiver of fear down my spine. If he knew I was in bed with his daughter, had sex with her last night, he would go ballistic. He had never been my biggest cheerleader, and once he had found out I had cheated on her, he was the first to put the boot in, and demand I 'fuck off and leave my daughter alone for good'. I reached a hand across and placed it on the top of her leg.

'That was quite a night,' I whispered.

'My head is going to hurt later.'

'Mine, too.'

I took in her face for a moment. She had shorter hair these days, a fringe that had grown out, and she had gone back to her natural darker colour. Her green eyes were still dazzling, as they always had been, and her skin still glowed with a youthful freshness. She hadn't really changed much over the years, at least in my eyes. She always thought her mouth was a little too narrow, her ears a touch pointy, and she often complained her skin was too pale, and prone, especially after a few drinks, to get a little rosy. I loved all these things about her because they were what made her perfect to me. The little mark next to her eyebrow from a childhood accident. Her perfect imperfections.

'I never imagined we'd be like this again,' I said.

'I'm as surprised as you, but you know you need to leave out of the window.'

'What?' I said louder, and Ash put her finger to my lips. 'I have to go out the window?'

'Yes.'

'But I'll break my neck.'

'Scott Laird did it.'

'Fine,' I said, leaning across and giving her one last tantalising kiss.

I quietly got dressed and gathered my possessions before I looked out the window. Her bedroom was at the front of the house, and under her window there were quite extensive eaves, and then perhaps a ten-foot drop to the driveway. It was obviously not that big a deal, and Scott had done it, so there was no way I wasn't going to attempt it.

'We can talk back in London,' said Ash.

'If I don't die escaping out of your window,' I said, before I grabbed one last kiss, and then I made my way out of Ash's bedroom window.

The first part was easy enough, clambering out of the window and onto the eaves, and they seemed reasonably solid. I made my way to the front, looked back, and Ash was watching me, wrapped in a bed sheet. I gave her a tentative wave, she waved back, and then I got to the edge of the eaves and peered down. It looked far higher than ten feet, and this was when the fear gripped me, but I knew I had to do it. I found my landing zone, a patch of grass to the left of the house, a softer landing than the gravel driveway beneath me. I took one last look at Ash, and then it was time. I jumped. Luckily, I hit the grass, but unfortunately, I twisted my ankle on landing, and then, without warning, I heard the front door of the house open, and had to scramble, with a twisted ankle, behind a nearby bush.

Fortunately, it was just Ash's brother and his fiancée. They closed the front door and set off for a walk, and after a minute I left my hiding place and hobbled to the nearest bus stop.

I couldn't believe I had bumped into Ash again, and we had spent the night together. It was magical, every kiss, touch of her body, and waking up together again like we had so many mornings before. It felt like a dream, and I had to pinch myself to believe that it had happened. Going to Southampton for the weekend had been something of an exercise in reliving the past, and trying to get something back I had lost, but along the way, perhaps I had regained the most important thing of all.

No. 88

Ash

Waiting for a sign from the universe

I had no idea what it meant because it was too hard to comprehend, like the size of the universe or cryptocurrency. I had spent the most incredible night with Charlie culminating in some amazing sex, but could we get back together just because we still had a physical attraction? We had been apart for so long, and just because we'd had one great night together, it didn't mean we could slip back into each other's lives as if nothing had happened. I wished it was that easy, but it wasn't because despite how wonderful it felt, he had still cheated on me. The strands of trust that had been woven into us had been pulled apart, tenuously stretched until they were barely strands at all.

A part of me longed to say, *Fuck it, move back in and let's see what happens!* Because what if it was the best decision of my life? However, another part of me, the boring, practical bit that paid my mortgage on time each month and organised complex and multifaceted publishing events, said I needed to think about it from every possible angle. The pain of having my heart broken again would be too much to bear, and there was also the question of time and age that had been tugging at my thoughts. I couldn't afford another mistake. I would be forty soon, and if I ever wanted a family, time was against me. Charlie hadn't been ready to have children before, and perhaps didn't want them at all, while I still longed for a family of my own. It was an important factor I couldn't leave out of the equation.

We were in The Windmill pub in Clapham. I hadn't been to that pub before, but it was Charlie's new local. It was a lovely gastropub, full of young professionals like us de-stressing after work with drinks and Instagram-friendly food. We were sitting at a table, my glass of Chardonnay and his pint of IPA in front of us. I looked across at Charlie, fresh from school in a crisp white shirt and a striped navy and silver tie, his red hair a little longer.

'I never stopped loving you, and I know I messed up, Ash. I made a terrible mistake, the worst, but surely the other night meant something.'

'Of course it did.'

'Then where does it leave us? I would love to take you out on a date sometime.'

I looked at him and laughed, tossing my head back as if he'd just told the greatest joke in the world. The idea of going on a date with Charlie felt ridiculous.

'You want to take me out on a date? I'm thirty-seven years old and damaged goods.'

'And yet still somehow the most beautiful woman in London.'

'Now you're just saying nice things to get back into my good books,' I said, taking a sip of my wine, and Charlie took a sip of his pint, too. There was still a distance between us, but we were more like the old us again, laughing, joking, and the attraction was definitely still there, bubbling away beneath the surface like an active volcano.

'I just want another chance to make you happy, Ash. To make up for what I did. I've changed so much. I don't even feel like the same person I was before. Maybe going through all of that with you and becoming a teacher was essential, but I feel like I can finally be the man you always wanted me to be. We've already lost so much time. I don't want to lose another day without you.'

He looked at me, and I could see the desire in his eyes, and I felt it as well. I could feel the power of his love for me, and

I wanted to feel it too, but something was holding me back. I knew this was a decision for the rest of my life, and I didn't want to rush it. It was clear we still had something, but the question I had to ask myself was whether what we had was enough. It would have been so easy to say yes, let's go on a date, pick up where we left off the other night, but I needed to know I was making the right decision. Time, age, and having children were still at the forefront of my mind.

'Charlie, the other night was incredible, but that doesn't erase all the things that happened between us. I'm not saying no, but I just need some time to get my head around this. My heart wants to say yes, but my head is telling me to pause, take a moment.'

'I understand,' said Charlie, but I could see the disappointment on his face.

'And also, I need to know how you feel about starting a family. It was something that came between us before, and I have to know it won't again. I still want children, Charlie.'

I looked at him, and I wasn't entirely sure what to expect as it wasn't something we had discussed in a long time, but when I finished speaking, he looked at me and smiled perhaps one of the loveliest smiles he had ever given me.

'I'm ready, Ash, and no offence, but we're not getting any younger, are we?' replied Charlie, and I could have leaned across the table and kissed him, but I held myself back and just smiled instead.

'So, you want children now? You're sure?'

'I am. Definitely one. Perhaps two. Although I think three might be pushing it.'

Knowing how he felt about children changed things in my mind. It wasn't the only factor, but it felt like one of the major hurdles that had been a challenge for us was gone, and it meant so much to me. I reached a hand across the table and placed it softly over his.

'That's good to hear, Charlie. I'm so glad, but I still need time to process everything, and it might sound silly, but I feel like I need a sign from the universe or something telling me that we should be together again. I'm sorry.'

'Don't be sorry,' said Charlie, smiling at me, but looking slightly crestfallen. 'I understand.'

'Thanks,' I said, and we sat for a moment, and took sips of our drinks. 'So, a teacher now? Do you love it as much as you always thought you might?'

'I do. I wish I had started earlier.'

'I mean, I don't want to be that woman, but I did tell you.'

'And you were right. Teaching history is definitely my thing.'

Charlie and I sat together and chatted, finishing our drinks before we stood up and got ready to head home. It had been good to talk and feel that connection again. When we broke up, it had all felt so sudden. One moment we were together, married, our lives so interwoven it felt impossible they could ever be torn apart, and then the next we were separated. The pain and the emotion of that time meant we couldn't really speak calmly about what had happened, and so this was the first time we had actually spoken about us. I knew he wanted to try again, and when we said goodbye, it was with a genuine feeling of affection and optimism. We hugged and his body pressed against mine felt warm and like something I had missed. I didn't necessarily believe in such things, but I longed for a sign from the universe to make me believe that we could love each other again. That it was possible for us to be happy, despite everything.

No. 89

Charlie

The day it happened, 8:04 a.m.

Most mornings at school started in the same way. I would arrive at about seven forty-five and head straight to the school staff-room for my morning coffee. As it was my first job in education, I didn't know if all school staffrooms had such decent coffee, but ours did. The headmaster, a self-confessed caffeine-head, had invested in a top-of-the-range Nespresso machine. So, every morning, I would get to the staffroom, pick my favourite pod and make myself a coffee.

It was a Friday morning in late November, I had just sat down, coffee in hand, and the staffroom was coming to life as more teachers arrived, itching to get the last day of the week over with before the blessed relief of the weekend.

'All right, fella,' said Josh, PE teacher and one of the loveliest blokes I had ever met. From day one, he had welcomed me to the school, offered to go out for drinks, invited me to join his fantasy football league and made me feel like a part of the family.

'Good, mate,' I replied, taking a sip of my dark and complex Napoli roast coffee.

Josh sat down next to me with his morning protein shake. Josh didn't have coffee like the rest of us but would have smoothies with things like kale, spinach and protein powder. They looked awful, but then again, Josh didn't. He had thighs like tree trunks, and upper body muscles I could only dream

329

about, although if it meant no coffee and an early morning green protein shake, then I was happy as I was. Josh was from Sevenoaks in Kent, had gone to public schools and then Lough-borough University. He had limitless energy, and due to his upbringing, we had one of the best secondary comprehensive rugby teams in the country.

'Ready for the weekend, Charlie?'

'If that means leaving work, then spending the entire weekend doing nothing, then I am one hundred per cent ready.'

Josh laughed. 'Classic. Well, a few of us are heading into Soho tonight, if you fancy it?'

Drinks in Soho with my fellow teachers didn't sound that enticing, but what else was I going to do? Wait in and hope Ash rang, which she hadn't since our meeting in The Windmill two weeks ago. She had texted that she needed some time and space to think, and I had told her to take all the time she needed, because what else could I say? So, I waited at home, praying she would call and tell me she was ready for that date. It had literally been my life for the past fourteen days, and so perhaps it was time to try a different approach.

'Sure, why not?' I said. 'Who's going?'

'Me, obviously. George, English, good bloke, loves a beverage. Laura, Art. Amelia, French. She's got a thing for you, by the way.'

'No, she hasn't.'

'Mate,' said Josh, looking around in case Amelia was nearby, which she wasn't. 'She told me herself. Can't get enough of the old gingers. Big Prince Harry fan.'

'Stop it.'

'Anyway, she's coming, and Will.'

'Geography Will or Maths Will?'

'Geography Will.'

'Right, good. Okay, I'm in.'

'I'm heading in after school, if you fancy it. Probs get some food first.'

'Sounds good.'

'Legend,' said Josh, standing up and gently slapping my thigh before he walked off, drinking his green protein shake, and it seemed like I had weekend plans all of a sudden. I was excited because the waiting was killing me. I understood Ash needed time and that she was waiting for a sign from the universe, but still, my heart ached to see her again, and every day we weren't together was another day that felt wasted. I was so close to everything I wanted, and waiting for that phone call was tearing me apart. A drink with Josh in Soho was probably just what I needed to take my mind off Ash.

No. 90

Ash

The day it happened, 9:27 a.m.

The morning meeting was brief, and I was soon back at my desk with my new protégé and Tim's replacement, Kate. She was straight out of university, lovely, although very green, but she was diligent, hard-working and never minded staying late. She reminded me a lot of myself at that age, and it made me yearn once again for youth. How happy I had been to get my first job in publishing! Moving to London had felt like the beginning of the rest of my life, and I thought Kate felt the same. She had gone to university in Sheffield, graduated with a first in English literature, and after a brief stint interning over the summer, earned her first job as my assistant. Kate was self-assured in the way you can only be when you're young, before life has taken chunks out of you, and I envied that about her.

'I'm so happy it's Friday!' she said with her usual sheen of enthusiasm.

'Exciting plans?' I said, taking a sip of my strong, dark builder's tea. It was the only tea I drank, while Kate took a sip of her floral Earl Grey. She drank Earl Grey in the morning and decaffeinated green tea in the afternoon. A classic post-Millennial.

'I'm off into town tonight for drinks. Oh, you should come! My friends would absolutely love you.'

'That's okay,' I said, even though I had no plans myself. My weekend consisted of shopping, cleaning and thinking about Charlie, and not necessarily in that order.

'Do you have plans?'

'No, not really, I just think—'

'Then you must come, I insist!' said Kate, clapping her hands in excitement, and I felt like she wouldn't let it go, and so I agreed to go for a quick drink. I would be in and out within an hour or two, and what harm would it do? Plus, I really could use the distraction. Thinking about Charlie and about us potentially getting back together had become something of a twenty-four-seven hobby. The thing was, until we met up by chance in Southampton, I hadn't considered us ever getting back together again. It wasn't even on my radar, but seeing my parents happy again had given me the thought, and then running into Charlie like that had nudged me closer. Now I was actually musing over the genuine possibility of giving it another go, but there was something else on my mind, too. Something perhaps even bigger than Charlie and me, but I couldn't think about that yet. It was too much on top of everything else, and so I had put it away for the time being, squashed down behind everything else.

Kate vanished for a meeting, which gave me time to reply to emails, and make a few phone calls, but then she returned while I was in the middle of reading an email about an upcoming book event in Bloomsbury, and she seemed excited.

'Are you okay?' I enquired.

'I messaged my friends about tonight, and they're literally so excited to meet you. I may have hyped you up a bit.'

'Oh God, Kate, what do you mean, hyped me up?'

'I just told them how bloody amazing you are,' said Kate with her winning smile. She had the sort of smile you would see on someone who had been named the most popular girl at school. Lots of straight, bright white teeth. 'It's going to be a fab night. Promise!'

'Right,' I said with the distinct feeling that popping out for one wasn't going to cut the mustard. Maybe I could stay for a few drinks, meet her friends and, who knew, perhaps it would help take my mind off Charlie and the other thing. I needed a distraction, and if Kate could put something down on her CV under 'special skills', it would be the ability to make people feel good about themselves and distract them from making tough decisions. She was a ball of bubbly, excitable energy, radiating happiness and positivity wherever she went. If you couldn't have a good time with Kate, I would imagine you were already a lost cause.

No. 91

Charlie

The day it happened, 1:12 p.m.

I had the same lunch of a cheese and ham sandwich with mayonnaise and cucumber, a packet of crisps and a chocolate bar of some variety almost daily. I had another cup of coffee, and I was sitting in the staffroom eating my lunch when Amelia came and sat next to me. Amelia taught French, and if I believed Josh, had a thing for me. She was actually quite attractive, with long brunette hair, dark eyes and a petite figure. She was mid-thirties, as far as I knew single, and the teacher all the teenage boys lusted after – especially if you read some of the graffiti in the boys' toilets.

'*Bonjour*,' I said when Amelia sat down.

She looked across at me and smiled. '*Bonjour*, Charlie, *comment allez vous?*' she replied in a flawless French accent.

I, of course, had no idea what she had said, and so I replied with the only other French word I knew except au revoir.

'*Oui?*'

'I asked how you were.'

'To which the correct response should have been?'

'Something like, *je vais bien, merci*.'

'Which means?'

'I'm good, thank you.'

'Then *je vais bien, merci*,' I replied, and she laughed.

'I wouldn't give up the day job, Charlie.'

335

Amelia took out a Tupperware container full of salad. There were a variety of salad leaves in varying shades of green, sliced cucumbers, cherry tomatoes, olives, hard-boiled egg and a creamy dressing. It looked a far healthier lunch than mine. She also had a reusable water bottle, which she carried everywhere. I admired her dedication to her health and the environment because I wasn't that organised or dedicated enough to my health or the environment to eat better or carry a reusable water bottle.

'I heard on the grapevine you're coming out tonight,' said Amelia, looking across at me.

'Umm, yes. Josh invited me somewhere in Soho. Are you coming?'

'I am,' said Amelia, with a tantalisingly coquettish grin. 'I'm looking forward to it. It's always good to let your hair down after hours.'

She looked at me and I definitely felt some friction in the air between us, and the way she said, 'after hours' certainly had a flirtatious ring to it. Perhaps Josh was right, and Amelia had a crush on me. I felt my cheeks redden slightly, and I didn't know what else to say because nothing could ever happen with Amelia. Since that night with Ash, all I could think about was her. Ash was my everything, and despite Amelia's attractiveness, she wasn't Ash. Luckily, before Amelia had the chance to say anything else, I got a text from my mum.

> Any word on you and Ash? All good here. Park run tomorrow. Gail from next door said hello. LOL. Your mum x

I loved a text from Mum because they always read like a shopping list of her thoughts, and I never corrected her use of LOL or that she always signed off with *Your mum x*, as if I didn't know whom the text was from. She usually texted about three or four times a week, just to keep me on top of the latest headlines. Her last text, two days ago, read:

> Going to Winchester to see the cathedral tomorrow. Thinking about visiting London. British museum? Could do a park run on Clapham Common? Hope it's sunny. LOL. Your mum x

When I had hobbled into her house after my night with Ash, she had asked where I had spent the night, and so I explained everything. Mum adored Ash and couldn't wait to find out what was happening between us. I replied to her text while Amelia tucked into her salad.

> Nothing yet Mum. Say hi to Gail. Speak soon. Love you x

I put my phone away and finished my lunch. Amelia and I were joined by a few other staff members, and then Josh, who had come blustering in, eating a protein bar while stretching next to the table, and then said he needed to do his lunchtime run, and left quickly. I finished my lunch and was packing it away when my phone buzzed with a message from Mum. It simply said:

> LOL. Your mum x

No. 92

Ash

The day it happened, 2:18 p.m.

I was walking towards Pret for lunch when I saw him. I hadn't seen Tim since we had broken up, and it took me by surprise. He was in a light grey suit, his incredible body stretching it out so you could almost see the muscles beneath, his hair was slicked back, and he was walking with a girl, who couldn't have been more than twenty-five. They were strolling together, she was smiling, and looking up at him in awe, it seemed, and he was talking animatedly about something. She was a stunning blonde, tall and slim in a tailored suit, and it was clear that, apart from me, he had a type. I stopped and watched them for a moment. They were across the road from me waiting to cross in the opposite direction, and luckily, he hadn't spotted me. The blonde laughed and then he leaned in and kissed her. They were obviously together, and a good match. She was exactly the sort of girl Tim needed. I just hoped she didn't want any children of her own.

There had been rumours flying around at work that Tim was almost ready to get his publishing business off the ground. I didn't know what to believe, but I knew Tim, and it wouldn't surprise me if he made an enormous success of it. Perhaps our professional paths would cross once again. If he ran a publishing house, the circles we moved in wouldn't be that far removed from each other. It wasn't that things had ended badly between us; they had just ended, and I missed Liv tremendously, and I hoped she was happy and didn't think badly of me. I broke up with her father, not with her, but obviously without him our relationship failed to exist. She was the closest I had ever come to being a mother.

The lights changed, and Tim and the blonde walked across the road together, while I continued on towards Pret. I got the sliced egg and cress sandwich and a lime and raspberry seltzer. I sat by the window, watching the world go by while I ate my lunch, thinking about how strange it felt seeing Tim again. I knew he wasn't The One, but it was more that he was there when I needed him, and I would always be grateful for that. If he had wanted children, perhaps we would still be together, but I didn't think he was the love of my life because that had always been Charlie.

The problem I had was that I always thought of Charlie like that, but what if there was someone else out there better for me? It was easy to look back fondly on my relationship with Charlie with huge dollops of nostalgia, and for the most part it had been wonderful, but the last few years had been difficult. I was doing my best not to forget about that. There was a fragility about Charlie, and the way he acted after our separation had shown me just how irrational he could be when the chips were down, but he seemed like a more confident, well-rounded version of himself now. Time and teaching had clearly changed him, and he wanted a family. Perhaps he was ready to be the Charlie I had always hoped he would become.

I was sitting by the window, eating lunch, when a woman walked in, pushing a pushchair. She looked about my age, dressed casually in denim dungarees, white trainers and a yellow shirt. She wheeled the pushchair in, had a quick browse but obviously knew what she wanted, ordering a coffee and a chocolate brownie, before she sat near me. I looked across and saw a gorgeous baby girl asleep in the pushchair, and the mum caught me eyeing her and smiled at me.

'You have to take a break while they're asleep,' she said. 'She's beautiful.'

'You should see her when she's crying her heart out. Lungs like Adele!'

I laughed. 'But still, being a mother is the best job, I imagine.'

She looked at me for a moment, probably trying to decide if I had kids, or was pregnant perhaps, but I had added, 'I imagine', and so she knew and didn't want to pry.

'It is,' she said, looking down at her daughter, asleep in her pushchair. 'The very best.'

I finished my lunch before I headed back to the office with all sorts of things rattling around my brain: Charlie, babies, Tim and his new blonde girlfriend, and what my future held.

No. 93

Charlie

The day it happened, 7:02 p.m.

I walked into The Blue Posts pub with Josh, ready for a night out. After school, we grabbed dinner at Nando's, had a couple of drinks in Clapham, and then we made our way into Soho. We were meeting the rest of the teachers there, and then, according to Josh, the night was ours. He had big plans to go on to other pubs, and then, potentially, a nightclub. It could be a big night ahead, although, to be honest, I wasn't sure I was in it for the long haul.

'Drink?' said Josh.

'A pint of something,' I replied, scouting out a table in the pub that was already filling up with a mixture of after-work suits, trendy Soho types and tourists. I scanned the room, but it looked like, for the time being, we would be standing. Josh returned with two pints of beer, and we stood against a wall, waiting for the other members of staff. Thirty minutes later, the rest of our group arrived, and we found a table that was just about big enough for us all to sit down, if not so cramped our legs were touching under the table. I was, of course, next to Amelia. It was the first round of the night, and I volunteered.

I squeezed through the crowds at the bar and waited. I had forgotten just how busy Central London got, especially on a Friday night. Every pub within a mile radius would be just as busy as that one. The wooden bar was lined with people, all jammed together, jostling for space. A man next to me in a smart suit got served three drinks, turned and left, and then a woman quickly replaced him, but there was something about her that looked vaguely familiar. I didn't know her exactly, but I was sure I had seen her face before.

'Sorry, do you know me?' said the girl suddenly in a bright, posh voice.

'What, sorry?'

'You were staring at me, so I wondered if you knew me, or perhaps you're just one of those men who stare at girls in pubs?'

'I'm sorry. I thought I recognised you from somewhere but couldn't place you.'

'So, you aren't a creep?'

'No, definitely not a creep. I'm Charlie.'

'Oh my God, Charlie!' came a fresh voice, and one I definitely recognised. I turned and saw Ash standing just behind me.

'Ash,' I said, astonished and shocked to see her. 'I was just… Do you know this girl?'

'She's my assistant, Kate.'

'That makes sense. I must have seen you in a photo with Ash.'

'Oh, you're Charlie,' said Kate with a knowing smile. '*Charlie*, Charlie.'

'That's right. I'm *Charlie*, Charlie but you can just call me Charlie.'

'What can I get you?' a barman said suddenly, appearing in front of us.

I let Kate order first, and then I ordered my round, which I took back to our table, before I excused myself and found Ash. She and I stood against a wall in the packed pub, and I looked at her and smiled, still flabbergasted we had bumped into each other again.

'You said you wanted a sign from the universe that we should be together. I think this might be it,' I said, and Ash laughed.

'You don't think this is just a coincidence?'

'Let me think. First there was Lanzarote, where we first spent time together. Then we met by chance in London while at university, when we first slept together. Then we met on the Tube years later, and that's when we got together. We slept together three weekends ago, after randomly bumping into each other while trying to relive our teenage years in Southampton, and now tonight. Do you know how many pubs there are in Central London?'

'Do you?'

'Well, no, obviously not, but there are a lot and you or I could have gone for drinks in any of them, but we didn't. I think the universe definitely wants us to be together, Ash.'

I saw Amelia walk past me, and towards the toilet. She smiled at me but looked disappointed. Perhaps Josh had been right, and she really had a crush on me and maybe she had thought something was going to happen. I had forgotten about the table of teachers I was supposed to be spending the night with, and Ash had abandoned her group of friends, too. As so often in our lives, when we were together, nothing else seemed to matter. It was always about us, and surely meeting like this was just the sign she had been waiting for.

'Maybe,' said Ash with a smile, and then took a sip of her orange juice. 'But I'm not promising anything.'

'That's fine. I'm not asking for anything,' I said, and then we both smiled at each other.

We stood and talked about our days and what our plans had been for the night ahead. Ash said she hadn't planned on staying out for long, and I said the same. When I actually thought about it, it truly was incredible how many times we had bumped into each other over the years. Like I said before, I didn't believe in some higher power moving us around like chess pieces on a board, but could it all just be chance and coincidence? Were we at the mercy of powers out of our control, or was our relationship just as tenuous and full of random inadvertent moments of luck as the rest of our lives? I didn't know the answer, but I knew at that moment as I stood against the wall of The Blue Posts pub that I believed in us and that somehow, for whatever reason, we seemed destined to end up together.

No. 94

Ash

The day it happened, 8:28 p.m.

'This is Josh, our PE teacher,' said Charlie.

'Absolute pleasure,' said Josh, shaking my hand. 'I think we're about to head off, mate, but I assume you're staying put.'

'I am,' said Charlie, who was sitting down with my group. He hadn't returned to his own friends since we bumped into each other.

'Then I'll say good night,' said Josh.

'Have a good one,' said Charlie.

Josh smiled, then walked away towards the group of teachers that Charlie had come with while we were sitting with Kate and her university friends. There was Chelsea, Liam and Jessie. They were all very nice, and fortunately didn't seem disappointed in me. Kate knew about Charlie, and she grilled him about his life as a teacher, and Charlie spoke passionately about his job, and it made me so proud of him. It had definitely been one of the contributing factors in the breakdown of our marriage. I had always been so intent on my career in publishing, but Charlie had stuttered after university and wandered into jobs he didn't particularly like and that resentment of my success and his lack of it, despite his love for me, had slowly worn us down. I had always encouraged him to follow his dreams, but he hadn't pursued it until after we had separated, but now he was happy, and it showed.

'Another round?' said Kate when we had all finished our drinks.

I looked at Charlie, he looked at me, and we both knew what the other was thinking.

'Actually, I think we might head off,' I said, and Kate instantly understood what I meant because she just smiled back and, when Charlie wasn't looking, she gave me a cheeky wink. We said goodbye to everyone, then Charlie and I headed out of the pub without a plan or an idea of what we were going to do next. It wasn't that late, and it was a nice Friday evening, and all of London seemed to be alive with people out to have a good time.

'Remember that night when we just wandered around London?' said Charlie. 'It was right after we got engaged, we met after work, had dinner at that little restaurant just off Tottenham Court Road, and then we strolled around for hours talking about the future.'

'I do,' I said, looking at Charlie, and I could feel the love again. It had been gone for so long, but I felt it once more. 'Everything felt so exciting then, so fresh, and like we had all the time in the world.'

We walked along Regent Street, through Piccadilly Circus and then through Leicester Square. We stopped in Leicester Square, grabbed a coffee, and listened to an incredible singer performing old classics before we kept walking slowly towards Trafalgar Square. We reached the steps that led down into Trafalgar Square and sat down for a moment and took in the view.

'Kate seemed nice,' said Charlie.

'She's lovely. She reminds me so much of myself at that age, all excitement, ambition, so much to look forward to and keen to get it all done.'

'And you don't have that now?'

'I do, but it's different, isn't it? You can never get that feeling back. The feeling in your twenties when London is all new, it's the beginning of everything, no baggage, and the world is at your feet. There's a freedom you feel then that you'll never feel again once it's gone.'

'So, what now? We are sitting in Trafalgar Square, looking at Lord Horatio Nelson himself, and I'm offering you a fresh start. Yes, we have more baggage this time around, and London isn't as new and shiny as it once was, but it could still be everything you wanted back then. We could still have the perfect life together, Ash. What do you say?'

I looked at Charlie, and I wanted to cry because he was right. We could have everything, and perhaps that was the scary part. I wanted to sink into him, tell him that, yes, of course, I wanted to try again and have everything, but there was that one thing holding me back. The thing that had come between us the first time and destroyed our relationship, and the thing that was on my mind again. I was a week late for my period, weeks after we had slept together. There was a chance I could be pregnant, but I couldn't tell Charlie until I was absolutely sure. I had been too afraid to find out because then I would be afraid of losing it all over again. He wanted children, I was desperate to start a family, and perhaps it was finally going to happen for us, it was all so tantalisingly close, but we had lost a baby once before and that thought had gathered in my mind and set up camp.

'Will you walk me back to Waterloo?' I said, standing up.

'Of course,' said Charlie, slightly deflated. He had told me he wanted me and was desperate to try again, and I had asked for a walking companion back to the train station. I just couldn't commit to anything until I knew whether I was pregnant or not, because that would surely change everything.

No. 95

Charlie

The day it happened, 9:46 p.m.

We walked across the Golden Jubilee footbridge, taking in the views of the river and the London Eye, which was lit up and looked stunning. We were almost back to Waterloo station, and Ash would be getting her train back to Kingston upon Thames to the house I had once called home. I was in a confused state of mind because, on one hand, Ash and I being thrown together unexpectedly for the night felt like a helping hand from fate once again, and surely we were on the cusp of getting back together, yet when I had floated the idea in Trafalgar Square, she had asked me to walk her back to the train station.

We walked into Waterloo station, and Ash checked what time her train would be departing. I would need to get the Northern Line Tube to Clapham Common, and so I would wait with her until her train departed. We stood in front of the departure boards in the station, looking up the way we had done so many times before, trying to find the times for the next train to Kingston upon Thames. Countless days when we had met after work and travelled home together, that seemed so ordinary then, but were now all I craved.

There was a South Western train departing in ten minutes, which didn't give us long. I thought of the great battles I taught in history and how crucial they were. Moments in time. When I taught history to my pupils, I always emphasised just how different life might have been for us if history had gone a different way. If Lord Nelson had lost the Battle of Trafalgar, if the Duke of Wellington had lost the Battle of Waterloo, and if the Germans had won World War Two. These were just the big moments in history, but there were thousands of small moments that had defined our small island, too. Moments could make us and moments could break us, like so many cliches that were so often true, and it applied to more than just history.

We strolled towards the platform where her train was departing from. The train was already there, and people were boarding. Some slightly drunk people walked past us, tapping their phones against the yellow card readers, and then stumbling off towards the train, fast-food burgers in their hands. Late night city workers in suits, speaking quickly on phones to loved ones, returning home after another long week.

'I'd better go,' said Ash.

'Ash, wait,' I said, reaching out and holding her hand. 'I wanted to say before you go—'

'Charlie, I—'

'Ash, please. I just want to say that I love you. I have never stopped loving you.'

She looked at me, tears beginning to form in her eyes, and smiled.

'I know,' she replied, before releasing her hand from mine, and then she dashed away through the barrier, tapping her phone against the card reader. She hadn't said she loved me, too. She had fled. For a moment, I thought about following her on to the train. I had to fight for her. I needed her to know I would do anything to be with her again, but she already knew that. I had told her I loved her, and she had said she knew. What else could I do?

I turned around and walked away, back through the station, and then outside. The earlier evening sunshine had been replaced with heavy clouds, and suddenly it was raining. Big,

349

heavy spots of rain that smacked against the pavement. I could have taken the Tube back to Clapham right there and then, but I needed a drink first to wash away some of the sadness. I put my earbuds in, and pressed play on my phone. 'Run' by Leona Lewis was the first song that came on, and I walked out of the station, and into the rain.

No. 96

The day it happened, 10:06 p.m.

I stumbled, crying, into the toilet of the train, and quickly locked the door behind me. It was unbearable seeing Charlie like that and having to walk away, and I hated myself for doing it, but what choice did I have? He had told me he loved me and all I could do was say that I knew. How terrible was that? Of course I knew, and I loved him, too. He must have felt awful but seeing him like that clarified everything in my mind. I was going to do the pregnancy test now, on the train, in the loo. It wasn't the most glamorous place in the world, but I had to know because then I could think with a clear mind. As soon as I suspected I might be pregnant, I went out and bought a pregnancy test, which I had been carrying around with me all week; a constant reminder of the other thing I might already be carrying inside of me. I took it out, opened the box and got myself ready. The only question I had was whether I had time to find out the results before the train doors closed and I would be shuttled off home.

Time ticked away as I waited for the answer, holding the white plastic stick in my hand. I wanted to be pregnant more than anything and yet it also terrified the life out of me because I had lost one baby before and couldn't stand the thought of losing another. Maybe I finally had the chance to have everything I had dreamed about since I was a teenager. I felt

351

the need for it heavy in my heart, and my whole body seemed to tense up, one giant muscle, just waiting for that moment to relax.

I waited and then I turned the stick over because I couldn't bear to watch it while I waited. One last breath.

Pregnant.

The word in black and white in front of me. The tears came again, but this time they were tears of elation and of overwhelming joy. I was pregnant with Charlie's baby! I had to tell him. I had to get off that fucking train!

I quickly picked up my bag, threw the stick inside and opened the door to the train that had slowly been filling up while I was in the loo. It was due to depart in less than a minute. A couple of drunk men in suits were standing outside the toilet, and I quickly brushed past them and towards the door.

'Watch out, love,' one of them slurred, but I was focused on getting off the train. I heard the beeping noise it made as the doors were about to close and knew my time was almost up. I saw a door, dashed towards it and jumped, the door snapping shut behind me. I stood on the platform for a moment, took a breath and then started walking back into Waterloo station. I had to find Charlie. It wasn't until I reached the card reader and scanned my phone, that I realised Charlie was probably already on the Tube heading towards Clapham. I could jump on the next Tube, but first I needed to call Charlie and find out where he was.

I stood in the middle of Waterloo station, under the big clocks that hung from the rafters, surrounded by people, my head spinning, and I called Charlie's mobile. It rang and then, after a few rings, he picked up.

'Ash?'

'Where are you?'

'Outside Waterloo, heading to the pub. Is everything all right?'

'Yes, perfect. Just stay exactly where you are.'

I couldn't believe it. Charlie was outside. I took a moment to compose myself. This was it. I was going to tell him I loved him, too, and that I was pregnant with our baby. The rest of our life together was about to begin. A second chance to get it right. To make it perfect. I started walking, faster and faster, towards the exit, and Charlie.

No. 97

Charlie

The day it happened, 10:16 p.m.

'Outside Waterloo, heading to the pub. Is everything all right?'
I said, probably sounding concerned because I was.

'Yes, perfect. Just stay exactly where you are,' Ash said, and
then she hung up.

I was standing in the middle of the road because that's where
I was when she rang and told me to stay exactly where I was. I
didn't know what was happening, but she sounded different.
There was an edge to her voice. The rain suddenly started
coming down harder, and I knew I needed to get back towards
the train station, and so I turned around and started walking.
I could barely see because it was darker now, the rain was
hammering down all around me, and I pulled my coat up
over my head to protect myself. A car was suddenly coming
towards me, far too fast, and I had to quickly manoeuvre myself
away from them and onto the pavement. They flashed past me,
sending a shower of rain in my direction that covered my back,
but I didn't care because all I could think about was Ash.

I reached the entrance to the train station, just as Ash was
coming out. She obviously didn't mind that it was raining
because she walked quickly towards me, her face lit up with
excitement. I had no idea what had happened between her
leaving me before, dashing through the barriers and onto the
train, seemingly desperate to escape and now, but clearly something had.

'Charlie,' she said when she reached me. The rain was still coming down, and was that a flash of lightning and a crack of thunder I heard in the distance?

'Are you okay? What happened?'

She was standing in front of me, and then she reached down and held my hands and I noticed for the first time that she was crying.

'Charlie, when you told me before that you loved you, I wanted to say that I loved you too. Of course I love you, Charlie. It's you. It's me. But I couldn't because, well, there was something I had to do first.'

'What?' I asked, genuinely confused and bewildered.

'I had to do a pregnancy test,' said Ash, and in that moment, I felt my whole life changing. My stomach flipped, and my mind was suddenly awash with thoughts and feelings. I understood what she had said, the words were clear and concise, but it made no sense.

'You had to... what?'

'I'm pregnant, Charlie!'

Ash and I stood in the rain, our hair dripping wet, and then she leaned in and she kissed me, and I heard a low rumble of thunder. Our lips joined together in the rain outside Waterloo Station, and I felt her body in my arms, and I knew that this time I wasn't going to fuck it up. This time it was going to be different because I was different, and she was having our baby. After a minute, I had to pull away because I had so many questions.

'How, Ash? I don't understand.'

'Well, when a man and a woman really like each other—'

'That's not what I meant and you know it!' I said, and she laughed.

'It happened the night in Southampton, obviously.'

'I know we were drunk, but didn't we use a condom?'

'I thought so, too, but obviously the universe wanted us to have a baby. I think I finally have the sign I was waiting for,' said

Ash, and I couldn't believe it. I was going to be a father. I was getting back together with Ash. All of it felt impossible.

'I'm going to be a dad,' I said, feeling tears in my own eyes.

'You are, and Charlie, this is it, okay? You and me forever. No more messing about.'

'Definitely no more messing about,' I said, and I kissed her again before she pulled away and looked at me in the rain.

'You know we're getting absolutely drenched, don't you?' she said.

'I do, and honestly, I don't care.'

'Me either,' said Ash, and this was how *we* once again became *us*.

2020

No. 98

Ash

The whole of the moon

The intensity of the pain was like nothing I had ever felt before. It shot through me and took me by surprise every time it came. How could something so wonderful, so beautiful, something I had wanted so badly, be so fucking painful?

'Hold my hand,' I said, and I reached across for Charlie.

'Just try and breathe,' said Charlie from underneath his mask before he proceeded to demonstrate the breathing exercises we had learnt at our antenatal classes, and despite everything, despite how happy I was, how much I loved him, I couldn't believe he was telling me to fucking breathe! I shot him a look of pure and utter disbelief.

'Breathe? Oh, I'm sorry I didn't realise that breathing would relieve the intense fucking pain of childbirth! And don't, for a moment, say anything about how painful being kicked in the balls is or I might do something I'll regret.'

Charlie looked at me, and obviously didn't know what to say.

'Right, Ash, almost there,' said the midwife, and I squeezed Charlie's hand just that little bit harder as another contraction came, and I was told to push again. *Push! Push! Push!* I closed my eyes and thought about how much I had wanted this baby. I tried focusing on the music we had brought with us. I had made a playlist for the birth and, at that moment, The Waterboys were singing 'The Whole Of The Moon'. I pushed and pushed with Charlie encouraging me, and despite feeling so drained, I knew I had to keep going.

'It's coming. One more big push!' The whole of the moon. 'He's a beautiful baby boy!'

I finally heard the words from the midwife, but I was so tired, so emotional, and just drained until I had nothing left to give. I slumped into the bed that was drenched with my sweat, and Charlie was crying, and I was crying, and then they put my baby boy on my chest, and I held him against me for the first time. Charlie and I had a little boy, who cried so loudly, the most wonderful noise I had ever heard. I looked down at him, at his almost impossibly small face and into his eyes, and I saw Charlie staring back at me. He looked just like his father, even down to his red hair and almost translucent pale skin.

'He's perfect,' said Charlie, sitting down on the bed next to me.

'He really is,' I replied, looking at Charlie, and all the frustration and pain I had felt just moments ago was gone, and all I felt and knew was love. I looked down at our little boy, wrapped up in my arms.

'So, what are we going to call him?' said Charlie.

We had spent hours and hours going through baby names together, jotting them down on our phones, and having summits before bedtime until, days before I went into labour, we had narrowed it down to two names. We had agreed on Harry and Jack but couldn't decide which one and so we had agreed to meet him first. We both looked down at our son, and then I looked at Charlie.

'I think he's Harry,' I said, and Charlie smiled.

'I think you're right.'

'Harry Talbot.'

'What about a middle name?'

'You wanted something cool,' I replied, and I paused before I said, 'what about Lennon?'

'As in John?' said Charlie, and even though he was wearing a face mask, I could see he was grinning from ear to ear.

'Harry Lennon Talbot.'

'I think it's absolutely perfect.'

Then we sat there with our son, Harry, and it was one of those moments I knew I wouldn't ever forget. We were a perfect little family, and the vision I had in my head as a teenager had finally come to be. I had everything I had ever wanted, and now was the time to decide what was next. I had spent so much of my life striving for things, making plans, and yet when it came down to it, most of this had come from luck, chance, or perhaps the helping hand of fate. So, perhaps the next part of my life was going to be about holding on to what I had. There weren't any next steps for the time being, no five-year plan, just quiet moments together. Who knew what was next, and perhaps for the first time in my life, I was ready to trust the universe.

No. 99

Charlie

All I want for Christmas is you

It was our first Christmas as a family of three, and it was just me, Ash, and Harry for the big day. Mum was in Australia with Alan, and we'd already FaceTimed with her and Ash's family. Harry was six months old now, and becoming quite the little man. He had swiftly moved from breast milk to food, and now had squidgy rolls of baby fat on his arms and legs, his strawberry-blond – definitely not a full-fledged ginger, despite what Ash said! – hair was getting longer, and our once little baby boy was growing up fast.

Ash was putting Harry down for his afternoon nap, while I was busy making Christmas dinner. The house had been wonderfully decorated by Ash, who was still on maternity leave, and there were decorations in every room, and, of course, the tree in the living room. For the first time, and because we had Harry, we had bought a real tree, and Ash had ordered decorations online and the whole house had a wonderfully festive feel to it.

In the kitchen, I was listening to a Christmas playlist on Spotify through the new Google Home speakers, while peeling potatoes and putting them in a large pan of salted water. I was making a traditional Christmas Day roast, with lots of soft vegetables for Harry. 'Mistletoe and Wine' by Cliff Richard had just ended and 'All I Want For Christmas' by Mariah Carey had just started playing, as Ash walked into the kitchen.

'Right, he's down, how can I help?'

Ash had been incredible since Harry was born, and had taken to motherhood like a duck to water, and I felt incredibly lucky she was my son's mother. Ash still had another three months of maternity leave before she would head back to work, and Harry would need to go to nursery. Luckily, there was a fantastic one in nearby Teddington, which had come highly recommended, and we already had Harry's name down for it.

'Fancy finishing these spuds because I need to crack on with the other vegetables, and make the Yorkshire pudding batter.'

'No problemo,' said Ash, and I looked at her and she smiled. 'What?'

'No problemo?'

'I remember you said that to me once,' said Ash with a smile.

'You remember that?' I said, walking across to the fridge and taking out the milk.

'Of course. One never forgets the time they've asked a young man, who is ridiculously nervous and quite clearly fancies them, to rub sun cream on their back, and the young man says, no problemo,' said Ash, giggling.

'I was ridiculously nervous back then, You were Ash Oliver, the hottest girl in college, and I was just Charlie Talbot, token ginger.'

'Hardly token ginger. I almost definitely fancied you too.'

'Almost?'

'Definitely,' said Ash, running the knife through a potato, and then popping it in the pan. I opened a fresh box of eggs, getting ready to make the batter for the Yorkshire puddings. Ash and I worked together in a peaceful harmony, listening to Christmas songs, making food, in our little bubble with Harry asleep in his bedroom. We had a baby monitor on the side in the kitchen so we would hear him when he woke up.

'Ready for a glass of wine?' I asked. It was just past two o'clock, and it felt like it was time for a drink. The turkey would be done at three, just before the Queen's speech, and we would eat at about three forty-five, once the turkey had rested and everything else was done.

'Maybe a small one,' said Ash. 'Don't want to go too early.'

'No problemo,' I said with a smile, walking across to the side where I had a bottle of red wine ready to go. I filled up two glasses, and then passed one to Ash.

Ash had always been the planner in our relationship. I would never forget the conversation we'd had in my old student house, when she had first mentioned her five-year plan. Her whole life seemed to revolve around a constant cycle of plans and goals, while I hadn't always been like that. I had tended, on the whole, to drift and let life take me where it wanted. However, at that moment, I realised that although I hadn't had a specific vision for my life, this was exactly what I had always wanted, whether I knew it or not.

'Merry Christmas,' I said, tapping my glass against hers.

'Merry Christmas,' Ash replied, before I leaned in and kissed her, as a sudden noise from the baby monitor pulled us apart. Harry was crying.

'That wasn't a very long nap,' I said, putting my glass of wine down on the side.

'Probably too excited for Christmas.'

We walked upstairs together, and waited outside of his bedroom door for a moment to see if he would stop crying, but he didn't. He was clearly done with his nap. Ash slowly opened the door to his room, which was dark except for the light from the white noise machine that reflected against the wall. Ash walked across and turned the noise machine off, and I opened the curtains, and then we met at Harry's crib and looked down at him.

'There he is!' said Ash, and Harry stopped crying, and gave us both a huge grin.

Ash reached down, picked him up, and he looked at me in her arms. My beautiful boy.

'Someone did a very stinky poo, didn't they?' I said to Harry, kissing him on the head.

'That's a bad one. Your turn, I believe,' said Ash.

'Why is it my turn?'

'Because it's Christmas and you love me very much.'

I laughed. 'Fine. Come here, wee man.'

Ash passed Harry to me, and I took him across to the changing table that Ash's parents had bought for us. I laid him down, unbuttoning his sleepsuit, and he was smiling at me, like he knew just how bad it was.

'Sure you don't want to do it?' I asked Ash.

'All I want for Christmas is you,' she said, and when I looked at her she smiled at me.

'So not the world's smelliest nappy then?'

Ash laughed. Harry giggled. I reached down, pulled his sleepsuit up, and then undid his nappy, the smell suddenly becoming even more potent. Ash took the moment to leave and escape downstairs. When I opened the nappy, I was greeted with perhaps the largest and messiest poo I had ever seen, and it was one Christmas miracle I could definitely have done without.

2022

No. 100

Ash

Everything I could possibly want

The warm Tuscan sun shone down brightly from the vast cerulean sky, as we sat in the most incredible vineyard, just outside the town of Siena. It was a quintessential Italian winery with rolling hills that seemed to stretch on forever, vast fields of short, wide olive trees, and the tall thin Cypress trees that marked a road up to a large stone house where some of the wedding party, including us, were staying. I was sitting next to Charlie, who looked so handsome in a white suit. Harry sat on his lap, behaving incredibly well, in an adorable little hat to keep the sun off his face, and we were watching as my parents finally had their second wedding. After COVID, when they had been forced to cancel their dream Tuscan wedding, it was finally able to go ahead, and so about fifty people were sitting in an Italian vineyard, on a gorgeous summer's day, watching them reaffirm their love for each other.

'So, once again, for the second time in your life, do you Hugh Alexander James Oliver, take Sarah Beatrice Oliver, to still be your wife?' asked Daniel, who was officiating the wedding.

'I do, indeed, with every ounce of my soul,' said Dad, who looked wonderful in a linen suit, much thinner these days. Apparently, he had been on a bit of a heath-kick and doing the Joe Wicks, The Body Coach, daily workouts!

'And do you, Sarah Beatrice Oliver, take Hugh Alexander James Oliver, to still be your husband, even though he can sometimes be a bit of a grumpy old bugger?'

Everyone laughed, and Mum wept.

'I do, yes, absolutely!' said Mum, wiping the tears from her face.

'Then, I am absolutely delighted to once again, and for the rest of your lives, call you still husband and wife. Dad, you may now kiss Mum,' said Daniel, and when they kissed, everyone clapped and cheered.

Once the ceremony was over, everyone got up and made their way through to the outdoor eating area, which was covered and shaded, and there were all sorts of wonderful Italian delicacies on offer. Plates of delicious breads, olive oils, cheeses, meats and fruits. Unfortunately, some of it, I couldn't eat.

'How are you doing?' said Charlie, his hand instinctively going to my belly.

'Okay. A little tired.'

'Being seven months pregnant will do that to you,' said Charlie. Harry was standing next to him, looking a little tired himself. We had only flown over yesterday and it had been a late night by the time we had got to the vineyard. 'We're going to get some food. Maybe have a sit down, and I'll bring you a plate.'

'Deal,' I said, and I wandered across and found a table in the shade. It was wonderful being pregnant again – planned this time – and knowing it was a little girl. Soon Charlie and I would have two children, and life would change once again. The last two years with Harry had been incredible, and so much had changed. Charlie was head of year at school, I was an editor with a long list of successful authors, and we had transformed our house with the loft and kitchen extensions. Harry was constantly speaking now, but his first word had been, 'mummy', although when he first said it, it had sounded like 'yummy', and so, of course, Charlie constantly referred to me now as 'Yummy Mummy'.

I watched Charlie and Harry walk across towards the food, Harry's hand tucked neatly in Charlie's, and then they were intercepted by Charlie's mum, Claire, and her boyfriend Alan. They had made the trip from Australia, and were spending almost three months in Europe and England, including, hopefully, being there for the birth of our daughter. Claire picked up Harry, swung him around, and he giggled and it warmed my heart to see them together. I saw Daniel and Gemma getting food, and I was looking forward to their wedding in Scotland next summer. I had heard a rumour that she might already be pregnant but it wasn't yet confirmed, so I would check in with him later.

I watched Charlie as he got a plate of food for Harry and another for me. I liked to watch him when he didn't know I was watching him. Like me, he was turning forty soon, and he was more handsome than ever. He had grown into his body and now it was like he was always the age he was supposed to be. Some people peaked when they were young – I think Scott Laird probably fell into that category – and others not until they were much older. I watched Charlie, his red hair that was still so thick and his sparkling blue eyes that I had always loved. He was slim, and had a confidence about him now that he had once lacked. We had spoken about what had gone wrong between us in the past, and he had taken the blame for the break-up of our marriage. He had never felt good enough, successful enough, ready enough, but now he was. He was a wonderful father and an even better husband.

I watched Charlie as he walked towards me with two plates of food, and then he placed them down on the table and looked at me.

'What?' said Charlie.

'Nothing. Just admiring my husband.'

'Oh yeah,' said Charlie with a smile, and then he leaned down and kissed me before he whispered in my ear. 'You know, I've never had sex in Italy before.'

I laughed. 'Well, if we can get rid of Harry for an hour then maybe your Italian dreams might come true!'

'I'll ask Mum,' said Charlie excitedly. 'Okay, going back in for round two. Need anything?'

I looked at Charlie, standing there in the shade of the old stone farmhouse, and then I heard Harry giggling, and when I looked across, I saw him on Daniel's shoulders. I put my hand to my belly and felt the life growing inside of me.

'No,' I said to Charlie. 'I have everything I could possibly want.'

A Letter from Jon

Firstly, thank you so much for buying and reading *One Hundred Moments Of Us*. As a writer, it always feels slightly strange to spend a year tapping away on a keyboard, inventing characters, dreaming up stories, and then one day, for someone like you, to read it. Writing is essentially a solitary process, but ironically, we do it with the intention of reaching as many people as possible.

Secondly, I wanted to tell you how this particular book came about. Like most of my books, this one started with the seed of an idea and a title. The seed actually came from my wife. There are two chapters in this book that relate to a scratch on a sideboard, well guess what? That actually happened! I am many things, but clumsy is top of the list. I did indeed scratch an actual sideboard we had just bought, and when I did it, I made a passing joke about if I died, she would see that scratch and it would remind her of me. This obviously became a chapter in the book. At the same time, I had a title for a book idea, *The Museum of You and Me*. The idea was about a relationship that had come to an end, and they were going through their house, and looking at all their possessions and discussing the memories of those things. Ultimately, it didn't work, but I liked the idea of a relationship told through things, and then the scratch on the sideboard happened, and then I thought, rather than possessions, what about moments? Thus, *One Hundred Moments Of Us* was born.

What I have tried to do in the book is capture a relationship through moments, some pivotal and life-changing and some every day, because to me this is what life is. It's a series of moments. It's a first kiss, it's getting engaged and walking down the aisle, but it's also sitting on the sofa and watching television together. It's as much about going for a walk with a cup of coffee, or waking up together every day, as it is watching someone you love pass away. Big moments, small moments, happy, sad, all captured and caught together to give us a whole relationship. It's an every-day love story.

So, I hope you loved *One Hundred Moments Of Us*, and it made you smile, laugh, cry, and feel all sorts of emotions – just like any good relationship should.

Acknowledgements

First and foremost, I'd like to thank my wonderful publisher, Hera, and especially Keshini Naidoo and Jennie Ayres, who have been instrumental in getting this book in the shape you see it now. If you haven't been through the publishing process – and I'm guessing you probably haven't – you won't know just how much work editors put into the book. When I first delivered *One Hundred Moments Of Us* to Hera, it was significantly longer, had a few more plotlines, and it needed some serious help. They obviously saw the potential in it, but also what it needed. With their help and guidance, we completely rewrote the book, and because of them, it is so much better now. So, thank you to them and all the team at Hera, who have been fantastic.

I have to say a thank you to my fellow writers, who have helped me along the way. If you aren't an author, you won't know this, but writers are the loveliest people. You might think that in an industry that is so competitive, so difficult, that authors wouldn't be so willing to help each other out, but you would be wrong. Authors are lovely, and so a special mention to Stephie Chapman (fellow Sotonian), Matt Dunn, Nick Spalding, Ben Hatch, Andy Jones, and I'm sure there are many others I have failed to mention, so thank you too. I would also like to thank the incredible book bloggers, who do so much just for their love of reading. The internet is full of book bloggers, who work so incredibly hard, so thank you! I would love to give a special shout-out to Juliette, who has for years championed writers on Twitter, including myself. When you work alone at a desk in your house, sometimes not speaking to anyone but your family for days, you really appreciate the connections you make online.

I have to thank my incredible readers. *One Hundred Moments Of Us* will actually, and rather incredibly, be my fourteenth novel, and I have some wonderful readers who have been with me since the beginning. So, if you are new to my work or this is your fourteenth book, thank you so much. I only get to do what I do because of you.

Lastly, and most importantly, I want to thank my family because none of this would be possible without them. My children are just so incredibly wonderful, and they love what I do. They always ask questions about it, know when I'm working and give me time and space, and they always have a kind, supportive word when I'm feeling down. Children have an incredible capacity for empathy and kindness, and it melts my heart every single day. I also have to thank my long-suffering wife. Being married to a writer is, I know, extremely difficult. We are often in our own heads, not always present because we are living another life, and yet our partners put up with us. When a book doesn't do well they understand and encourage us to keep going. I know this to be true: behind every writer is a very patient and loving partner. So, to my wife, thank you for everything. None of this would happen without you. I'm publishing a second book with Hera, out next year, and it's another cracking love story! So, until then, thank you all for letting me live my dream.